I0681207

Prophet Wacko

Glory is yours
(for a slight hole in the head)

Prophet Wacko

Thomas Leo

KIKIRUKA PUBLISHING

Thomas Leo

Printed in the United States of America.

Kikiruka Publishing
kikirukapublishing@yahoo.com

Trade Paperback 978-0-9898535-0-7
E-book 978-0-9898535-1-4

Cover design by Devi Jaya DeLavie
Book design by Catherine Leonardo

This edition was prepared for printing by The Editorial Department
7650 E. Broadway, #308, Tucson, Arizona 85710
www.editorialdepartment.com

To Kyoko

Tree

and

Juju

Prophet Wacko

Chapter 1

"They destroyed the whole planet."

The speaker was Fumb fo Jelpmittlebong, a diligent young business manager at Eeftwat Avatars Company Limited. He had few flaws, save for the increasing number of voices in his head, which, depending on perspective, wasn't really a flaw, but a tell-tale sign of telepathic promise.

"The Horde," he said. "They've destroyed the Qanjivians' home planet."

Jelpmittlebong had never met a Qanjivian, but he did have a unique familiarity with their proclivities for interior design. The Qanjivians had built the Sphere, which in addition to being an architectural wonderment imbedded in the gas-giant planet L'goth, was home to all Eeftwat Avatars employees, Jelpmittlebong included.

Eeftwat fo Malgorp spit a mloshfruit pit into his palm and chucked it behind him.

1

"Uh-huh," he said.

Malgorp was the Topmost Executive Xenkonian of Eeftwat Avatars, and Jelpmittlebong's immediate superior.

They were standing on an observation deck that ran along the inner perimeter of the Sphere. Below them was an equilibrium barrier between the viscous methane-ammonia ice of L'goth's mantle and the artificial nitrogen-oxygen gas bubble that constituted the upper half of the Sphere's internal environment.

"The Hoo'qqai may react unfavorably," Jelpmittlebong said.

The sanctums of the Hoo'qqai perforated the aqua surface of the equilibrium barrier in no apparent pattern. Tethered within some of the pools, massive bodies of Hoo'qqai floated like round icebergs. The pale glow of the observation deck reflected off the sticky vapor that rolled from their backs. Xenkonian laborers hovered about.

Malgorp popped another mloshfruit in his mouth and sucked on its fibrous pulp. Various shades of blue rippled over his face like reflections from an underground lake.

"Who says they need to know?"

Jelpmittlebong looked at his boss. The Hoo'qqai were the only known channeling species in the galaxy, and would have undoubtedly detected the collective suffering of the dying planet.

"TEX," he said, "the Hoo'qqai are masters of extrasensory perception. Surely they—"

"Look out there," Malgorp said.

Jelpmittlebong followed his gaze.

"How many occupied sanctums do you see?"

"Can't tell from here," Jelpmittlebong said, squinting his dominant eye. "But there are currently twenty-three active charters, so I assume—"

"Twenty-three?" Malgorp said. "We have nearly a hundred

2

sanctums down there, Jelp. I don't consider less than a quarter occupancy good business. Do you?"

Jelpmittlebong scratched his chin and wondered how anyone could so easily dismiss the obliteration of one of the galaxy's more august civilizations.

"Well?" Malgorp said.

"No, TEX." Jelpmittlebong said. "I don't think it's good for business."

"And you call yourself a marketeer?"

"Not really. Although I did a marketing internship at the asylum—"

"Snap to it then, shall we?"

"Yes, TEX."

Malgorp chunked his foreclaws over his nostrils and blew, spewing a yellowish blueberry glob over his silk sash. The Sphere's methane and ammonia kept his membranes in a constant state of inflammation.

"Shit!"

He wiped his sash and turned.

"Now, then," he said, "we all set to start the corporate brainwashing?"

Jelpmittlebong nodded. "The program's ready. All you have to do is push the buttons like I showed you."

"That's my boy."

Malgorp took wing and hurried toward the Sphere's central hub, where the new recruits were waiting. His underbelly jiggled with the effort. Jelpmittlebong extended his wings and followed.

———————

Malgorp alit on a mezzanine dais that jutted from the wall, his sweat gleaming under the fluorescent lights. He scanned

3

the assembled recruits. They gaped at the hub's towering cobalt ceiling, darting, shouting, and pointing at the immensity of their new surroundings.

Malgorp pushed a button on the wall behind him and said, "Hologlobe."

The overhead lighting dimmed, and a glowing, three-dimensional image of L'goth materialized in the center of the room. The image was huge, still to Qanjivian scale, with L'goth depicted in its current physical state. All weather patterns, atmospheric currents, mantle ripples, methane-ammonia streams, plasma eddies, magnetic fluxes, even planetary rotation, were simulated on a real-time basis. The opacity of the aqua planet was diluted, made translucent for better internal viewing.

"Recruits," Malgorp said, all four foreclaws uplifted, "I give you L'goth."

The recruits flocked into the air. Most of them headed into the holoimage toward the core to get a closer look at the legendary Labyrinth of L'goth.

"The Labyrinth," Malgorp said, "is recognized as one of the greatest mysteries of the galaxy."

The recruits oohed and aahed. Many hovered around the Labyrinth's mouth, others flew over the branches that coiled in an ever-tightening whorl of canals into the core.

"It's so gnarly," said one recruit. "Is it really made of dark matter?"

"Is it really conscious?" asked another.

"The Hoo'qqai call the Labyrinth their Mother-God," said a pert recruit hovering a little too close to Malgorp.

Malgorp stared at him. The recruit inched away.

"That's what the Hoo'qqai claim, yes," Malgorp said. "But I've never had a conversation with it."

"Is it really the conduit for their galactic channeling?" asked another recruit.

"The exact mechanics aren't known," Malgorp said. "But our engineers consider the Labyrinth critical to the process. And surely you read in the orientation manual that during absorption, a Hoo'qqai's hyperbolic noggin connects to the Labyrinth with a steady stream of electrons."

"What about the Sphere?" another recruit asked. He was hovering around the holographic Sphere and observing it through a thick monocle.

"It enhances the natural carrying capacity of the channels," Malgorp said, "but I'm told it's not responsible for their original linkage. Think of the Sphere as a massive amplifier for the Hoo'qqai's natural channeling abilities."

"Why'd the Qanjivians build it?"

Malgorp chortled.

"Ah," he said, "for that you'd have to ask a Qanjivian. But I'm afraid they're indisposed."

"Don't the Hoo'qqai know?"

"Ah yes, our beloved Hoo'qqai." Malgorp ran a foreclaw over a digipad imbedded in the wall behind him. "Shall we meet them?"

Miniature fluorescent replications of the tagged Hoo'qqai appeared in the hologlobe. They looked like tiny jellyfish ghosts in an oversized fishbowl, despite each being over a kilometer in length and having an average girth of a few hundred meters. The recruits went silent, transfixed by the strange, ancient creatures.

Malgorp dabbed his glistening forehead with his sash, then pushed another button. A soft, theatrical sonata commenced, over which a baritone narrative resounded.

"The Hoo'qqai," the narrator said, "the enigmatic, indigenous behemoths of L'goth. The only known organic telepathic channeling species and, arguably, the most mysterious creatures in the galaxy."

The narration paused, and the incidental music swelled to a quick crescendo that trailed into a soft, reedy resonation.

"For over eleven millennia," the narrator continued, "the Hoo'qqai-Qanjivian God-Making Cooperative imposed its narrow vision of Providence upon countless sentio-intelligent species throughout the galaxy. This morally questionable practice ceased with the conquest of the Gwoonpee Zone by the Great Intrepid Horde of Xenkon V'rpq. Today, the mechanics of the Cooperative have been retooled to facilitate the more pragmatic goal of God charters for a profit."

Malgorp rolled his foreclaws toward the hologlobe and smiled.

"The Cooperative's initial purpose," the narrator said, "was to provide pointed impressions of love and hope to any sentient creature within range of a channeling Hoo'qqai.

"As the Cooperative evolved, it learned to invoke the existing mythologies and folklore of the relevant civilization and foster within recipients a strong belief in a powerful, divine guardian. In essence, they manufactured God.

"Although the Hoo'qqai channel is normally received at the subconscious level, on rare occasions it is perceived at the conscious level. Such recipients are hyperintuitive galactic anomalies known as *seer minds*. From the beginning, the channeling Hoo'qqai were able to communicate with seer minds. The Cooperative, in due course, learned to establish and maintain prolonged relationships with many seer minds, who often went on to exert significant influence on the cultural development of their home world.

"Fast forward to today."

Prophet Wacko

The corporate logo of Eeftwat Avatars began blinking in neon symbols on the simulated Sphere in the hologlobe.

"Confiscated by the Great Intrepid Horde and granted to the commercial sector in accordance with the Xenkon V'rpq Plunder Grant, the Sphere is now operated by Eeftwat Avatars Company Limited. Under the visionary guidance of Topmost Executive Xenkonian Eeftwat fo Malgorp, whole worlds can now be manipulated regardless of the presence or absence of a seer mind. Whatever the purpose—enslavement, animal husbandry, sport—Eeftwat Avatars guarantees successful manipulation of any sentio-intelligent species predisposed to believe in a Supreme Being."

The music built to another crescendo, then stopped. Malgorp's huge face filled the hologlobe.

"Eeftwat fo Malgorp," the narrator said, "the epitome of the corporate vision. Eeftwat Avatars Company Limited, the paradigm of success."

The recruits burst into applause. Malgorp bowed from his pulpit.

The hologlobe flickered, and an image of L'goth returned. The Hoo'qqai, the Sphere, and the Labyrinth were each highlighted with fluorescent markers.

Pyrotechnics exploded around the main chamber. Multi-hued fumes of dry ice blasted through the holobasin's floor like geysers.

Malgorp stood on the dais like a messiah, arms outstretched, foreclaws upturned.

"Recruits!" he said. "Welcome to Eeftwat Avatars Company Limited."

7

Chapter 2

"Cuz!" said a lanky Xenkonian, his voice like burnt oil. He was standing in a wet sauna, a damp towel crowning his head and violet beads of sweat bathing his gaunt cheeks. An achromatic mist wafted around him.

"I was stoned out of my gourd."

Kiku fo Swaq, standing Lord of the Great Intrepid Horde of the Great Empire of Xenkon V'rpq, was on the other end of the holoscreen. He crossed thick limbs over his breastplate.

"Humph," he said.

"I mean," the lanky one said, "how can I be held to a contract in that condition?" He held out four empty foreclaws. Steam roiled around his body.

"I was smashed. Cracked. Lacked the proper state of mind. Couldn't manifest the intent. You know, all that legal twaddle. I mean, nobody in their right mind would agree to a long-term output contract for sea stars at that price."

Swaq scowled.

"Cuz?! Don't tell me you're gonna pull that I-can't-be-bothered-because-I'm-the-ultimate-badass shit on me. Now listen. This bridge," he poked his chest with two harried foreclaws, "ain't burnable. *Comprende?*"

Swaq lifted his brow.

"What were you on this time?"

"Sea stars. What else? I mean, had to sample the goods. And," the skinny one cleared his throat, "maybe a little residual alfifi resin from the trip over." He planted his foreclaws on his hips. "But for your information, I've been clean since Jivropt Seven, so back off, yeah?"

Swaq straightened his back and scrunched his neck into his broad shoulders.

"Qoohx, you're a fuckup." He grinned. "But it'll be like old times."

"That's my Cuz!" Qoohx said, swirling the steam with his arms.

"Fuck you," Swaq said. "If you weren't kin—"

"Yeah, yeah."

"And send me some more of that prototype."

"The Mind Whopper?"

"Whatever you call it. You're getting close. The telepathic portals are staying coherent longer. I can sometimes make out three or four voices at a time. But the distortion's still a bitch. And do something about the side effects."

"Palsy? Foaming at the mouth?"

"To a weaker mind, perhaps."

"The few telepaths we've tried it on report the same thing. They start ticking or barking like rabid aasmamyl bucks. Some have even ripped off their own heads. Nothing like that from the non-tellies. For them it's just a big, wild trip."

"Well, fix it. It's not going to work if it fries my brain in the process."

"Oh," Qoohx said. "I can do even better than that. You won't believe what your little band of warrior-scientists has been up to. They can be nifty at times."

"Don't get too attached—they're still mine. What have they done?"

"I'll give you a one-word clue." Qoohx widened his dominant eye. "Vivisection."

Swaq stared. "Explain."

"Call it serendipity. A saunter through the Mhowr revealed a backwater species that synthesizes a molecule with the same chemical composition as the one we're developing, but with a mind-twisting kick in the eye." The last words were delivered with the zest of a true narcotics connoisseur. His dominant eye began pulsing in the heat of the sauna.

"Residual psychic energy in their subatomic chemistry reflects their brain images, or something like that. And the more fantastic the images, the more wild the ride."

Swaq gurgled. "You're talking shit," he said.

"Now, now," Qoohx said, wagging a foreclaw at the holoscreen.

"Say it straight."

"You have to promise all commercial benefits fall to me, and I have sole discretion over marketing decisions. Your soldiers are driveling clods when it comes to presentation."

"That's always been the arrangement, provided no military strategy's compromised—and that includes controlling access to the portals."

"Nothing military about it. And I wouldn't know a mind portal if it bit me on the ass." Qoohx tilted his head. "How's it we're kin, but you're telepathic and I'm not? Huh? Not fair, not fair."

"Natural mutation. And it's your job to amplify it."

"Humph!" Qoohx knew not to push the issue beyond the confines of a lighthearted tease. "Anyway, I may need some strings pulled with one of the commercials." His tone had shifted to that of a regular customer making a peculiar—and perhaps grubby—request of his supplier. "Ever heard of Eeftwat Avatars, the Hoo'qqai charter outfit in the Rahzelav-Nalk System?"

"Sure. It's run by a self-indulgent doofus named Eeftwat fo Malgorp. He's using that Sphere to turn the God-Making Cooperative on its head and churn a profit. We've got undercovers there."

"You think you could arrange a discount for their services?"

"Why?"

Qoohx grinned. "No can do, Mr. Badass. Have to wait 'til we're in person. Classified stuff, you know."

Swaq's mouth tightened.

"You're a stupid fucker."

"Oh, Lord Swaq. Ye of little—"

Swaq terminated the transmission by shoving the holoscreen to the floor. Sparks and blue smoke dispersed from the smashed interface. He brooded for a moment then twirled to another holoscreen behind him and punched in a secure code. A stumpy horder with a crinkled head stared back.

"A biological source?" Swaq said.

"My lord?" the horder scientist said.

"The flaming idiot just told me you found a species that produces the same molecule as the prototype."

"Yes, my lord. They're one of those rare species that requires sleep. The hormone that regulates the entrainment of their circadian rhythms perfectly matches the prototype's molecular chemistry. Tests indicate that when harvested from an unagitated specimen, the hormone is more effective than the prototype—and without the disagreeable side effects."

"And when harvested from an agitated specimen?"

"We suspect accumulated psychic energy in their subatomic fabric carries emotional memory that somehow interacts with a Xenkonian's mental state—"

"Spit it out."

"If the specimen's agitated, the side effects are worse."

"But either way, the mind portals open?"

"In tellies, yes."

Swaq's dominant eye drifted sideways in contemplation.

"Do you think it's worth pursuing?" he asked.

"Yes, my lord, if we can learn to control their emotions. Interestingly, they assume a peculiar psychological state when they sleep that's not unlike that of a meditating mute monk, though, unlike the mutes, there's no indication they're conscious—it appears to be just a sporadic succession of involuntary images."

"The mutes are wily bastards. They probably mucked up those test results intentionally."

"Yes, my lord."

"Who are these creatures? What kind of civilization?"

"They're called Humans. Level one, maybe two, if you ask me. But their social dynamics appear complicated."

"Which is why Qoohx is looking to subcontract the avatar engineers ..." Swaq's voice trailed off in thought.

"That's right, my lord."

"Keep me apprised." Swaq reached to terminate the transmission.

"My lord?"

Swaq raised his brow and sniffed an impatient bolus of snot down his throat.

"What?"

"I know this mission needs to be conducted through the pretense of a commercial enterprise, but is Zoggop Recreational Substances the best—"

"Qoohx is kin," Swaq said, clenching his dominant eye into an irritated squint. "So he's a stupid fucker. Deal with it. He's adequate cover—"

A sharp sense of insolence jabbed at him from the direction of the holoscreen. Swaq drew in a breath and let it dribble out as he conjured up a more collaborative spirit.

"If you wish to conceal something," he said, "you only have to create a lack of interest in the place where it's hidden. My public dealings on Qoohx's behalf create the image of a magnanimous lord indulging his cousin. Do you not agree that no one will suspect anything otherwise?"

The horder flashed a grin at this candid sharing of strategy.

"Yes, my lord." He bowed. "Your bounty is unsurpassed."

A little over a week later, a small team of horders barged into the boardroom of a large sea star manufacturer on Seventh Moon, Gwod-Cunk'r. In their wake strode Swaq in full Horde regalia. He tromped to the head of the table and ordered the Topmost Executive Xenkonian to his feet.

"Lord Swaq!" the TEX said, frozen to his seat. "We weren't expecting—"

"Up."

The TEX trembled to his feet, his face just reaching Swaq's collarbone. The other board members gawked.

Swaq flashed a copy of the contract.

"The price terms of this contract will be revised, and you will immediately withdraw your breach of contract claim against Zoggop Recreational Substances." He thrust the contract into the TEX's shaking foreclaws. "Do you agree?"

"L-l-let me explain," the TEX said.

"Do you agree?"

The TEX twitched a pleading dominant eye at his colleagues.

"A resolution is required for—"

"Are you not the TEX?"

"Y-y-yes, your eminence, of course."

"Then answer."

The TEX swallowed. "A-a-agreed."

Swaq grinned, then squinted his dominant eye.

"Good," he said, severing the TEX's head with a swift swoop of his foreclaw. The small band of horders grunted as the torso crumpled with a leathery thud.

Swaq turned to the board members, the TEX's head in his grip. He shook it, then circled the table shouting obscenities in his unique version of the Horde victory stomp.

The exposed vertebrae flapped.

Chapter 3

The Hoo'qqai Ulluoi is the second-eldest living Hoo'qqai, junior only to the Hoo'qqai Chubij. She'd been gliding on a soft current under L'goth's ancient triple-storm system when the Xenkonians invaded the Sphere. A tiny bundle of dormant root neurons sparkled to life, triggering a hitherto fallow instinct that caused her to change course.

At first she interpreted the summons as her time to retraverse the fibrous canals of her birth and surrender to its creative powers, so that another Hoo'qqai could be born to carry on the traditions of her species. Instead, the Labyrinth directed her to a warm eddy of ammonia sloshing in a membrane sac under its yawning mouth. Surrounded by a crib of gnarled branches and aerial roots, the eddy would be her refuge during the Xenkonian infestation.

A watery sequence of hoots echoed from the zenith, separated by a few seconds of silence, then repeated. Chubij stirred from his drift through the murky lower reaches of L'goth's mantle. He severed his connection to the Labyrinth and began to unwind his body.

Ulluoi normally would have sent a stream of configured electrons, which, given the high electrical conductivity of L'goth's interior fluid, would have reached Chubij in seconds. It was, after all, the natural way for Hoo'qqai to communicate. But, not wanting to risk detection by the Xenkonians, she resorted to simple acoustic bursts instead.

Chubij's glob of entwined membranes prickled and protested as he loosened them with strategic combinations of thrusts and stretches, as if unwinding a large ball of tangled rubber bands. Hours later his tail limbs streamed hundreds of meters behind him as he set out in the direction of the hoots.

Swooshing along, he recalled the visions he'd been channeling. Some of the creatures he'd encountered in the past, others he'd never seen before. Some were catalogued on the Mhowr, others not. But they all suffered. He was tormented that the Sphere was no longer at his disposal, so he could soothe them or channel more intricate messages of inspiration, as he would have during the days of the Cooperative.

As the atmosphere became increasingly cerulean, he settled into a smooth rhythm, propelled by his long tail limbs, moving almost perpendicular to L'goth's magnetic field, counter to the planet's rotation, guided by Ulluoi's faithful hoots.

He could get no closer to the Labyrinth of L'goth than the plasma bubble shield—surgically imposed by the Xenkonians under his outer cephalic membrane—would allow. But he could still discern its throbbing force. He found a soft current flowing in its direction, and positioned himself in it, so that he was pushed against a similar shield surrounding the Labyrinth, thus remaining as stationary as possible. He lowered his head and let out a short burst of hoots, announcing his arrival.

Ulluoi responded in low, guttural vocalizations that any non-Hoo'qqai eavesdropper would easily mistake for the muffled rumbling of methane stormbolts.

"Chubij, my patriarch."

"Ulluoi, my fond sister."

Being genderless, these designations were purely symbolic. The elder Hoo'qqai is always referred to as the patriarch and the younger as the indulged sister.

"You are well?" Ulluoi asked.

"As well as can be expected. I carry on with my channeling, unaided of course by the technology. I've encountered some remarkable seer minds, incredible souls." Chubij was silent for a moment. "But I regret not being able to channel meaningfully with them. The Xenkonians herd us like animals, forcing us into unwholesome unions."

"Even you, my patriarch?"

"Not anymore. I disrupted a couple of their charters, as only an elder would know how to do." He hooted a laugh. "They no longer consider me reliable."

Ulluoi let out a small series of mirthful hoots.

"But," Chubij said, "I digress, my sister. How are you?"

"I'm taken care of, my patriarch." Her voice seemed far away, as if fighting a current. "But truthfully, I'm bored. I dream of frolicking in the currents of our home planet and channeling across the galaxy."

"My sister, the Mother-God surely has a purpose for your seclusion. Please have faith."

"Yes, my patriarch, faith will prevail."

"I know it will. Now, what is the reason for your call?"

"I must tell you," Ulluoi hooted, "the Great Intrepid Horde destroyed the Qanjivians' home world. Few have survived. I'm afraid their great civilization is no longer."

"I didn't sense anything."

"Perhaps you weren't in absorption when it occurred, or the channels weren't aligned."

"I should have sensed it."

"My patriarch ... the Labyrinth ... it shuddered when it happened. Actually, it began before ..."

Chubij was silent.

"Patriarch?"

"That is distressing," Chubij said.

"It's said the Xenkonians have no sense of ethics as we know it."

"So it seems."

"I remain in contact with a small band of surviving Qanjivians," Ulluoi said. "They've infiltrated the Xenkonians' communication systems. Duplicate streams of all transmissions to and from the Sphere are now diverted to them through me."

"Their technical prowess is unmatched."

"Yes, my patriarch."

"Sister," Chubij said, "I must go. They will become suspicious if I remain too long in this location so close to the Labyrinth."

"I'm sorry the news is not better."

"Do not despair. It's when evil emerges overwhelming that we must be most brave. We must not lose faith in our Mother-God."

"Yes, my patriarch. I will so endeavor."

"Hope be with you."

"And you, my patriarch."

Chubij turned and, lacking the energy to swim, sought the outflowing current of a quick ammonia stream he sensed was nearby.

Chapter 4

Two horders trundled through a poorly lit corridor. Gutted and skinned aasmamyl carcasses hung from meat hooks connected to an idle conveyor line along the ceiling. Hoisted hindquarters up, they were so close together that many were joined at the ribcage by frozen body grease, their broken forelimbs stretching toward the floor. Lard deposits clung like icicles from the tips of their skinned heads.

The horders walked side by side in synchronized strides, their exhalations freezing in midair. Lord Swaq's holographic portrait shimmered on their breastplates.

"Why'd they put the fucker here?" the little short-necked horder asked with a grunt as they marched.

"Thought it'd break him," the old one said.

"'Cause he's a mute monk?"

"Yeah. They say pointless brutality fucks with their heads. This place is one of the oldest slaughterhouses in the system. They

23

don't do stunnin' here, and the bloodlettin' machines ain't the best. So lots of these critters is still alive when they're skinned and gutted. Anyway, he's been in this shithole for years. Every so often he's told to repent his idiot religion. When he don't, we tear off his head."

"Humph," the little one said. "If it don't work, why don't they just kill the fucker?"

"Got me," the old one said. Then after a moment, "Something to do with a fate worse than death. They be teachin' a lesson to every mute monk with the nerve to challenge the Horde. That's the reason they put in the holocameras. They broadcast his crappy life in regular showings on the Mhowr."

"Ppppth! Guess they don't be knowin' mute monks don't pay no attention to the Mhowr, or any other kind of media."

"Mmm. Guess not …"

"Besides, mute monks ain't religious. They be antireligious if anything. Hell, they be anti-everything, as far as I know."

"Well, I don't know much. Just do as I'm told. Maybe they be tryin' to teach anybody who be watchin' the Mhowr. But, what you know about mute monks anyway? Seem mighty informed for a recruit … Or you just puffin' shit?"

"Born and raised in the Gok'l Nebula," the little one said. "Used to see the scrawny fuckers every once 'n a while. Saw one down in a rock fissure in the Great Maze-Jungle on Hurm IV. He was meditatin' on a ledge about a nanometer from a twenty-kilometer drop. Local dude who pointed him out said he'd been there like that for at least two seasons, maybe more. Saw another on the bank of a mud canal during the dark season on Gwod-Cunk'r. Had to use infrareds to see him. Snuck up and tried to talk to him, but all he did was laugh like an idiot. That's all I know."

"Well, this fucker's the only one I seen, and he don't laugh much. But he sure is weird ... Always talkin' in riddles and shit."

The passageway began to incline and narrow, causing the horders to shift into a single-file procession. The older one stepped forward to take the lead. Their black metal pauldrons rammed the carcasses aside.

"Not sure why they call 'em 'mute monks,'" the older one said with a pant, as he drove his shoulder into a dead aasmamyl. "Sometimes he jabbers on like an old slink lizard, but, like I said, he don't make much sense."

"Called *mute* because if ya ask 'em something about their secret ways, they just clam up and smile like idiots. Cagey little bastards."

"Well, he seems harmless to me ... No doubt this shithole fried his brain."

The horders came to the end of the corridor and burst through a series of creaky doors. The sounds of machinery and squealing aasmamyls grew louder as they passed through each dividing compartment. By the time they reached the slaughter hall, the temperature had gone from subfreezing to sweltering. Thick, red sweat beaded on their heads like mercury and slithered down their necks.

"How long you say he's been here?" the recruit asked.

"Least as long as I been stationed on Mwookt Qor, coming up on nineteen seasons. Ain't nobody been here longer than me, and they don't keep good records around here. They say mute monks can live forever. That true?"

"Shit if I know."

As they approached the exsanguination area, the stench of excrement mingled with the syrupy smell of fresh blood. The bleeding machines sat atop grated flooring, through which the blood slopped into a deep trough that ran under the main slaughter hall. The churning cascade of body fluids all but drowned the frightened cries of the aasmamyls and the relentless din of the slicing apparatuses.

The older one held up a foreclaw and pointed ahead.

The recruit followed his companion's finger. In the distance a mirage-like speck floated in the air, but he couldn't make out what it was. He pointed at it and yelled something.

The older horder just nodded.

Zawt sat cross-legged on a small, open platform suspended over the frenzy of the slaughtering. The platform was of the free-hovering type, and programmed to take him on regular tours of the abattoir so as to observe all of its ruthless operations. He was currently floating above the carcass-dumping hole, which was the default site when not touring and, when necessary, the point of horder embarkation. The thuds of carcasses emanated from the chasm below.

"Hello, fucker," wheezed the old horder, alighting onto the platform. He stepped to the side, lowered his head, and dug his foreclaws into his sides to catch his breath. The recruit landed behind him, stared at the mute monk, and scratched his crotch.

Zawt eyed them.

"How straight they flew," he said, "circling the tree."

"Uh-huh," the old horder said, stretching out his neck. "Well, asshole, the new head be lookin' fine."

"Clearly," Zawt said, pointing at his head with a willowy foreclaw, "I am in the midst of birth and death." The chains around his limbs jangled with the movement.

"Looks to me like you're in the midst of death and more

death," the horder said. "Don't see much birthin' goin' on 'round here."

"If there's even a particle of dust in the eye," Zawt said, "flowers are seen dancing in the air."

"Shiiiiiit," the old horder said. "See what I mean?" he said to the recruit, but with his eye trained on Zawt. "He's one weird mother—"

"Holy shit," the recruit said, who had turned to gaze over the sweeping panorama presented by their lofty vantage. The outer walls were kilometers away, and the area in between was a dark-red ocean speckled with black metal and blurry steel islands of old machinery. It exuded a holistic ambiance of bone-crushing efficiency.

"Welcome to my abode," Zawt said, cracking a wild grin at the recruit. Then he turned to the old horder. "You're here for the head, I presume. Shall I save you the trouble?"

In the past Zawt had indeed torn off his own head, much to the consternation of the old horder.

"What? And deprive an old Xenkonian of his only pleasure in life?"

"When I'm hungry, your eating of food will not fill my stomach," Zawt said.

"Fuck you, mute head." The old horder's face phased from violet to crimson. "Guess you're not in the mood to repent your idiot religion today, heh, fuckwad?"

"It's repented and lonely. It's squalid and splendid in the cold night air. I had nothing to do with it."

"Well, that ain't how Lord Swaq sees it." He pulled out a digipad. "Okay, same drill, fucker. What're the political intentions of the mutes?"

Zawt stared back with a smile and said, "I bet I can remove

my head faster than you can." He seized his cheeks with his fore-claws and stretched them at acute right angles to his head.

"Oh no you don't," the old horder yelled.

In one quick motion, he tossed the digipad to the recruit and lunged at Zawt's head, snapping it from the neck like a dry winter twig. He straddled over Zawt's flinching body and spat, but the spittle stuck to his dehydrated lips and dribbled down his chin. He wiped it with his forearm.

The recruit stared at the still-twitching face that dangled from the old horder's foreclaw. Part of the spinal column had come off with the head, and the upward-curling chain of exposed vertebrae glistened like resin in a scrimshaw pipe.

"Watch this," the old horder said. He placed Zawt's head face-down near the platform's edge and, stepping back a few paces, wrapped his tail around his side. "This fucker's gonna splat." With a yelp, he jumped and twirled toward Zawt's head, whipping his tail around. Just before impact, the head's lips puckered against the floor, pushing it out of the path of the whiffing tail.

The horder landed on his belly halfway off the platform.

Zawt's head rolled over the edge and into the shadows of the carcass hole, blinking as it dropped. It pinballed off the jostling carcasses, then rolled up against the leg of a janitorial laborer, who picked it up and tossed it in a nearby black metal offal container on a conveyor belt rumbling toward the subterranean ice hall.

The horders stared into the carcass hole from the edge of the platform.

The old horder rattled his head as if warding off glipflies.

"Shit!" he said. "They're gonna kill me for lettin' his head get away like that."

A few hours later, a laborer stuck a label on the offal container that contained Zawt's head.

It read "Eeftwat Avatars Company Limited."

Chapter 5

Jelpmittlebong bent over a holoscreen imbedded in a bow-shaped table. His four foreclaws swarmed over a flickering terminal. He simultaneously monitored the status of the absorbed Hoo'qqai and the locations of the inactive Hoo'qqai, as well as arranged team schedules for pending charters. Cooling fans hummed and droned on either side of him, sputtering frigid clouds of ice crystals over his station.

A small hologlobe hovered in his dominant line of sight as he worked. Inside, the smoldering surface of Qanjiv floated against the hoary backdrop of its star. Its largest moon glowed with Swaq's vandalic scowl—the notorious stamp of Horde conquest. Jelpmittlebong felt a tightening in his gut with every replay of the annihilation.

Below the simulated destruction of Qanjiv streamed the real-time entries of a species-rights site he often visited.

FatherDoogl: *Qanjiv lies in ruins, reduced to a charred and life-less planet. And for what? What threat exactly did the Qanjivians pose to the Xenkonian Empire?*

Kah-Mutt: *Doodly-squat.*

QeepPopDaal: *Exactly!!*

SoftBrain2: *I find this hilarious and a waste of good ammunition.*

Dipamp: *The Qanjivians were pompous assholes. Good riddance!*

FatherDoogl: *Am I the only one who thinks the Horde's imperialistic activities are a blatant affront to all sentient beings' accepted standards of decency—not to mention a plethora of galactic laws?*

SoftBrain2: *FatherDoogl = dipshit peacenik fuckwad!*

Jelpmittlebong commandeered the hologlobe closer and spoke clearly in its direction. His words entered the blog-stream under the name FumbfoJelp.

FumbfoJelp: *Fellow Xenkonians, all indications are that Lord Swaq is on a warpath whose goal is nothing short of galactic domination. He must be stopped.*

SoftBrain2: *It's Fumfo-Dolt!*

Kah-Mutt: *Yo, Fumb! You wanker! The Xenkonian Empire Rocks. We'll soon rule the galaxy.*

SoftBrain2: *Yeah! So piss on your fuckin' peacenik parade!*

Jelpmittlebong sighed. The voices in his head, telepathic or not, paled in comparison to the intrusive, bottom-of-the-barrel voices from cyberspace. Undeterred, he spoke again to the hologlobe.

FumbfoJelp: *Unfettered aggression without purpose seems unworthy of praise. Are Xenkonians the chosen species?*

Prophet Wacko

Dipamp: *Hell yes!*
FatherDoogl: *Hallelujah, Jelp! Good to see your rational voice join the fray. But what drives Swaq's fury?*
SoftBrain2: *Damn straight we're the chosen species, but only if we're willing to shit on our neighbors! Ha!*
Kah-Mutt: *LOL!! Lord Swaq Rocks!*

Jelpmittlebong shooed the hologlobe away and closed his dominant eye. Through the fog of the injudicious stream of comments shined FatherDoogl's. *"Indeed,"* he thought, *"what does drive Lord Swaq's fury?"*

A sudden emptiness filled his mind, from which a clear voice arose.

"My student, it's his nature."

It was the voice of his overseer at Toq, Pwond fo Niukah, and it was as though Niukah were standing right behind him.

Jelpmittlebong spun around and scanned his station. No one was within earshot.

He contemplated the disembodied statement—not so much the content as the medium. The voices in his head were not infrequent lately, but they were generally incoherent, which he considered a consequence of work-related stress.

Then again, Niukah had often referred to Jelpmittlebong's inchoate telepathic ability as unprecedented. Toq was an obscure but legit learning institution for young brood with a shadow curriculum for potential telepaths. But Jelpmittlebong doubted his own qualifications, despite Niukah's unwavering conviction that his telepathic puberty would transpire. The only question was when.

Jelpmittlebong closed his dominant eye and wondered.

"Overseer," he thought, *"is it happening?"*

31

He tilted his head in concentration.

The ensuing silence was interrupted by the rotund face of Malgorp jiggling in the upper corner of the holoscreen.

"Jelp," Malgorp said. "Turn around."

Jelpmittlebong looked toward the door. Malgorp stood in the doorway, foreclaws on hips.

Jelpmittlebong leaped up and scurried over.

"Humph," Malgorp said, waddling off with a flick of his hand. He gestured for Jelpmittlebong to follow.

"Must I always call repeatedly?" Malgorp asked. "And what's wrong with your lateral eyes?"

"Nothing, TEX. Apologies. I was going over the charter schedules."

"Seems like you're always preoccupied with something these days," Malgorp said as he strode.

"My duties, TEX." Not only had he been more productive lately, but the intense concentration also helped quiet the voices.

"What can you tell me about a company called Zoggop Recreational Substances?"

"Zoggop?" Jelpmittlebong pinched his chin. "Runs the Eyes of the Morinurk chain of inhalant dens in the Hurmoodily System. Fairly profitable, I believe." He gazed upward. "Also involved in narcotics R&D. Its most successful product is the *Fwap!* brand of hallucinogen lozenge, distributed in localized pockets throughout the Empire, but without mass appeal. Zoggop fo Qoohx is the TEX, who's probably more renowned than his products—occasionally on the gossip sites, involving scandals and celebrities—"

Malgorp held up a hand to stop. They were at the entrance to the passageway to his quarters.

"Bear your formidable marketing acumen on it and tell me: do you think we should grant a charter to this Qoohx?"

"A charter?" Jelpmittlebong drew in his lips. "Why would a narcotics tycoon need to charter a—"

"Why do any of them need a Hoo'qqai?" Malgorp asked. "I'm sure he has his reasons. It's not our place to probe the motives of our clients, beyond what the law requires. It's bad for business. There could be a dozen reasons why he'd want to exploit the religious disposition of a species. What I want to know is whether or not he can pay."

"I'm not aware of anything that questions the soundness of Zoggop's financial condition." Jelpmittlebong paused. "But, TEX, Qoohx counts Lord Swaq as kin. A failed charter may bring unwanted Horde scrutiny to our enterprise, perhaps, given Qoohx's reputation."

"Reputation?"

"He's well-known to imbibe narcotics himself."

Malgorp frowned. "And he's Lord Swaq's kin?"

"Yes, TEX. And Swaq's use of the Horde to intervene in Qoohx's commercial affairs is not unprecedented," Jelpmittlebong continued. "He recently—and personally—beheaded the TEX of a sea star manufacturer on Seventh Moon, Gwod-Cunk'r—"

"So Lord Swaq's been known to rip off the heads of anybody unlucky enough to get on the wrong side of his fuckup junkie cousin?" Malgorp snorted. "How do you know all this, anyway?"

"It was in the news—on the Mhowr—mostly because the TEX's head failed to regenerate properly. His dominant eye didn't seal and turned into a clot of natal agar."

Malgorp waved a foreclaw.

"These things happen. Listen, Lord-of-the-Horde connections or not, we need the business. I want you to respond to this Zoggop. Tell them we're happy to accommodate their charter request. Be enthusiastic, but not overly so. We don't want to guarantee success, only commercially reasonable efforts."

"Yes, TEX," Jelpmittlebong said, twirling to leave. But after two paces he stopped.

"Umm," he said, turning around, "do you have the NAD tube?"

"I gave it back to the mipoon messenger," Malgorp said. "His ID recall is 99-23, I believe. Must I do everything?"

Jelpmittlebong coiled his lips in preparation of making a point, but stopped.

"No mind," he said with a diagonal tilt of his head, and departed.

The diversion to the message chamber was an inconvenience. But the mipoon in question didn't respond to transmission requests, and company protocol required that charter requests be handled by the mipoon receiving the request.

Jelpmittlebong peered into the dark, yawning cavern. A haze of vapor fumes blanketed its upper reaches. Laborers and—to Jelpmittlebong's uninitiated eye—general miscreants rumbled about in a swarm of activity. Multilevel communications machinery rose from the floor and extended to the far wall. Mipoon messengers sat in random attendance, their bioengineered foreclaws jammed into blinking interfaces. NAD tubes poked from their lateral eye sockets.

Jelpmittlebong took a step into the throng, and was nearly trampled by a red-eyed fellow with a vapor bong strapped to his chest like a bagpipe. The fellow stopped and looked at Jelpmittlebong. Blue-silver fumes billowed from his bong.

"Who are you?" the fellow asked.

Jelpmittlebong tugged at his red sash.

"Oh, one of them sexless tush lickers from front-side, eh? Life's tough, eh? You come all that way just to show us that?"

"Pardon me?"

"Bugger off," the fellow said, trudging on.

Jelpmittlebong watched him disappear then rubbed his chin with a puzzled foreclaw.

"Havin' trouble with the locals, eh?"

Jelpmittlebong turned and glared down at a mipoon messenger.

"Excuse me?" he said.

"At least he didn't spit on ya," the mipoon said with a grin. The kaleidoscope ends of NAD tubes protruded, like rainbow antennae, from where his lateral eyes should have been.

"Ahem," Jelpmittlebong said, retreating a step and dropping his face. "I am Jelpmittlebong, from the House of Fumb, presently in the employ of your TEX, Eeftwat fo Malgorp."

"Is that right?" the mipoon said. "Well ya got my attention. Mipoon 8-1-21, at ya service—maybe, depends on what ya be wantin'."

"I'm looking for a mipoon messenger with the ID recall of 99-23. But, it must be a mis—"

"Ain't no such mipoons 'round down here. Mipoons' ID recalls consist of a string of numbers. First number identifies the specific row." He swung a stunted, bioengineered foreclaw in the direction of the interface row behind him. "Second number's the level, and third's his seat. It's like a nifty three-dimensional coordinate system. Got that? There be lots of rows here, but ain't no way they add up to ninety-nine."

"Yes, I know all that. I also read the internal operations manual."

"Then why ya be lookin' for a mipoon that don't exist?"

35

Jelpmittlebong sniffed and pulled on his sash.

"That's how it was communicated to me," he said. "I've deduced that the mipoon in question must be 9-9-23. Do you know where I might find him?"

"Clever tush licker, ya be," 8-1-21 said. "If ya can figure that out, ya can surely figure out that 9-9-23 means ninth row, ninth level, twenty-third stool. Come on, I'll show ya." 8-1-21 pulled Jelpmittlebong down one of the aisles, and stopped in front of a small panorama of glowing interfaces. He pointed at the faded numbers stenciled in what appeared to be crayon above his own screens. "This be my station—first level of the eighth row, twenty-first stool."

"Clever indeed," Jelpmittlebong said, looking up at the numbers.

"Now, follow me." 8-1-21 flew up into the wispy darkness that enveloped the interface column. Jelpmittlebong flapped into his swirling wake.

The chamber at level nine was dimmer. The fog thickened, and many of the surrounding fluorescent tubes had burnt out and not been replaced. They landed on the ledge and walked to the far end, through a web of blinking interface emissions, stepping over a lifeless mipoon slumped against a stool, at which Jelpmittlebong stared, swiveling his dominant gaze as they passed.

"Too much of the bubbly mixed with the inhalants," 8-1-21 said, as if reading Jelpmittlebong's mind. "And maybe even some of the good stuff mixed in for good measure. He be tuned totally inward—top to bottom, front to back. Who knows what he be seein'? About as close as a Xenkonian can get to sleep, whatever that is."

"*Good stuff?*"

"That's what they tell me."

"I mean, what do you mean by the *good stuff*?"

"Here ya go," 8-1-21 said. He'd stopped in front of a messy interface, the blanched numbers *9-23* just discernible. An empty vacuum flask was overturned on the desk, and brown dregs had gelled over the touchpads.

"Looks like your fella's been imbibin'," 8-1-21 said, setting the vacuum flask upright. "What kinda business ya got with him?"

"He delivered a message to our TEX, Eeftwat fo Malgorp. A request for a Hoo'qqai. I've come—"

8-1-21 laughed. "Ya say that like he had the honor of haulin' around Lord Swaq's jockstrap."

"Excuse me?"

"Why didn't ya just use the internal message line? No need to come all this way to talk to a mipoon."

"He didn't answer." Jelpmittlebong said. "And corporate protocol provides that only the transmitting mipoon can respond to a request for a Hoo'qqai."

"Obviously some manager's brain cramp," 8-1-21 said.

"The policy's sound. There's been double-booking, even double-billing, in the past, due to multiple transmission streams."

8-1-21 stared then shook his head.

"Yeah. Okay then. Shoot ya'self."

"Look, Mipoon 8-1-21, do you know where he might be?" Jelpmittlebong gestured toward 9-9-23's interface.

8-1-21 smiled and pointed down the passageway. "Puttin' two and two together, I wouldn't be surprised if that's him back there."

Jelpmittlebong swiveled. "Him?"

They hurried back. 8-1-21 rolled the unconscious mipoon over.

"Is it him?" Jelpmittlebong asked.

37

"Can't tell. All us mipoons look alike." 8-1-21 looked up with a roguish grin. "Ya know, since we're all from the same genetic mutant pool, and all."

"Then how can we tell?"

"Relax, tush licker. I can—"

"Stop calling me that." Jelpmittlebong put his foreclaws on his hips. "I'm Fumb fo Jelpmittlebong."

"Whew! Ya be mighty huffy too." 8-1-21 twisted his head and squinted at Jelpmittlebong. "Say, are you related to FumbfoJelp the blog-ranter?"

"Um, yes, that's me."

8-1-21 slapped his forehead. "Well, I'll be damned. Ya one crazy Xenkonian, rantin' off on Lord Swaq like that. Don't be thinkin' the Horde ain't watchin' the blogs."

"Well, I—"

"Maybe I'll just call ya *Lordy*." 8-1-21 grinned. "But ya got my vote. He's one mad horder. Drivin' the whole damned galaxy straight into the shitter. Ya just better watch ya back, Fumb fo Jelpmittlebong."

"Yes, I'll do that. But right now I need to send a response to a client, and this unresponsive mipoon has the key sequence."

"Okay, okay," 8-1-21 said, yanking a NAD tube out of the unconscious mipoon's head. He stuck it in his own lateral socket and stretched his lips into a pucker. He closed his dominant eye in concentration. "Charter request, you say," he said. "Hmm … Zoggop Recreational Substances?"

"Yes."

8-1-21 opened his eye. "Okay, Lordy. I can send the reply for ya. But you'll have to override the idiot internal policy that only the receivin' mipoon can send it. Can't do that myself."

Jelpmittlebong nodded.

Chapter 6

Malgorp was reclining in his private quarters under the artificial rays of a Xenkon V'rpq solar simulator when the transmission panel bleeped red.

"Speak," he said without bothering to remove the slices of mloshfruit from his face.

"Malgorp TEX, sir," a voice said through the interface, "a live transmission holding for your attention."

"Who is it?"

"Not sure, sir. Only said it was a friend. Normally it'd be discounted as a prank transmission, or at least one unworthy of your distraction. But it's been piggybacked by a unique sequence of fractal logarithms—"

"What?"

"It assessed our own security barriers before self-decrypting, typical only of conglomerate or Horde transmissions. We don't get many calls from the Horde, so high probability it's from a conglomerate, Malgorp TEX, sir."

"Why didn't you just say that?" Malgorp asked, pulling off mloshfruit and stretching his face in an attempt to rein in the flaccidness of his head skin, which under the solar simulator had slunk to his neckline like melted candle wax.

"Say what, Malgorp TEX, sir?"

"That it's from a conglomerate. I didn't understand one word of that mumbo jumbo."

After a few moments of low-dissonance static, signifying Malgorp had been put on mute, the mipoon on the other end responded.

"Yes, sir. Sentiments have been logged for future reference. Apologies. But not one-hundred percent positive of the source, sir. Only a high probability."

"Yes, yes, I heard you." Malgorp shuffled in front of the Eeftwat Avatars logo engraved in precious stones on the wall, and pulled a distinguished air. "Transmission on," he said.

Within moments, a life-size holoimage of Lord Swaq in Horde combat regalia materialized in the middle of Malgorp's private quarters.

"Eeftwat fo Malgorp, I presume."

Malgorp swallowed and blinked.

"Did I catch you at an odd moment?" Swaq asked.

"No, no ... your, er, lordship," Malgorp said. "Just startled to be graced by your eminence, my lordship. I was expecting a conglomerate call."

"Yes," Swaq said. "They no doubt use similar algorithms. In any event, this is, indeed, a sudden intrusion into your profitable enterprise, so I will endeavor to occupy as little of your time as possible."

The image flickered and began undulating, causing Swaq's

face to stretch and swell as if reflected in a fun-house mirror. The mipoon in the message chamber adjusted the frequency margins to steady the image, but the comical effect eased Malgorp's jittery nerves.

"My time is yours, my lordship," he said with fresh poise.

Swaq scrutinized the room.

"So, this is the lair of luxury … Cozy, if you like that sort of thing. I personally eschew such comfort, as it tends to distract my meditations. And a properly maintained meditative mind is, of course, the noblest state of Xenkonian consciousness. At least"—he paused—"that is my philosophy." He squinted his dominant eye at Malgorp and tilted his head. "What is your philosophy, Eeftwat fo Malgorp?"

Malgorp let out a nervous laugh. "Admittedly, my lordship," he said, gesturing at the various gadgets in his quarters, "it's one of accumulation."

Swaq stared back without expression.

Malgorp pulled at his sash. "But, your lordship … I … um … agree that meditation is—"

"Good," Swaq said. "It's upon agreements that relationships are built. And I'm here to build a relationship of sorts. You've recently received a business proposition from Zoggop Recreational Substances. A request for a Hoo'qqai charter, I believe."

"Yes, your, er, lordship."

"Zoggop fo Qoohx is my cousin."

"Yes, my lordship. I've heard."

"Your cooperation in this regard is greatly appreciated."

"We at Eeftwat Avatars always strive for the success of our clients," Malgorp said, regurgitating his marketing materials.

"Yes, so I'd imagine. Otherwise how would a TEX remain a TEX?"

"Well, yes, your lordship. There's always that."

Swaq drew in a long breath and crossed his forelimbs over his black breastplate.

"It's either *my* lordship or *your* lordship, but not both."

"Excuse me."

"The purpose of my call is twofold." Swaq chomped his fangs. "First, I expect a generous discount for your services. Second, I've lent some horders to Qoohx. They have excellent technical skills, and they'll be involved in this little God-making project. You'd gain my gratitude—which is another way of saying you'd avoid my disappointment—if you showed them the proper respect."

Swaq lifted his chin and drilled his dominant eye into Malgorp's skull.

"Umm," Malgorp said. "Yes, of course, your ... er, I mean, my lordship."

Swaq straightened his back. "You're not as dumb as you look, Eeftwat fo Malgorp."

"Thank you, my lord—"

"But looks can be deceiving."

Swaq's scowl dissipated into the air.

Chapter 7

Arabella Paasikivi sat with her four housemates in a century-old pub in Eugene, Oregon. Microbrews and a basket of breadsticks crowded the tabletop between them. Midterms were over, and a week of spring freedom loomed.

"Teach," she said. "Or write." She leaned with her elbows on the table, a pint in her hands.

"Or flip burgers," Rock said.

"But don't you have to have a PhD to teach?" Carmen brandished a breadstick like a wand. "And exactly how many folklore programs are there? I mean, *where* would you teach?"

"It's a good interdisciplinary curriculum," Arabella said. "A lot of alums go on to get PhDs in religious studies or anthropology. Some even study film. I'm sure I could use it as a stepping-stone to something."

"Flipping burgers," Rock said.

"Knock it off," Carmen said. "If anyone's going to flip burgers, it's you."

Masa wiped suds from his lips with his sleeve. "What mean, Rock, *flip burgers?*"

"It means welcome to the welfare state," Rock said.

"Don't believe him, Masa," Carmen said. "He's full of shit, and jealous. It's a common trait in English majors."

"Full shit?"

"You guys," Leah said, "Masa's not going to learn proper English if you keep talking like that." She turned to Masa. "*Flipping burgers* means being employed as a cook at a fast-food restaurant."

"Thank you, Leah. So kind."

Rock laughed and grabbed a breadstick.

"Well, everybody's got to make a buck, don't they? Masa says Buddhist monks in Japan drive around in Bentleys—some of the richest bastards in the country. Maybe I should become a monk."

"But then you'd have to actually commit to something," Arabella said with a laugh. "I don't see it."

"You know," Carmen said, finishing her beer, "we should go on a trip. We've got a whole week."

"Camping," Rock said.

"We could go somewhere on the coast."

"The Dunes."

"Yeah," Carmen agreed, nibbling on a breadstick. "What do you say?"

Leah finished her mineral water and stood. "Fine with me," she said.

"Where are you going?" Carmen asked.

"Bible study. We're reading about Jesus' ascension into heaven tonight. Since the Feast of the Ascension is almost here."

"The Ascension?" Rock said, rippling his nose. "Bella?"

Prophet Wacko

"I think according to scripture Jesus' ascension was a literal, bodily return to heaven. He rose from the ground and disappeared into a radiant cloud. Some angels appeared and promised Jesus' return in the same way—I mean, from a radiant cloud."

"Sounds a bit tawdry."

"It's probably just a fabrication of the Christian community in the Apostolic Age, based on visionary experiences or hallucinations."

"Yeah," Leah said, pulling her sweatshirt over her head. "I'll be sure to bring that up when we get to that part."

Carmen groaned. "I thought you were giving up cult headquarters."

"It's not a cult. It's Glory to GOD Faith Center, and everyone there's really nice."

Masa burped as he set his glass on the tabletop. His face glowed scarlet.

"What mean, *cult headquarters*?"

"That's Carmen's way of saying she doesn't like religion," Rock said.

"But *cult* has lots of meanings," Arabella said. "It could just mean something weird."

"*Ah-so*," Masa said. "Like *Rocky Horror Show*?"

"Yeah, something like that." Carmen laughed.

"I want go."

Leah ran her arm through the strap of her backpack.

"Bible study's not a movie. We go to learn about Jesus. In America, Jesus is our savior."

"Speak for yourself," Carmen said.

"In Japan, Buddha," Masa said with a smile. "Also, Japan, Shinto."

Leah smiled. "You can come if you want. It'll probably help your English."

45

"Not to mention soften your brain," Carmen said.

Masa downed his pint and smiled. "Next time go. Tonight beer soften brain."

Leah snickered. "See you guys."

Carmen blew at her bangs as her little sister skipped off. "What does she get out of that crap?"

"She's just exploring," Arabella said, "like when she got so caught up in Ayurveda last year? Give her credit for pushing her boundaries."

"Yeah," Rock said, "and if that's any indication, she'll lose interest in the big JC in about six months." He pointed at the breadbasket and grinned. One breadstick remained. "Rock, paper, scissors for that?"

Carmen swiped the breadstick and broke its tip with her teeth. "I win," she said with a gleam.

"You guys are so juvenile," Arabella said. "We can always get some more."

"You haven't been here for a while, have you?" Rock said.

"Why?"

Rock flagged his arm toward the bar. Moments later a stout man with long, stringy hair that didn't quite hide his bald spot approached the table.

"Yeah?" he said.

Rock lifted the empty basket. "May we have some more of these scrumptious breadsticks?"

"Sorry, only one basket per table, unless you want to pay for them, five bucks a basket."

"Five bucks?" Carmen said. "But they taste like pencils."

The man looked at her. "Then why do you want more?"

"Because they're free," Rock said.

"No they're not. I just told you." The man wrung the bottom of his apron with beefy fists.

"It's okay, we're fine," Arabella said, before her companions could respond. "Thank you."

The man loosened his grip on his apron and smiled.

"You're welcome," he said. "Anything else?"

"Four more microbrews, please," Rock said. "And we'll pay."

"Yep," the man said, and disappeared behind the kitchen door.

"See?" said Rock.

"What a jerk," Carmen said. She sat back in her chair. "You know, it really bugs me watching Leah go down this path. I mean, to so willingly let herself be brainwashed."

"What makes you so sure she's being brainwashed?" Arabella asked.

"Isn't that what all religions do?"

"Religions don't have a monopoly on thought control," Rock said. "Governments do it all the time. So does the media."

"Not to mention parents," Arabella said.

"Yeah, but religions are more creepy about it."

Arabella laughed. "True."

"Religion creepy Japan too," Masa said.

"Really?" Carmen asked. "Do you follow Buddhism or Shinto?"

"Both, but mostly neither." Masa smiled. "Japanese just do mostly."

"Uh-huh," Carmen said, scratching behind her ear. "Well, looks like it's up to me and Bella to maintain the rational, atheistic line of thought."

"Actually, I'm agnostic," Arabella said. "But, I think I'd accept anything as true if it could be verified with objective empirical evidence, even God. It's the ultimate open mind."

"Sounds like the ultimate straddle," Carmen said.

Arabella laughed.

47

"No," she said. "It's just that I really don't know. And I don't really have a need for faith—I mean, I actually don't like the idea of faith. Kills the brain, you know. But I am intellectually curious."

"Well, I'm curious too."

"But both theists and atheists take a side without really knowing if their belief is true," Arabella said. "Think about it, what would you do if a reputable, scientific study came out that proved God's existence?"

"Yeah, right." Carmen snorted. "I'd ask what they meant by *God*. I mean define it. If we're talking aliens or bigfoots, then at least we'd have something concrete to look at. But an omnipotent being? What the hell is that?"

Masa leaned toward Rock and said, "*Bigfoot?*"

"Neanderthals in the woods," Rock said. "They're cool."

"*Ah-so*," Masa said.

"Bigfoot's a myth," Arabella said, "a combination of folklore, wishful thinking, and hoax. At least that's what the evidence indicates."

"In other words, they're not real," Carmen said.

"My brother's a hardcore atheist too. We've had tons of conversations like this. Now he lives in the woods like a hermit 'cause he can't stand all the daily feel-good religious crap of the moral majority."

"I'd love to meet him," Carmen said.

"But what if someone could convince you with objective evidence that an omnipotent being exists?" Arabella asked. "Wouldn't you be compelled to believe in it?"

"I just don't think anyone could prove such a thing."

"And can you prove there is no God?"

"It's a dumb question." Carmen tightened her lips. "Replace God with bigfoot or aliens in that sentence, and I'd agree. I just don't think it's possible to define God."

"Here we go," the waitress said. A tousled ponytail spilled from the bandanna tied around her head. "Four refills of microbrews." She placed the pints on the table, then whisked a fresh basket of breadsticks from her tray. "On the house."

They looked at her questioningly.

"Don't worry about him." She flicked her thumb in the direction of the bar. "He's a stingy fart, but it's no biggie. Just don't tell him, okay?"

"Deal," Rock said.

"Thank you," Arabella said, reaching for a breadstick.

The waitress smiled as she stuck the tray under her arm. "Anything else?"

"What you believe bigfoot?" Masa said with a laugh. "They cool hoax myth, no?"

The waitress chortled. "They've got horrendous table manners, I hear."

"Like your manager?" Carmen said.

"You could say that." The waitress started retrieving the empty glasses from the table. "But, I know some people who think bigfoot's more than just a cryptid."

"Cryptid?" Rock said. He looked at Arabella. "Bella?"

"A creature whose existence hasn't been confirmed by science."

"That's my nerd."

Arabella grinned. "You know," she said to the waitress, "I've heard there are Chinook legends that suggest contact with bigfoot."

The waitress's eyes flashed. "That's what my grandmother told me too. She was part Shoshone and Chinook. I wrote a paper on it for one of my undergrad classes—a long time ago."

"Really? How'd you find any material? I'd have thought it's all based on oral history."

The waitress smiled. "I interviewed some elderly Chinooks in a nursing home in Astoria. Anyway," she said with a thoughtful gaze, "probably the weirdest thing they told me was that bigfoots can camouflage themselves as trees."

Carmen nearly choked on her breadstick.

"Trees?" she said.

"That's right," the waitress said. "Little Douglas firs, to be exact, which is why they're so hard to find."

Carmen scoffed into her microbrew.

"Did you major in folklore too?" Rock asked, gnawing a breadstick.

"Kimani!" the manager suddenly bellowed from the bar.

"Something like that," Kimani said, then looked over her shoulder. The manager nudged his chin in the direction of some new customers. Kimani acknowledged them with a wave of her hand.

"Cultural anthropology," she said, turning back, "which is why I work here." She laughed.

"Kimani!"

"Oops." Kimani winked. "Gotta go." She pranced away with crisp bounces of her high-top sneakers.

Chapter 8

"The Skooks are the closest advanced civilization to this planet." The speaker was Goonhopple fo Gargado, senior target world analyst at Eeftwat Avatars Company Limited.

"The hairy tree cloakers?" Malgorp asked.

"The very same."

"They were quite helpful on the Pilt-Zax charter," Jelpmittle-bong said.

"Well, throw them a bone," Malgorp said. "Legal tender. Hard nuggets. Whatever they want. Find out what they know about this Earth."

"Way ahead of you, TEX," Gargado said. "Called our Skook contact and worked some lines. They have a scientific expedition right on the ground. But it's small, and their leader's not one to covet cash or commodities."

Malgorp narrowed his gaze.

"What could possibly be better?"

"Information, allegedly. He's a grizzled, old malcontent with an austere bent. His name's Pomple-phat, and it seems his only passion is information."

"Well," Malgorp said, "that should cut down on costs." He inhaled with a loud snoot. "Offer him something unclassified—anything that can't be twisted into a military gadget."

"He's a social scientist," Gargado said.

"So?"

"He's not interested in technology."

Malgorp flicked his wrist and fleered.

"Then some anecdotal crap from the Imperial Tomes," he said. "Whatever."

"TEX," Gargado said with a slight bow. "His team's been observing Earth for a few local centuries. He describes Humans as a 'study in contradictions.' Something to do with an unhealthy attention to self despite their very social—"

"Gargado," Malgorp said. "Can you rely on this Pomple-phat to help us with the charter?"

Gargado set his digipad on the table and crossed his arms.

"I'm confident," he said, "that we can add significant value with respect to the manipulation of the distinctive cultural and philosophical characteristics of the target civilization."

"Excellent. Say nothing of your Skook contact to Zoggop's team. I want them to think our research skills are so outstanding as to border on the mysterious."

"Your bounty is unsurpassed," Gargado said, bowing his head.

"What about linguistics?" Jelpmittlebong asked.

"Umm, er, yes," Gargado said. "I've delegated that to Skro-Skro-Bleep, who should have no problems with—"

"Malgorp TEX," SkroSkro said, the left head of the two-headed Xenkonian anomaly known as SkroSkro-Bleep. The Siamese entity stood. "There are a few dominant languages, and we can start with them. There's no uniform writing system, so we'll have to analyze each one separately. I'd say a few days to analyze and a couple more to develop the initial programs."

"That's too optimistic," Bleep said.

"What?" SkroSkro said, squaring a dominant glare on his neighbor.

"There are too many dialects and sublanguages, even for a species so geographically scattered."

"What are you talking about?" SkroSkro said. "It's not like there's no interaction between their separate nation states. Look at the specs." The left head turned to Malgorp. "TEX, apologies. We can do it in—"

"You're assuming a highly dispersed vehicular language," Bleep said, scanning their digipad. "I don't see any data supporting that. I'd say at least ten days to master all languages on this planet."

"Would you pull your head out of that abstract ass of yours?" SkroSkro said with a sharp clip.

Bleep looked up from the digipad. "My ass is your—"

"We're not trying to communicate with every subunit of the species." SkroSkro bristled. "We just want to allow the avatar to communicate within the major languages. The trickledown to the more inaccessible populations will happen naturally via local channels."

"There's no need to cut corners. The avatar should be conversant in all vernacular subtleties. Malgorp TEX, I suggest ten days."

"You insufferable pedant." SkroSkro was growling. "We can't program every argotic detail. The avatars are designed to pick up social and linguistic idiosyncrasies as they go. Not read fucking poetry."

53

"Obfuscation," Bleep said, "is the common claim of the simpleminded."

"You asshole!"

Bleep stretched his head as far away as he could from his neighbor to avoid the imminent head-butt.

"You'd think a linguistic expert could think of a more sophisticated retort than that," he said.

"Enough!" Malgorp said. "Just make sure it's full linguistic mastery. I want all corners covered on this one."

Gargado and Jelpmittlebong exchanged glances.

Malgorp slid from his stool and waddled to the glass wall with his foreclaws clasped behind his back, grinding his jaw. He gazed out over the sanctums.

Jelpmittlebong sensed urgency, but nothing about this charter indicated anything extraordinary, except perhaps Qoohx's connection to Lord Swaq. Still, Jelpmittlebong thought, maybe it would be worth designating an elder Hoo'qqai for the job—Chubij, if he could be controlled. But he'd need a big enough incentive. He was always requesting unfettered access to the Labyrinth. Maybe it was time to cut their losses and give him what he wanted, on the condition that he first contribute to a successful charter.

"Maybe," Malgorp said in a tone suggesting sudden inspiration, "we should give them the old patriarch himself."

Jelpmittlebong looked up.

"Chubij?" Gargado said. "I thought after the last time—"

"I know," Malgorp said. "But he's the best."

"If we can control him," Gargado said.

Malgorp snorted. "Obviously the stick doesn't work with him. But perhaps a big enough carrot ..."

"TEX?"

"He's always asking for unfettered access to the Labyrinth. Let's give it to him, on condition that he help out on this charter. Afterward, he can destroy himself in the time-honored way of his species."

"TEX," Gargado said, "is there any particular reason why this charter should be any different from the others?"

Malgorp sighed.

"The client's had some help," he said. "Horder help."

Jelpmittlebong stared wide-eyed.

"The Great Intrepid Horde?" Gargado said.

"Is there any other?" Malgorp said. "Got a transmission from Lord Swaq himself."

Jelpmittlebong gulped.

Chapter 9

Zoggop fo Qoohx—Topmost Executive Xenkonian of Zoggop Recreational Substances Manufacturing Corporation and Lord Swaq's kin—strode into the charter room. The rainbow lace of his magenta sash flapped at his temples. His lateral eyes were gyrating slowly in their sockets. A smattering of alfifi resin was smeared along his nostrils.

Behind him marched four horders. Shiny mucus adorned their heads with the iridescence of an abalone shell. A holographic insignia of Lord Swaq decorated their aasmamyl hide breastplates. They hopped onto their seats and crossed their arms.

Jelpmittlebong eyed them with a furtive glance.

Qoohx's bloodshot dominant eye scurried around the room. He gripped the edge of the table with his lower foreclaws and stood on the tips of his hindclaws.

"I believe," he said, "you've all reviewed these bland specs." He waved a digipad in the air as if it smelled, then dropped it with a thud on the tabletop. "Now for some much-needed color. This," the image of a planetary system materialized in a hologlobe over the center of the table, "is our target."

A three-dimensional image of Earth, with its moon by its side, rotated inside the hologlobe.

"This image is delayed by about seven or eight compressed light days," said a stodgy horder scientist, "but it shows a typical diurnal pattern. The dominant species is a bipedal primate type, mammalian in basic physiology, warm-blooded, and consisting of two sexes."

The horder scientist cleared his throat with a protracted honk.

The room darkened, and the hologlobe took on the impression of a crystal ball with a dull, red glow around its edges. Earth and its moon disappeared, and in their place was the three-dimensional equivalent of a blank screen. From a single point in the center appeared the image of a female Human face, her skin unblemished to the point of robotic.

"The most salient fact," the horder said, standing, "is that nearly all organisms on this planet experience biochemically inspired endogenous circadian oscillation. It's modulated by the diurnal cycle caused by the planet's axial rotation. In the higher animals, this translates into regular periods of rest afforded by a suspension of consciousness and voluntary bodily functions."

As he spoke, the focus in the hologlobe penetrated the woman's face at the crux where nose meets forehead and traversed through the fibrous tissue of her meninges. It proceeded through the dark crevice of her hemispheres into a narrow groove that marked the joining of her thalamic system, and stopped before a tiny cone-shaped pod tucked in a small crimson furrow in her brain.

"Ain't that a mouthful," Qoohx said, with a flutter of his wings. "Now, what our horder friend forgot to say was that in the target species this *suspension of consciousness*"—he mocked the horder's matter-of-fact tone—"is marked with off-the-chart brain activity. From all indications, these ugly creatures spend more than a third of their lives in a biological stupor of phantasmagoric hallucination."

The horder scientist coughed.

"They dream," he said.

"Damn straight they do," Qoohx said. His dominant eye widened. "One of those rare species that sleeps."

The focus accelerated toward the glistening pod and drilled through its structure in successive magnitudes of tininess until finally penetrating a random cell. Molecules drifted in the medium like plankton in a pelagic zone. One of them enlarged in the center of the hologlobe, under which a chemical formula materialized in plump, convex Xenkonian symbols.

$C_{13}H_{16}N_2O_2$.

Melatonin.

The scientist horder pointed at the hologlobe.

"This is the molecule we wish to harvest."

Qoohx's lateral eyes gyrated.

"Narcotics connoisseurs throughout the Empire will stampede over this little glob of atoms," he said.

Malgorp coughed.

"Very impressive, Qoohx," he said. "But, um—"

"It's a hormone," the horder scientist said, "markedly similar to a prototype narcotic Zoggop's been developing called the Mind Whopper. They share the improbable characteristic of corresponding functional-group reactivity mechanisms, although there are some subatomic spin differences that we can't explain."

"The next generation of narcotics," Qoohx said as if announcing a beauty queen.

"We've found it in most of the creatures we've vivisected," the horder said, "from unicellular organisms to the higher animal forms. The output levels vary with the planet's diurnal cycle, which leads us to believe its purpose is related to the regulation of their chronobiological functions. But in the target species—the Humans—it displays more varied and pronounced subatomic spins. We suspect accumulated psychic energy in the quantum fabric of the molecule that carries emotional—"

"So you can't just cultivate a tub of protoplasm," Qoohx said, "if that's what you're thinking."

"The plan is to market it as a natural, sentio-intelligent source from exotic alien beings," the horder said in a civilized timbre.

"We've even thought of identifying batches as being harvested from particular individuals," Qoohx said, "and suggesting flavors of associated mental states. The marketing possibilities are endless."

"But," Malgorp said, "why a charter?"

Qoohx stared at Malgorp, then sighed and flicked a fast foreclaw at the horder.

"The harvesting process will be intrusive," the horder scientist said, punching some buttons.

An emaciated Asiatic black bear popped into the hologlobe, strapped and listless in a soiled cage barely bigger than itself. An opaque tube poked from a festering incision in its abdomen, from which greenish-yellow bile dribbled into a metal basin on the floor. A swarm of flies lifted into the air as a woman reached into the cage and funneled the contents of the basin into a plastic jug. The bear jerked its head against the cage and fell to chewing its paw. The holodemonstration flitted and started again from the beginning.

"We'll need to insert a permanent tap into the gland for regular milking." The horder scientist pointed at the hologlobe with a brawny foreclaw. "A process with which—as you can see—Humans are already familiar."

The bear was chewing its paw again.

"The trick for us is to avoid the type of hostile objection this lowly creature's expressing. We've learned that the quality of glandular output is most effective when the specimen is unagitated and stress-free."

"Blissful," Qoohx said.

"Thus," the horder said, "we dismissed military force and trauma-induced behavioral shift. Mass hypnosis and controlled disease remain credible second options. But since we need them in a constant state of natural bliss, we decided on religious exploitation."

"And also because, well," Qoohx said, "we thought it might be fun." He pursed his lips and slaked his eye across the room. The horders croaked like toads. "It will be fun, won't it?"

"So," Malgorp said, "you want to farm this particular hormone from live Humans on an ongoing basis, and you need them to cooperate as you do it?"

"They have to willingly accept holes in their heads," the horder said. "And a Hoo'qqai charter appears to be the best option for success."

"So, Malgorp TEX," Qoohx said, "can you help?"

Malgorp smiled through curled lips.

"Absolutely," he said.

———————

"Manipulation of an intelligent species' spiritual philosophies," Gargado said in a natural academic brogue, "is a tricky business.

But, I agree with this approach vis-à-vis the target species. Humans have managed some rather insightful technological advances—did you know that they've set foot on their only natural satellite and accomplished nuclear fission? And their theoretical physicists have accurately predicted black holes, dark matter, the big bang, and the multidimensional nature of the physical universe. They also have a solid understanding of biological evolution and genetic transmission."

Qoohx stared.

"But despite all that," Gargado said, "they still linger in the story-bound narrations of their ancient mythologies. As a matter of fact, most of them believe an omnipotent being has written a treatise just for them and is obsessed with their personal fates."

Snickering trickled through the room.

"Frankly, so many of their belief systems eschew reason and scientific scrutiny that it's a wonder the few rational thinkers among them have been able to usher the planet anywhere near technological enlightenment. Even the most powerful nation-states are heavily influenced by faith-based folklore regarding an imaginary deity of one form or another.

"The unavoidable conclusion is that Humans are remarkably susceptible to suggestions from any putatively divine source, and will submit to the most bizarre forms of guidance when faced with something not easily explained.

"Did you know that ardent disciples of some religions are in the habit of exploding their own bodies in order to destroy the bodies of others who belong to a different religious tribe, a practice which the disciple believes will garner lots of amazing prizes in a blissful afterlife? It should be emphasized that this is not conducted as part of a larger warfare strategy in a time of open hostilities, or even in defense to a perceived threat. It's driven entirely by the religion-generated delusions inside the disciple's head.

"In any event, for the stated purpose of this charter, I would posit that it's not too enthusiastic to assume that many Humans would welcome the introduction of artificial cranial tubing if convinced it was commanded by their particular tribal God. If my understanding of their religious philosophies is correct, they'd probably view a hole in the head as a small price to pay for an eternity in paradise.

"The variety of their disparate religions may prove troublesome, but isn't insurmountable. And, frankly, I relish the challenge. Who would've thought that plate tectonics and prehistoric nomadic migrations could result in such a fractionalized state of myths and God fantasies? As you know, most surviving sentio-intelligent species in the galaxy were quick to discard—"

"Ahem," Malgorp said.

Gargado stopped. All dominant eyes were staring back, glazed.

The bile bear banged and gnawed in the hologlobe.

"I'm afraid I've blathered on a bit," Gargado said. "Apologies … TEX … sir—"

"Who would've thought all that?" Qoohx asked with a bawdy smirk. "Aren't they just as gullible as a virgin slink lizard in heat?"

The recruits in the room giggled.

"Umm," Gargado said. "I'm afraid I've never knowingly encountered a slink lizard in heat."

"Professor, you don't know what you're missing," Qoohx said. "But you've certainly done your homework. Please continue."

"Yes, well, um," Gargado said, "anyway, your specs suggest a certain amount of initial groundwork. Can you let us know what steps have been taken thus far?"

"Of course," Qoohx said, clasping his foreclaws before him and straightening his back. "Well, let's see ..." He gazed at the ceiling. "We've drafted a basic foundation message." He smiled. The horders sat like stone.

"What does it say?" Gargado asked.

"It's a beaut," Qoohx said, as if waiting for just that question. "If I do say so myself. Short and pithy. It goes like this, 'Oh, Human! I command thee! A hole in the head!'"

Silence.

"That's it?" Gargado asked.

"That's obtuse," SkroSkro-Bleep said from both heads.

"Can you work with it?" Malgorp asked.

Gargado nodded.

"Needs some tailoring ... But it's a start, Malgorp TEX, sir."

"Thank you," Qoohx said, taking his dominant eye off the two-headed Xenkonian.

"Due to the fractionalized nature of their religions, the message will have to persuasively foretell their unification," Gargado said. "That's the critical first step. And we also have to make sure it's time-displaced, so it's interpreted as originating within a certain geological timeframe, otherwise it may be misconstrued as—"

"Okay," Malgorp said in his patented abrupt tone. "We have a little work to do." He turned to Qoohx. "Qoohx TEX, I've arranged a tour of the sanctum for your charter."

Qoohx bowed.

"Gargado, show Qoohx's team around and make them feel welcome."

The horders grunted.

Malgorp and Qoohx departed shoulder to shoulder.

Gargado smiled at the horders.

"Come on, I'll show you how we make an avatar vehicle."

He motioned for them to join him, and they walked single file in his direction.

"First," he said, leading them out the door, "we send a gelatinized mass of aasmamyl offal to the target world—already embedded with the bionic nano-lattice, of course. Then we activate and monitor it using wormhole scanning."

"Fascinating," the horder scientist said.

As they marched past Jelpmittlebong, the last horder stopped.

"What're you looking at, fuckwad?"

Jelpmittlebong stared. "Excuse me?"

The horder jutted a stiff chin.

"You're one stupid, blog-ranting dipshit," he said, then plodded out the door.

Chapter 10

A gamut of channels vibrated through Chubij's network as he bobbed in the shimmering methane of sanctum twelve. A few channels were projecting the mental imagery of faraway beings. Some were cohesive, but most quickly broke into degraded incoherence.

His instinctive reaction was to open up to the more coherent impressions and respond to the extent he could with a benign message of emotional identification. But he needed to keep himself ready for the channel from Earth. So he watched and listened as a remote observer.

Through the cascade of voices and images a faint but familiar burst of hoots emanated like scattered shouts in the wind.

"... you must ... Sphere by now ... I know ... can't respond, but if ... hear me ... tapped in and acting as conduit ... Horde aggression increasing ... Lord Swaq seems determined ..."

All channels suddenly went silent. For an instant Ulluoi's voice boomed through clear as light.

"… still very bored. Perhaps it's my destiny to remain inoperative. But don't fret about me, my patriarch. I'll be fine. I'm praying for your protection and safe return. Just think, soon you'll be able to give yourself up to our beloved Labyrinth. How glorious, my patriarch, to pass in such honor. I'm so happy for you. Let's just hope the Xenkonians keep their promise. This Earth charter seems ordinary on the surface, but I sense pitfalls given the Horde's involvement. I'll try to maintain an independent channel—"

The hoot sequence gave way to a stumpy electronic voice.

"Hoo'qqai Chubij," it crackled. "Prepare for dimensional shift passage."

───────────

Chubij's mind gushed into the multidimensional galactic mesh like dust in a vacuum. It plopped light-years away into a chunk of gelatinized aasmamyl offal in the Three Sisters Wilderness of Oregon that, against astronomical odds, contained Zawt's head.

A faint, phosphorescent sheen glistened across the surface of the jiggling pile of guts as it steadily transformed into the corporeal facsimile of a nude Human male.

───────────

After an hour of lying motionless, the vehicle began heaving in shallow, rapid gasps, then sprang from the forest floor. Pine needles and cones scattered. It landed on the balls of its feet in an ungainly squat, its knuckles squared into the topsoil.

"Do ya think it's supposed to do that?" said one of the recruits on visual monitor duty, stretching his neck for a closer look at the hologlobe.

His companion joggled his head but kept his eye on his digimag. "Do what?" he said.

The first recruit gripped the base of the hologlobe with his foreclaws. "Is that normal?"

"Hell if I know," his companion said, putting down his digimag. "Gargado said it'd be out for hours."

The vehicle wobbled, then shifted into a more stable kneeling position. It raised an arm to block the intermittent sunshine and darted wide-eyed looks at the branches overhead.

"Maybe we should call Gargado."

"Relax, will ya? We can't be callin' him over every little thing. He'll think we don't know what we're doing."

"But we don't know what we're doing."

"Yeah, but he don't need to be reminded of it. Let's just watch and see what happens."

The vehicle twisted its face skyward and began rocking its head back and forth. It smiled and began tweeting and chirping toward the branches, occasionally stopping to nod or close its eyes.

"What's it doin'?" the first recruit asked.

"Got me. What's the specs say?"

The second recruit whipped out his digipad and began flipping through holopages.

"What the hell's it doing now?" the first recruit said.

The vehicle was standing and flapping its arms toward the treetops.

"That definitely ain't normal—"

The vehicle sucked in a deep breath, then tilted forward, stretching its leg in a rubbery stride. Its other leg followed, and it was soon zooming through the forest in an abandoned zigzag that culminated in a face-first collision with one of the trees. It crumpled into the shadows of a verdant bed of ferns.

"Holy shit!" the recruits said in unison, their dominant eyes distended and glued to the hologlobe.

The first recruit leaped from his stool.

"I'm gonna get Gargado."

Chapter 11

A hooded individual stood in Jelpmittlebong's doorway, his face shrouded in darkness. A faint neon glow shimmered through the narrow slit of a black cape that flowed to the floor. The stranger closed the gap with an unhurried tweak of the cloth. A soft flurry of condensed water vapor seeped from under the hood.

Jelpmittlebong eyed the stranger with a lift of his chin. He seldom received visitors, but when he did it was at least someone with whom he was acquainted. He was just about to inquire as to the stranger's purpose when his tongue went numb and his mind blank.

Inside his head a voice said, *"Greetings, my student."*

Jelpmittlebong leaned toward the figure.

The stranger peeled back his hood. An ashen and pale face revealed itself. The dominant eye that stared back was ovoid and pinkish.

"Overseer?" Jelpmittlebong said.

"Fumb fo Jelpmittlebong," said Pwond fo Niukah with a gentle nod. He extended two bony foreclaws through his cape and let down the hood, exposing a blotched crown and taut facial skin.

Jelpmittlebong blinked.

Niukah chortled from his gut. "Not even a failed head regeneration could turn out such intricate disfigurement," he said. His eye pulsed with a purposeful verve. "May I come in?" He slipped inside, and the door latched softly behind him.

A shadow settled over Jelpmittlebong's face. "Is it really you?" he asked.

"I simply zapped some melanocytes to create the blemishes," Niukah said. "The scabs weren't much fun, but do you like it? The rest I entrusted to the steady scalpel of an old quack I know in Toq." His cheeks sported sharp creases that reminded Jelpmittlebong of pleats. "What do you think?"

"Scary comes to mind."

"Ha!" Niukah said, gliding to the glass wall that overlooked the Sphere's equilibrium plateau. "I think I look rather charming." Gleams of lapis flushed across his face. His breath seeped from his lips like dry ice.

"If deception is your purpose," Jelpmittlebong said, stepping beside him, "you have achieved it. But why?"

"Ever the master of understatement, my student." Niukah tugged the cape around his shoulders. "And you still like it cold." He tilted his head and looked out over the sanctums. "My purpose was camouflage—and to a certain extent, an attempt at fashion." He flashed a mischievous grin.

"But surgical transformation is peculiar—"

"Life itself is peculiar, my student."

Jelpmittlebong inhaled deeply and clasped his foreclaws across his spine. His thoughts churned in an attempt to fathom the sudden presence of his overseer. Niukah seldom did anything without a purpose, but Jelpmittlebong discerned no recent circumstances in his life that would warrant an unannounced appearance, except—of course!—the voices. But before he could ponder further, distant memories surfaced and brought with them gentle waves of nostalgia. He looked at Niukah and felt the same electricity he always felt when in his overseer's proximity.

Niukah's dominant eye tracked the green vapor from a distant Hoo'qqai lifting into the darkness of the sanctuary's ceiling, then back down to the absorbed Hoo'qqai from whence it rose.

"Amazing creatures," he said. "To think, interspecies telepathy ..."

Jelpmittlebong followed his gaze. "Their channeling ability is extraordinary," he said. "And they've done much to create a peaceful galactic community."

"Yet Eeftwat exploits them."

Jelpmittlebong looked down. "It's difficult to reconcile, I admit. But I felt drawn to them."

Niukah remained silent.

"Overseer," Jelpmittlebong said, looking up, "are my lessons unfinished?"

"Lessons are never finished."

"But why are you here?"

"To help you make sense of the voices in your head."

Jelpmittlebong smiled. "That's what you said when you arranged my internship at the insane asylum."

"Yes, and the principle still holds."

"But they're largely incoherent, just as then."

"That will soon change. Your telepathic puberty has begun."

"But I—"

Niukah let his cape slip from his shoulders. The faint neon glow revealed itself to be a Lord Swaq chest insignia worn by rank-and-file horders.

"I arrived here aboard Swaq's frigate," he said.

Jelpmittlebong's dominant eye swelled. "Swaq's frigate?"

"Yes." Niukah traced a foreclaw across the glowing profile on his chest. "There are holes in his security—if you're crafty."

Jelpmittlebong gulped as he recalled his recent conversation with the horder on Qoohx's team. Had he indeed ranted against the Horde once too often? Surely Swaq hadn't come to the Sphere because of him ...

With his next breath an incongruent calmness climbed from his gut, circled his throat, and entered his mind, followed by an image of the Horde's destruction of the Qanjivians' home planet. He closed his eye and felt a surge of indignation.

"There are many in the galaxy who share that sentiment," Niukah's voice said. *"But only* we *can do something about it."*

"What can we do?"

"First things first. You're on the brink of telepathic puberty, but it needs kick-starting, I'm afraid. Are you willing to let me help you?"

Jelpmittlebong opened his eye and straightened up.

"Of course, my Overseer," he said. "When shall we start?"

"We just did," echoed Niukah's voice in his mind.

Jelpmittlebong stepped away from the glass and scanned the room, but his overseer was not to be seen. He'd taken a step toward the adjoining room when there was a rap on the door.

Another visitor! This was surely a record.

"Lordy?" a crabby voice said from the other side. "You in there?"

"8-1-21?" Jelpmittlebong unlatched the door, and the mipoon hurried in. "How'd you find me?"

"Mipoons know where everybody is in this big ball. It's our job." 8-1-21 took Jelpmittlebong by the shoulders. "Lordy, listen! Lord Swaq's here, in the Sphere. There's horders spillin' from the landin' bay. Ya better watch—" He stopped as his dominant eye

Chapter 13

The charter team sat around a conference table in the charter room for sanctum twelve.

Malgorp thwacked the tabletop with a clenched foreclaw and said, "If this is Chubij trying to sabotage another charter, so help me ..."

Gargado ran a foreclaw across his chin. "Never can tell with him, but his own puzzlement seems genuine."

"A seer mind?" Malgorp asked.

"It would be extraordinary for a natural seer mind to go undetected. And I don't think Humans have the requisite neural wiring."

"Could it be one of those hairy tree cloakers?"

"A Skook?"

"Whatever they're called."

"I doubt it," Gargado said. "There aren't that many of them on Earth, and they seem otherwise unremarkable. But if a seer mind's really causing this, it must be one hell of a mind to conceal itself so thoroughly."

"Shit!" Malgorp said. "Of all the charters."

"TEX," Gargado said. "I suggest we concentrate on other aspects of the charter. If this vehicle proves unsalvageable—and I admit it would be an unprecedented step—there's nothing inherently amiss in sending another Hoo'qqai to the same target world."

"Let's not give up just yet," Malgorp said. "What parts of this charter have yet to be activated?"

"Well, for example, the foundation message has yet to be sent," Gargado said.

His recruits looked at each other, bug-eyed.

"We've determined that a backdated placement in strategic places on the planet would be the most effective. As soon as you approve the content, we could go ahead and disseminate it."

The recruits fidgeted on their stools.

Malgorp chuckled. "You've never sought my approval before."

"I thought, given the unprecedented circumstances, you'd want to be in the loop, so to speak."

"Yes, yes," Malgorp said. "Can I see a draft?"

One of the recruits jabbed the other in the ribs, causing Gargado's lateral eyes to narrow in their direction.

"Of course," Gargado said, handing a digipad to Malgorp.

The TEX read out loud:

> *All big gods will unite (and the lesser godheads too)*
> *under the blessed hand of a multilingual beacon!*
> *The chosen Humans will find paradise*
> *through his merciful and most wise counseling!*
> *Glory is yours (for a slight hole in the head)!*
> $E=mc^2$*!*

"Catchy," Malgorp said. "But may I suggest deleting the parentheticals? They seem, well, rather extraneous."

The other recruit poked his companion in the cheek.

Gargado raised a foreclaw.

"TEX, your point is well taken. By way of background, the 'hole in the head' statement is a retention from the draft Qoohx brought us. We wanted—"

"Delete it," Malgorp said. "It's stupid."

"Yes, TEX," Gargado said. "The other parenthetical is a reference to the numerous secondary deities prevalent throughout their religions. This is my proposal for how to deal with the—"

"Delete. As a matter of fact, delete all the punctuation. It just makes it look cluttered."

"But—"

"What's this last bit?" Malgorp asked, pointing to the $E=mc^2$ formula.

"That's the equation Humans use to designate the concept that any mass has an associated energy, and vice versa. They've only recently discovered that the equivalence of mass and energy is a general principle in the physical four-dimensional universe and a basic consequence of the symmetries of space and time."

"Why's it so short?" asked SkroSkro and Bleep.

Gargado coughed.

"Not sure, really," he said. "Probably because ours delineates all the possible energy forms that make up natural phenomena." He was squinting. "Ours also anticipates certain standard frames of reference. This is actually a cleaner version." He flipped a foreclaw at the digipad. "More general, but less complicated. That's my guess."

"Thank you," chimed SkroSkro-Bleep with a tandem nod.

"In any event," Gargado continued, "this little expression has a special place in the imaginations of most modern Humans. But ancient Humans would have had no inkling of it, which is why we're confident it will be interpreted by modern Humans as having come from a higher intelligence. If they remain true to their cultural history, they'll attribute its presence in an otherwise prehistoric message to the divine guidance of their tribal Gods."

"The hook?" Malgorp said.

"The hook," Gargado said.

"Well done. Make the changes and send her off. At least something on this charter is going smoothly."

As soon as Malgorp was out the door, Gargado twirled toward his recruits.

"What the hell's up with you two?" he said.

The recruits exchanged glances.

The first one said to the second one, "You tell him."

"No, you tell him. It was your idea."

"Bullshit! You're the one who—"

"Enough!" Gargado said. "You," he said to the recruit closest to him. "What's going on? Now!"

"Team leader, sir," the recruit said. "We ... um ... we ... I mean ..."

"What?"

The recruit pointed an implacable foreclaw at his companion.

"He already sent the message."

Chapter 14

In a sweltering coastal town on the island of Borneo—approximately two hours from the archaeologically significant Niah Caves—a man with bushy, white hair and a walrus mustache staggered into his hotel room. In his hands were a custom-made Deering Banjosaurus and a brown bottle of cloudy rice wine.

Professor Elgin P. Tilford nudged the door shut with his boot and plunked into the musty cushion of the room's only chair. A plume of dust billowed over the bamboo coffee table and the photographs spread across its surface.

With one blithe motion of his arm, the banjo lay across his lap, and he was wiping the perspiration from his brow with the sleeve of his multihued cowboy shirt. Patches of sweat issued from his armpits in dark, flaring circles.

Above him in the dinner hall of the flimsy wooden structure, a noisy team of Nippon Oil geologists, finishing up a two-week exploratory sojourn of natural gas fields in northern Sarawak, continued carousing without him. Their laughter and off-key karaoke penetrated the ceiling as if it were made of papier-mâché.

Professor Tilford smiled and poured himself another cupful of local brew. His cheeks flushed red, and his gin-blossomed nose warbled as the alcohol scorched his throat.

"Ahh!" he said, slamming the plastic cup on the coffee table. "This tuak'll burn ya a hide of steel," he hollered up at his new friends on the other side of the ceiling. "Who says the Ibans have stopped headhunting?"

Without understanding a lick of the esoteric choice of words, but appreciating the emotional gist with which they were uttered, the geologists replied through the ceiling with guffaws and broken English.

"*Sensei*!" they shouted. "Another song pu-reez."

"Ain't y'all got an off switch?" Professor Tilford shouted back. "Ever heard of sleep?"

"Maybe," said a voice filtering through the laughter, "something for our sleeping."

Professor Tilford ran his fingers over his whiskers and pursed his lips, as he pondered through his repertoire for an apt sleep-inducing melody. An impish grin spread across his face.

"Okay," he finally said. "Got just the lullaby for you wannabe cowboys."

He saddled the pot of his banjo under his arm, and slid his palm into the smooth, worn spot on the back of its blond maple neck. With the sudden aplomb of a veteran high-wire artist, he straightened his spine, shook off his sottishness, and leaped into a bluegrass-inspired version of Japan's national anthem. "*Kimigayo*" had never been rendered quite so evocatively, its haunting gaps interspersed with the clear trills of a musical genre from the foggy mountains of a far-off land.

Prophet Wacko

Stillness hovered in the air as the last notes waned like the resonations of a temple gong, causing the professor to think that perhaps he'd succeeded in charming his audience to sleep. But then the geologists whooped and pounded the floor.

"*Sensei!*" they called. "*Sugoi-naaah!*"

The ceiling began to wobble as if they'd fallen to sumo wrestling. Professor Tilford laughed, then poured himself another drink.

"Goodnight, y'all," he said as he leaned the banjo against the wall.

He sat feeling his whiskers and pouring an occasional drink, as the commotion upstairs subsided. The last ten days had been a blur of planes, buses, jeeps, and trekking that had taken him far from the American Midwest into the tropical rain forests of Sarawak.

He looked at the single bed across from him. It smelt as if it had never seen the light of day. But right now it was as inviting as the great bed at Versailles.

He sighed. Despite his fatigue, the diligent scholar in him would not let the article he had to write wait any longer.

The ancient cave writing was brought to his attention by an archaeologist friend from the University of Sydney. He'd immediately recognized the absurdity of such a discovery, assuming both the translation and the radiocarbon dating results were accurate—his friend assured him they were.

It also appeared to be similar in content to a recently discovered Nez Perce cliff drawing in the Snake River Canyon that someone had, unfortunately, vandalized with a large swastika before it could be deciphered by archaeologists. The implications being too tantalizing to ignore, he finagled a trip across the globe, as he was wont to do, bequeathing the rest of that term's teaching schedule to a trusty grad student.

He began organizing the photographs on the table. Next to the photos he placed a notepad that had the original ancient Malay above the modern English. He reread the message, then picked up his banjo and fingered the fret board in dampened scale progressions as he thought.

From out of the glaring religious overtones of the message, two lines in particular garnered the majority of his focus. Because of the immense time displacement that it implied, the last line of the message was the more unsettling.

That line was "$E=mc^2$."

It was also the same in both languages, which in and of itself was no small feat, considering that no known stretch of world history placed a native from ancient Borneo in contact with the Western alphabet twelve hundred years ago.

The other line—in parentheses—left Professor Tilford scratching his head. He was almost inclined to dismiss it as the juvenile graffiti of a mischievous prehistoric Malay teenager, but for the sinister insinuation in the otherwise inspirational context.

That line read "(for a slight hole in the head)."

It was eleven p.m. local time when he started typing his article. Hours later he stowed the substantially finished product on a USB drive.

When he allowed himself the clammy comfort of the old, rickety bed, the cocks of Sarawak were crowing.

———————

Eighteen hours later, from a rental Internet cubicle in Changi International Airport, Singapore, the professor hastily uploaded the new article on his website, www.nirvana-thru-bluegrass.com. He entitled it "Is God an Alien?"

Prophet Wacko

He closed the website on his laptop, then opened it on the rental computer to confirm the article was properly uploaded. Satisfied, he picked up his gear and headed toward his gate, not bothering to close the website.

———

Arabella was a regular visitor to *Nirvana Thru Bluegrass*, and an occasional contributor to the professor's blog posts. She found his articles refreshing and original, and a treasure trove of obscure folklorish information.

Despite his hillbilly façade—his childhood years were spent as Pickin' Elgin, a banjo prodigy who regularly appeared at the Grand Ole Opry and other celebrated country music venues— Professor Tilford was a well-respected scholar of comparative religions and tenured professor at Indiana University.

It seemed he published something every few weeks or so, with amusing titles such as "Religious Adultery: Worshipping in Two Faiths," "Pope Spelled Backward Is E-Pop," "Now, Where Did I Put My Soul?" "God, There's an Atheist in My Soup," etc.

Arabella read every one.

She was the second person to come across "Is God an Alien?" The first was a bemused businessman from Mumbai who sat at the same computer at Changi International Airport that Professor Tilford had used. Whereas the Indian man's reaction was to scoff and quickly navigate to the live cricket scores, Arabella snickered.

In an oversized walk-in closet in her bedroom that doubled as her study, she clicked on the title and began reading about the ancient cave writing that referenced Albert Einstein's $E=mc^2$ equation.

91

The crux of the article was that, while Einstein first proposed his theory in 1905, radiocarbon dating indicated that the ochre scribble on the cave wall was nearly twelve hundred years old.

Professor Tilford offered some plausible reasons for the discrepancy, such as sample contamination or faulty laboratory techniques, then concluded with some preposterous—and extraterrestrial—speculations, all assuming the radiocarbon dating was accurate.

When she finished, Arabella looked past the closet door and into the darkness of her bedroom. Light from a full moon spilled through the shadows of an old oak tree outside the window, casting a silver puddle across the hardwood floor.

She nibbled on the inside of her cheek and wondered.

A few minutes later she commented "Wow!" on Professor Tilford's ongoing blog post, and logged off.

Chapter 15

Niukah sat on the floor in Jelpmittlebong's quarters, next to a smoldering vapor bong. Jelpmittlebong sat across from him.

"Do you remember the games we used to play in the jungle when you first came to Toq?" Niukah asked.

Jelpmittlebong smiled.

"'Cover eyes, where is it?'" he said. "Of course." He drifted back to the Great Maze-Jungle on Hurm IV. They'd bring him to the jungle at dawn, when the heat was not so unbearable, drape a cover over his head, and ask him questions about things in the surrounding rain forest.

"Where's the toy dune hopper now?"

"Which way is Overseer Twip pointing?"

"In which direction is the nearest mloshfruit vine system?"

And so on. It was one of his favorite pastimes while in Toq.

"You were quite good," Niukah said, "even as a hatchling. That's how we assessed your telepathic faculties." He picked up

93

the bong and rubbed his foreclaws over the protruding orifice of its carburetion ports. "You were exceptional."

"I don't feel exceptional."

"Yes, well, as I've told you before, the natural development of telepathic ability—for those predisposed to it—includes an interim latent period. Hatchlings can read minds to varying degrees. But for some reason, the ability only resurfaces in a handful of adults. You're just coming back into it, but, unfortunately, we don't have the luxury of waiting for it to develop on its own." Niukah straightened his spine. "We must coax it along."

"I don't understand."

"My student, there's a threat to the social stability of the galaxy, and you, of all beings, are best placed to counter it."

"Me?"

Niukah moved the bong's mouthpiece to his lips. "Do you remember, from your history lessons, the origins of the Empire in its current form?"

"The Empire in its current form was established fourteen thousand and twelve seasons ago," Jelpmittlebong said, as if conjuring up a flashcard from his rote memory, "by a small band of astute Xenkonians who united the various factions striving for power at the time. They achieved social stability by influencing the probability restraints through strategic manipulation of the leaders of the day."

Niukah rippled the surrounding haze with a shake of his head, his pink dominant pupil cutting through like a fog light. He flapped into a low hover and poked his face into the space between them.

"Where do the mutes come in?"

Jelpmittlebong narrowed his dominant eye. "Mute monks?"

Niukah nodded.

"Umm ... I thought they were just crazy—"

Prophet Wacko

"Crazy is relative." Niukah alit back to his spot on the floor, and cleared his throat with a cough that released a thin flurry of vapor. "This is a favorite mute maxim, but I'm sure you've already deduced its underlying logic, or will, once you get around to looking hard enough."

Jelpmittlebong crossed his foreimbs and frowned.

"Fumb fo Jelpmittlebong, I'm going to say it straight. You are projected to become a mute monk of unprecedented ability and rank."

Jelpmittlebong stared. "Come again?"

"The voices in your head," Niukah said, sucking on the bong, "are the thoughts of others." Vapor twirled from his mouth as he toked. "They enter through what experienced tellies call the mind portals—usually one-way. Many tellies of lesser fortitude succumb to the cacophony, unable to filter them out or live with the constant mental intrusions—auditory hallucinations, as you say. You no doubt met some in the insane asylum. But there are a handful who, with practice and resolve, are able to not only master the broader Xenkonian collective consciousness—which is in essence what it is—but also even traverse the other way, probing others' minds and projecting thoughts into theirs."

Jelpmittlebong rubbed his chin.

"So," he said, "you're a member of a powerful, clandestine group of tellies of which I'm destined to join—after I snuff Swaq?"

"Something like that." Niukah rested his foreclaws in his lap. "My student," he said, his dominant eye narrowing, "the Horde's a dangerous force. It needs careful handling. It can't be disbanded. Practically, that would be impossible. Besides, it serves an important stabilizing function, under normal circumstances. But under Swaq, it's become recklessly unpredictable and aggressive."

Niukah sighed and set his bong on the floor.

95

"Indeed," he continued, "Swaq's disrupting the very social fabric of the galaxy. Already the probability restraints predict a seventy-seven percent likelihood that he will rule the galaxy within six seasons, resulting in a long reign of tyranny. Basic rights are being shredded like a hatchling in a morinurk's maw."

Jelpmittlebong frowned. He knew Niukah was right. It wouldn't take a supertellie to see the swath of Swaq's destruction.

"But am I really the best option? I mean—"

"Yes." Niukah smiled. "I think so. A mute Lord of the Horde would present certain advantages, not least of which would be a constant check on the Horde's aggressive tendencies, which Swaq has exploited so brilliantly."

"But—"

The door burst open.

8-1-21 hurried in.

"Voilà!" he said, holding up a translucent satchel of whitish liquid. "Got ahold of some good stuff—the organic variety from them ugly two-legged critters." He tossed the satchel to Niukah. "That there's guaranteed from a blissful specimen—some floozy abducted in the middle of a sex ritual."

"Ha!" Niukah said. "That would do it."

8-1-21 laughed. "Don't think she's so blissful anymore."

Niukah held the satchel up and squinted at it.

"What's so special about that stuff, anyway?" 8-1-21 asked, taking a seat on the floor. "The junkies tell me it can be a major trip, but don't seem like no military secret to me."

"Military's in the eye of the beholder," Niukah said. "But this pearly substance represents a shortcut to the mind portals. I have no idea how."

"Ya tellin' me Swaq's a tellie runnin' amok, and that stuff's the reason?"

"Well, it's more multifaceted than that, but yes."

"Now that's a big, meaningless word," 8-1-21 said, curling his nose. "*Multifaceted.*"

"You've just stated the obvious, mipoon. There's hope for you yet."

"Overseer," Jelpmittlebong said, "what drives Swaq to conquer?"

"He's just a mean bastard," 8-1-21 said, waggling his head. "I heard he's a mutant."

"An aggressive mutant," Niukah said. "Swaq was an abandoned brood who spent his childhood in the Yonkoo Forest. He went unnoticed by us, but obviously had natural telepathic abilities. Legend has it a lunatic mute monk guided him through the portals—and by *lunatic* I mean a monk impervious to the need for psychological balance. Swaq was never taught to balance his aggressive nature." Niukah turned to Jelpmittlebong. "But it doesn't matter now how he came to be what he is. He must be stopped."

An unwelcome image of Swaq tearing off his head suddenly flashed into Jelpmittlebong's mind. He shook his head in an attempt to force the image out. It slowly vanished from his thoughts.

"I thought so," Niukah said.

"Thought what, Overseer?"

"If you can push out an image like that, you can handle a mind probe. But we'll need to be a little less conspicuous about it. Swaq mustn't know you're deceiving him."

"A mind probe?"

"Yes. Chances are he won't attempt it in the company of others, as I understand he's not perfected it, and he prefers minimum distractions."

"But when—"

Just then Jelpmittlebong's wrist monitor began to vibrate. He picked himself off the floor and tapped his monitor.

"Jelp, where the hell are you?" Malgorp was teething on mloshfruit rinds and spraying pulp, not bothering to make eye contact through the holoscreen. "The Earth avatar's acting up. I've had to call in biological systems. Must I do everything?"

"Sorry, TEX, I—"

Malgorp cut the transmission.

"You'd better go, my student," Niukah said.

8-1-21 threw up his arms. "We're sittin' here talkin' about how he's gotta save the galaxy, and now you're tellin' him to go kiss that fat bastard's ass?"

Niukah smiled.

"He needs to keep up pretenses—for a bit, anyway. Besides, mipoon, you and I have work to do."

Chapter 16

Zawt frolicked through the night, soaking in his new surroundings. His peculiar ability to mimic the cries of the forest's nocturnal animals inspired more than a few self-congratulatory touchdown signals. Daybreak—and the sun's dissipation of the surrounding shadows—incited further escapade. But the avatar vehicle didn't seem to share Zawt's eagerness. It collapsed at the foot of an old ponderosa pine and settled into an autonomous biological rhythm that completely disengaged him from the external environment.

Bemused, Zawt scanned the charter notes. Sleep, he learned, was a regular Human attribute, necessary for the processing of memories and the proper maintenance of the immune system. As he settled into a meditative state to wait out the imposed physical inactivity, a violent flow of thoughts and images gushed from a dark crevice of the vehicle's brain and swept him into the bewildering, psychedelic world of dreams.

Meditation had never come so easily.

———

Hours later, Chubij couldn't remember how the vehicle came to be trekking along a mountain path, but he felt alive as he sucked in a mouthful of the balmy, sun-baked air.

He looked up and down the path. Both ends trailed into a similar maze of old-growth forest. For no particular reason that he could discern, he picked one and ambled off in lanky strides. He was soon tacking at a brisk pace.

As he huffed over the undulating terrain, he became aware of a slight, unbalanced impression in his brain, as if a large weight were leaning against the opposite side of a thin wall that he himself was also using for support. He waggled his head, as if trying to remove water from his ears, but the sensation persisted.

"You're a tricky seer mind," he said. "Perhaps you'd like to show yourself."

Zawt sat atop Chubij's mind like a ghost rider on his mount, expending little energy so as to fully take in the details of their new surroundings.

"If you say your mind is still uneasy, my lovely," he said, "that is up to you."

Chubij discerned only a soft mental waft of air.

———

They heard them long before they saw them. Chubij slithered the vehicle up the path and caught a glimpse of their backsides and the muddy soles of their hiking boots as they trekked. The pre-programmed cultural database identified them as Caucasoid, thirty-five to forty years old, female.

Chubij and Zawt eavesdropped on their banter. The autonomous functions of the vehicle zoned in on the local inflections, downloading and incorporating them into its neural lexicon catalog.

Light-years away, employees of Eeftwat Avatars stared at their holoscreens.

———————

"No! ... Did she really?"

"Yes!"

"Sassy bitch!"

"I'll say ..."

"What did Sylvia do?"

"It was hilarious. She called her a *conniving little cunt.*"

"Oh my God. No!"

"Oh shit!"

"What?"

"Did we lock the car?"

"I don't know. You drove—"

Neither Chubij nor Zawt could extrapolate the context of the discussion from the massive amount of linguistic and cultural data stored in the vehicle's network. SkroSkro-Bleep was hard at work dissecting the input and refining the preprogrammed linguistic conjecture parameters.

———————

The hikers came to a large Douglas fir that had fallen across the trail, its upper branches bent against the trunks of trees on the other side, so that it spanned a meter or so above the trail floor. They clambered up and sat straddling the log, facing each other.

One of the hikers drew a pipe from her backpack and began stuffing it with the leafy contents of a plastic bag she'd unrolled. They were soon alternating tokes of a sticky bud of Hawaiian Haze.

Chubij snuggled the vehicle against a large stone in the cover of trailside ferns some twenty meters away. He was watching from the shade of the undergrowth as the hikers chatted and passed the pipe, when he suddenly felt woozy, then faded into unconsciousness. This coincided with the avatar's face smacking against the stone, opening up a sizeable gash.

Seconds later, the buck-naked avatar leaped from the fronds like a gazelle and galloped up the trail. He waved his arms in a crisscrossing pattern above his head as if trying to flag down a lorry. Blood trickled down the bridge of his nose.

"Yoni, yoni, yoni," Zawt said in greeting.

The stoned couple stared.

Zawt stretched his arms and shouted a phrase from the avatar lexicon database in the vehicle's neural network.

"Crucify him!"

The couple sat motionless on the downed Douglas fir.

Zawt stopped about four meters away, and beamed a hearty smile. He was waving his hands like a schoolgirl at a parade.

The couple's silence did not match any of the anticipated responses in the vehicle's database—unless they were dead or sleeping, neither of which seemed applicable—and their behavior was registered for future reference. The database then suggested something designated as very meaningful in its extensive greeting catalog.

"Thou shalt not kill!" Zawt said, lifting his upturned palms toward the sky. He stretched his red eyes wide in a gesture of friendship—as any well-mannered Xenkonian would do in like circumstances.

The couple rocketed down the mountain and alerted the nearest ranger station of a naked maniac harassing hikers on the French Pete Creek Trail.

———————

Rummaging through the hikers' abandoned backpacks, Zawt found a pair of sweatpants that squeezed the vehicle's calves just below the knees. A short, baggy T-shirt drooped over his torso to just above his navel. He also found a butane lighter, a dog-eared book of day hikes in the Three Sisters Country, some homemade granola, an apple, a flashlight, a compass, a water canteen, some marijuana paraphernalia, sunglasses, a crinkled tube of petroleum jelly, and a large dildo with the words *Anus Hercules* embossed along its ergonomic rubber grip.

Zawt stuffed all the items into one backpack and sauntered down the trail. He was mimicking the whistles of the warblers in the trees.

Chapter 17

Jelpmittlebong hastened to the charter room for sanctum twelve. He found Malgorp and the charter team huddled around a hologlobe, watching the avatar vehicle wandering through the woods.

He'd circled around to the opposite side of the hologlobe when the door crashed open. All dominant eyes turned.

"Lord Swaq," Malgorp said with a gulp, "we weren't expecting—"

In three powerful strides, Swaq stood over the TEX, nostrils flaring. He gripped the flaccid skin of Malgorp's crown and yanked him off the ground.

"You," he said, "are fat and stupid."

"I ... er—"

Swaq ripped Malgorp's head from his shoulders and flung it into the corner. He turned toward the table. An entourage of horders fanned out behind him.

"What a bunch of fucking idiots," Swaq said, folding his forelimbs over his chest. "You!" He pointed at Jelpmittlebong. "Front and center."

Jelpmittlebong raised his chin. His dominant eye widened and settled into a shimmering pool of dread. He shuffled toward the Lord of the Horde, the thought of his own severed head hitting the floor dictating his gait. He stopped an arm's length away. They were eye to eye. Jelpmittlebong extended his spine, prepared to meet his fate with at least a sense of decorum.

"For a blog-ranting marketing fuck, you got balls." Swaq flashed a crocodile grin. "I'm making you the new Topmost Executive Xenkonian of Eeftwat Avatars." He turned and threw an errant foreclaw toward the conference table. "I expect all of you fuckers to show Fumb fo Jelpmittlebong the proper respect. Anybody don't like it, talk to me."

No one stirred.

"You," Swaq said, pointing at Gargado, "what's the present status of this Earth charter?"

Gargado stood, clamping his foreclaws to the table to steady himself. "Umm, well … the, um …" He stared as if Swaq were a charging morinurk. "The channeling Hoo'qqai has only been reachable intermittently. There's been some limited contact with the target species that didn't go well … It, I mean the avatar vehicle, acted outside of parameters. We're, uh … troubleshooting …" Gargado coughed and ran a shaky foreclaw across his chin. "And I'm afraid the foundation message was sent prematurely, which is unfortunate—"

"You stupid fuckers." Swaq glared. "This charter's barely off the ground, and you've already fucked it to its knees."

"But, your highness, if I can—"

"Shut up," Swaq said. "Here's what we're going to do." He

raked his dominant eye over the room. "Eliminate the current vehicle and send a new Hoo'qqai."

Silence.

"All clear?"

Silence.

"All right then. Hologlobe."

A miniature Earth appeared over the holobasin in the middle of the table.

"The current avatar vehicle's here," he said. A red prick of light began blinking in the northwest part of North America. "Adrift in a mountainous forest with no foreseeable way to reset its bearing. Why the hell it was placed in such a remote area is beyond me." He threw a sharp glance at Gargado. "But we'll not get mired in the assumptions that went into that questionable tactic."

Gargado's lips turned ivory.

"The more sensible location would have been here," Swaq continued. Another red prick of light began blinking in northeast Asia. "I understand the nation-state known as China will be the most dominant social force on Earth in the near future."

"Um … We also scrutinized that probability," Gargado said. "But our poli-sci statistical analysis concluded that the Chinese have a propensity for snuffing social movements with excessive force—"

"Damned smart policy," Swaq said. "Remind me to study their system later. Now, our tactic's twofold. We send a new vehicle to this China, channeled by a young, healthy Hoo'qqai, then cut the power to the sanctum of the current Hoo'qqai—which, from all indications, is infirm and incompetent." He looked around the room with a determined squint of his dominant eye. "Any questions?"

"Your lordship," Gargado said, "that would disconnect the wormhole tether and result in the loss of the channeling Hoo'qqai."

Swaq rotated his head like a crane.

"So?"

"Your lordship," Jelpmittlebong said. A calmness stroked his nerves, which he attributed to Niukah, despite the unfamiliar vibe that accompanied it. "The loss of the channeling Hoo'qqai could have an adverse impact on the Sphere's operations, particularly since the Hoo'qqai in question is of such high stature."

Swaq snarled.

"Then what do you suggest?"

"Corporate policy is to have a contingency plan for every charter," Jelpmittlebong said, "which includes vehicle salvage."

A pudgy Xenkonian with sagging, gray skin appeared in the hologlobe. He pulled himself into a standing position and blinked at the faces staring back.

"Gwoot fo Krog here, Reconnaissance & Contingency." He turned his gaze to Swaq and asked, "Who y'all?"

Jelpmittlebong leaned forward.

"This is his eminency, Kiku fo Swaq, Current Standing Lord of the Exalted Chamber of the Great Intrepid Horde."

"Huh?" Krog said.

"This is Kiku fo Swaq—"

"I heard ya the first time. Where's Malgorp TEX?"

"I'm the TEX now. Fumb fo Jelp—"

"Ya don't look like the TEX."

"Well," Jelpmittlebong said, "I am. And Lord Swaq has a vested interest in a particular charter that we'd like to discuss with you."

"Eh?"

"Old little creature," Swaq said, "we have a problem that requires your expertise."

"My name's Krog, from the House of Gwoot, currently in the employ of the TEX, Eeftwat fo Malgorp."

Swaq's inclination to tear off Krog's head—and maybe even Jelpmittlebong's for good measure—was countered by an annoying intuition that counseled diplomacy. He tensed his jaw.

"My condolences," Swaq said. "Your TEX is indisposed."

Krog's face loosened, and his skin turned violet.

"'Tis okay, Swaq, TEX," he said. "So, then, y'all got a problem with an avatar vehicle, eh?"

It was explained that the current vehicle was dysfunctional and needed to be decommissioned as inconspicuously as possible.

Krog nodded and made a gurgling sound.

"Well then," he said, "if the vehicle ain't open to suicidal suggestion or easily tricked—which it sounds like it ain't—then ya gonna have to kill the bastard."

He squinted his dominant eye at the group.

"Best way to do that is with an old-fashioned assassin—but can't be masquerading as a member of the same species. I mean, it can't be murder or no such thing, 'cause that'd draw undesirable attention for sure, which I'm guessing we don't want either. I suggest we send an agent in the form of one of the local fauna—"

"You mean a wild animal attack?" Gargado asked with a nervous laugh.

"Yessir, that's exactly what I mean."

"But—"

"Stupendous," Swaq said. "I like your style, Gwoot fo Krog."

"Obliged," Krog said. "Now, let me pull the diligence file on this world—Earth, you say? Should have a sample of some of the critters from the particular locale where the vehicle finds itself."

Krog disappeared from the screen, then stumbled back with a bundle of NAD tubes threaded together on a string and began mumbling names of target worlds. He raised more than a dozen to the light, then brandished a nondescript tube at the holocam with a whoop.

"Can y'all correlate a channel from here to that hologlobe up there?" he asked.

The hologlobe in the charter room flickered, and the Earth disappeared. In its place began a rapid holoslide show of all the animals native to western North America: hundreds of separate species of mammals, reptiles, and birds.

"Stop," Swaq said after it had gone through a couple of cycles. The slide show stopped on a picture of a western big-eared bat roosting in a dark rock crevice.

"Not there. Back."

A large northern elephant seal basked on a rock in a dark-green sea.

"Back."

The hologlobe flashed back another frame.

"There," he said. "That's it."

Krog twisted his head at the glowering image in the hologlobe, then began flipping through a digichart.

"Says here that that particular creature is known as …" He looked up. "It's a critter called bigfoot, your lordship."

"Bigfoot?" Swaq said.

"Yessir, bigfoot," Krog said, folding away the digichart. "Lives in the mountains. Solitary type."

"Excellent. Perfect for a predator, don't you think?"

"But—" Gargado said.

"Yessir, an excellent choice," Krog said.

"That's a Skook," Gargado said. "They're not indigenous to Earth. They're hairy tree cloakers from—"

"Gwoot fo Krog," Swaq said, "please arrange for one of these bigfoots to go avatar hunting—promptly."

Krog beamed as his image disappeared from the hologlobe.

"Okay," Swaq said. "If there are no other business issues, let's—"

"Your lordship," Gargado said with an awkward combination of nervousness and persistence.

In three powerful strides, Swaq's breastplate was chafing against Gargado's chin.

"You," he said with a glare, "are trying my patience."

An unfamiliar voice swelled in Jelpmittlebong's mind with such a whoosh that his head reeled.

"Show your worth, neophyte," it said.

Against his own volition, Jelpmittlebong leaped like a marionette and thrust himself between Swaq and Gargado.

An old, decrepit horder limped forward from the group of horders behind Swaq. He assumed what appeared to be a feeble defensive posture, but his expression suggested serene concentration.

"Bloodletting without purpose," Jelpmittlebong said, "is undesirable." He felt like he'd just kicked a sleeping morinurk, but a strange, overriding sense of composure kept his body from wilting.

Swaq eyed Jelpmittlebong with a tight curl of his lip.

"Are you challenging?"

Jelpmittlebong's mouth said, "I mean no disrespect, but he's the best target analyst in the Sphere. Lose him, and we'll be set back indefinitely. As the Topmost Executive Xenkonian of Eeftwat Avatars and the appointed custodian of Zoggop Recreational Substances' business objective, I'm merely thinking of my client's best interests."

Swaq bristled and stretched his dominant eye as if trying to penetrate Jelpmittlebong's skull with his vision. After a long moment, he sighed.

"Logic tames the morinurk," he said.

The horders in the room grunted. The old one dropped back.

"Consider this a lucky day, Goonhopple fo Gargado," Swaq said with a sniff.

Gargado swallowed and blinked several times.

Jelpmittlebong wanted to pee. He remained until he was sure his legs wouldn't fail, then backed away. In his mind he sensed a vacuum.

"Umm," Gargado said. Purple beads of perspiration drizzled from his pores. "The, uh, issue of the foundation message remains outstanding ... your lordship—"

"So what's the problem?" Swaq asked.

"There are, um, two separate issues, your lordship. The first is that, um, well ... it was inadvertently sent to Earth too early, and contained some content that should have been deleted." Gargado shivered as if something inside was trying to wiggle out. "But," he hurried, "I believe this is of negligible significance. I mention it only in the spirit of disclosure, so that—"

"You talk too much."

Gargado swallowed.

"What's the second fucking issue?"

Gargado gulped. "Umm, the message is not attracting their attention. We used time-wrinkle technology to place it well before materialization of the avatar vehicle, and configured it to look like ancient Human etchings and fool their carbon-dating techniques. But, it's ... umm ... not being discovered as quickly as we'd expected. And when discovered, it's often not recognized as meaningful. It's even been vandalized. We think—"

"Vandalized? How?"

"They, um, painted a controversial emblem across its center."

112

Swaq gurgled in appreciation.

"Outstanding," he said. "Show me."

"Your lordship, I, um, we … don't have a copy handy—"

Swaq stuffed his arms across his chest.

"You're a total fuckup," he said.

Gargado cheeped.

"Here's what we're gonna do," Swaq said. "Delete the parts that should've been deleted, and resend it using a distribution method that ensures mass delivery."

"Mass delivery?"

"I assume the Humans have some sort of postal system, don't they?"

"Are you suggesting we mail the message?"

"It would achieve the objective, no?"

"Umm—"

"Your lordship, sir," Jelpmittlebong said, his mind still charged but once more synchronized with his own will. "The postal services of most of the major political and cultural subdivisions are state-run. It might create confusion among the masses if it appears the governments are involved in the charter mission, given what we're trying to achieve."

"Then drop them from the fucking sky like confetti," Swaq said. "Just get it done."

He marched toward the door.

Chapter 18

In the predawn hours of what would be a cloudless blue day, in the lower reaches of Earth's stratosphere above Portland, Oregon, space-time burped.

Little strips of paper spewed out of the dimensional aperture, hit the atmosphere spinning, and scattered on the wind. As quickly as it opened, the aperture closed, and the scores of paper strips descended over the city.

One strip, separated from the pack by a random sequence of gusts, swirled on a southward air current along the rugged coast. By the time gravity had its way, the slip of paper had traveled hundreds of kilometers to a low stretch of coast where, near the bend of a meandering creek shouldered by dunes on its way to the ocean, the paper landed on Arabella's arm.

She raised her eyes from her studies. A breeze fluttered the thin piece of paper as if in greeting. She reached over and pinched it between her thumb and index finger. It was about the size and shape of the slip of paper in a fortune cookie. Its texture looked grainy, like that of a grocery sack, but was smooth to the touch. A faint phosphorescent sheen glistened from its edges.

Crammed across its rectangular surface, in crisp red letters, was this:

ALL BIG GODS WILL UNITE UNDER THE BLESSED HAND
OF A MULTILINGUAL BEACON
THE CHOSEN HUMANS WILL FIND PARADISE
THROUGH HIS MERCIFUL AND MOST WISE COUNSELING
GLORY IS YOURS
$E=MC^2$

Arabella stood and reread it. The day had shifted into mid-morning, and sunlight was charging down at steeper angles, shortening the trees' shadows over the sand. She puckered her lips and closed her eyes.

"What is it?" she said.

Her musing was disrupted by the whir of distant dune buggies. She shook her head and turned back into the shade to start packing up camp.

Two dune buggies jolted to a stop in front of the tree island.

"Bella," Rock shouted, shutting off the engine and standing on his seat. "You missed one hell of a joyride. Woo-hah!" He jumped into the sand and jogged into the shade. Masa remained in the passenger seat, still gripping the base of the roll bar.

Arabella smiled in Rock's general direction and continued rolling up a sleeping bag.

Carmen and Leah disembarked from the other dune buggy. Rock already had the cooler open and was fishing for a Heineken.

"Arabella," Carmen said. "You should've come. The sunrise was awesome."

"The sunrise here was nice too," Arabella said. "And besides, I really did have to finish my reading."

"You know what they say," Rock said, throwing a beer to Masa as he stumbled out of the dune buggy. "All work and no play makes Bella boring as hell."

"Well, if I'd gone on your little pleasure trip, I'd be less versed in contemporary Hindu eschatology and wouldn't be able to tell you how Kalki, the tenth incarnation of Vishnu, will someday come riding on a white horse with wings to end the sleaze and debauchery of the present Kali Yuga. Now that's worth a dune buggy excursion, don't you think?"

Rock swigged on his bottle and said, "You're the nerdiest nerd I know."

"Oh, and this too," Arabella said, reaching into her pocket. She brandished the slip of paper. "What do you make of this?" she asked, handing it to Carmen.

"What is it? Where'd it come from?" Carmen said, passing it to Leah.

"Just fell from the sky. Landed on my arm."

"Is it some kind of advertisement?" asked Leah, handing it to Masa. He mumbled in his native Japanese and handed it to Rock.

"Another religious kook peddling his wares," Rock said, returning the thin piece of paper to Arabella.

"But there's something ... well, odd about it," Arabella said. "Don't you think?"

"Like what?" Rock said, unfurling the sleeping bag Arabella had packed. "No punctuation?"

Arabella frowned. "What're you doing? I thought we were leaving before noon."

"Waiting for Kalki to end this debauchery," Rock said.

The others laughed.

"Come on," Carmen said. "Leah and I'll show you this amazing view of Tahkenitch Creek and the ocean from the top of that dune." She was pointing to a round erg in the distance. "It's just a short drive, and these slobs can pack up while we're gone."

"Don't count on it," Rock said, lying down on the sleeping bag and throwing his forearm over his eyes.

Masa squatted in the sand next to Rock. "What mean, *slob*?" he asked, wiping beer suds from his lips with the sleeve of his sweatshirt.

Arabella laughed.

"Okay, what the hell."

She hopped in the buggy and fastened her seatbelt. While she was waiting for Carmen and Leah, both of whom had disappeared behind some trees, she looked down at the message in her hand. She twirled it for a moment, then looked again at the red script. Her mind stopped at the equation "$E=mc^2$."

"Wait a minute," she said, remembering Professor Tilford's odd article. She reread the entire message from the beginning. "No!"

Chapter 19

Chubij was on his hands and knees, foraging through the un-derbrush. He'd been walking all night along the banks of a stream and was famished. Zawt watched from his hidden mount while Chubij plowed the topsoil with the vehicle's fingertips, its snout close to the ground like a rooting pig, popping small in-sects and grubs in its mouth.

Neither of them noticed the man resting against the trunk of an old western hemlock. He was tall and thin, with brown dread-locks drooping over his shoulders to the middle of his back. The dreadlocks were adorned with baby pinecones and little bells. A scraggly beard outlined his weathered face.

Chubij grabbed the man's tattered hiking boot and tried to lift it to look underneath for earthworms.

"Whoa, dude. Relax on the boot, man," the owner of the boot said, shaking his dreadlocks with a jingle. The avatar vehicle shot to his feet and backpedaled. The man squinted one eye and raised the eyebrow of the other.

"Why the shock, Spock?"

Chubij managed a few vowelless groans before a ringing in his head drowned out his voice. A presence scrambled over him as he fell.

The vehicle convulsed in a way that appeared to an outside observer as a chicken pecking the wind, then straightened and signaled a touchdown.

"Yoni, yoni," Zawt said.

"Uh-huh," the man said, not the least bit flummoxed. "Is that right?"

"Thank you, I'm well," Zawt said with a grin.

The man stood and brushed his jeans with his hands.

"That's good to know, brother," he said. "I'm feeling a-okay myself." He raised his chin and swallowed a lungful of air. "Ah!" he said. "Nothing like morning mountain air to kick-start the ol' noggin, eh?"

Zawt imitated the man by inhaling through his mouth.

"Or I could just be talking shit," the man said.

"Talking shit," Zawt said.

The man laughed.

"So, what's your name?" he asked.

Zawt had recently discovered the divine-incarnation status of the vehicle, as programmed in its databanks. He stretched his arms parallel to the horizon and winked.

"I'm the savior of this planet," he said. "I speak on behalf of Jesus of Galilee, Buddha of the Bodhi tree, Muhammad of Mecca, Abraham of Canaan, Lao Tzu of the Tao, Confucius of Lu, Black Elk of the Oglala, a nameless Zen master, and Krishna, to mention just a few."

The man bobbed his head and grinned.

Prophet Wacko

"Big kahunas, eh? Right here in the buffalo home on the cascade range?" the man said, breaking into wild laughter.

Zawt's eyes gleamed with admiration.

The man stepped forward with an extended hand, took Zawt's, and they shook.

"Frick's the name," he said.

"Good morning," Zawt said.

"So really, brother, what's your name?"

"Who is it who now repeats the Buddha's name?"

Frick smiled. "Shit, dude, you're a casebook example, all right."

Zawt nodded.

"Okay, man," Frick said with a chuckle, "if that's the way you want it. It's wacko, but whatever ... I gotta call you something, though ..."

"Wack-oh," Zawt said. He fell silent for a moment, then whispered it again. "Waack-ohhh." He smiled and shouted, "Wacko!"

Frick laughed.

"Wacko?"

Zawt waggled his head.

"Okay, brother," Frick said. "Wacko it is."

"Wacko!"

They looked at each other, then burst into laughter.

"Nice to meet ya, Wacko," Frick said.

―――――――

Frick led Wacko—with Zawt at the wheel—along the stream to a point where it was joined by a smaller creek, then morphed into a rapid-flowing channel that tumbled through the forest. They walked along the bank of the reinforced waterway in single file.

121

"This stream feeds the McKenzie South Fork," Frick said as they maneuvered through some moss-covered boulders. "And the McKenzie joins the Willamette just north of Eugene, where they flow together all the way to the Columbia, which pours into the Pacific." He waved to the west. "You piss here, and it can end up in the belly of some whale on its way to Alaska."

"McKenzie," Wacko said with a huff.

"Yeah, named after some fur trader who explored the Willamette Valley about two hundred years ago. Before that, the Kalapuya lived here for over eight thousand years. Pretty sure they called it something besides McKenzie, so go figure, huh?"

About half a kilometer along the small rapids, in a spot where the stream slowed and formed small eddies, Frick turned into the woods. They scrambled up an incline and came to a level piece of ground, stopping at the foot of two western red cedars.

The trees stood five meters apart, but shared a thick branch some fifteen meters up, their joint bark fusing over the improbable linkage, which created the appearance of two giants holding hands. A ladder made of stripped branches ascended from the earth into the dark underbelly of a simple wooden structure that straddled the branch and spanned the space between the trees' trunks.

Frick clambered up the ladder and disappeared. Wacko twisted and craned his neck from the ground below. After a moment, Frick dropped two metal pails from the opening and climbed back down.

"Come on, Wacko," he said, scooting a pail in Wacko's direction with his boot, "let's catch some crawdads."

———

The charter members watched from the Sphere as the avatar vehicle traipsed with his new companion through the creek, overturning stones and laughing. SkroSkro-Bleep was busy adjusting the vehicle's linguistic gradations and speech patterns to match those of Frick's, while Gargado analyzed Frick's cultural allusions in an attempt to identify his particular societal status and philosophical leanings.

Though they couldn't contact Chubij, it almost appeared as if the vehicle were operating normally, until the avatar vehicle jumped into the creek and began high-stepping about in a knee-deep eddy.

"Oh, this one rare occurrence!" Wacko said as he splashed, twirling his hands in the air.

———————

"Why does it keep saying weird shit like that?" SkroSkro said in the direction of the hologlobe.

The recruit sitting beside the two-headed linguistic specialist flushed.

"I don't know, SkroSkro-Bleep, sirs, er ... sir," he said.

"It's quite uncharacteristic," Bleep said, running foreclaws over two digipads simultaneously.

Chapter 20

"My standard reaction to your kind of insolence," Swaq said, "is to rip off your head."

He and Jelpmittlebong were in Malgorp's quarters, with the former TEX's luxury knickknacks tossed in a corner. Swaq's personal envoy—the same frail horder Jelpmittlebong noticed from the charter room—stood in the shadows behind him.

"Thank you, my lordship," Jelpmittlebong said, "for ... er ... not."

Swaq shot into the air and landed centimeters from Jelpmittlebong's face. He ran the back of his foreclaw across Jelpmittlebong's cheek.

"Most blog-ranters are craven dipshits," he said. "But you've got pluck. My intuition tells me that a few scars to that pretty face would make you a decent horder."

Jelpmittlebong bit his lip.

Swaq grinned.

"I've studied you, Fumb fo Jelpmittlebong," he said, "at the behest of a trusted advisor." He gestured toward the aged envoy as he seated himself on the edge of the desk, his knees eye-level to Jelpmittlebong. "Born in Cityplex Stratum Four on Xenkon V'rpq Proper in squalid conditions, the sole survivor of your pod. Tested unprecedentedly high in the newborn analytical reasoning assessment, and removed to the Toq Conservatory for Exceptional Brood on the outskirts of the Great Maze-Jungle, where you excelled in every subject—particularly abstract mathematics, history, and political philosophy. At Toq you were personally tutored by one Pwond fo Niukah, who took you under his wing for the bulk of your studies and found you to be of superior stock. After Toq, you were inexplicably placed in an intensive marketing program despite the obvious fact that your skills lay elsewhere."

Jelpmittlebong felt the mind probe descend as Swaq's words filled his ear. He tried to focus his thoughts into the stream of the conversation so as to minimize his own mind chatter, as Niukah advised, when another presence appeared—the same one that calmed him as he challenged Swaq over Gargado in the charter room. It had the effect of veiling the probe, as if through a gauze.

"Overseer?" Jelpmittlebong thought.

"What's that?" Swaq asked.

Jelpmittlebong resisted the urge to blink. He noticed the old envoy staring at him from the shadows, who nodded slightly in his direction. He felt a sudden bond of accomplice.

"Overseer Niukah is a wise Xenkonian," Jelpmittlebong said, looking up at Swaq. "I'm sure he had his reasons."

Swaq reached for a smoldering vapor bong on the wall. The gray cinders in the bowl glowed orange as he toked.

"Did you know Niukah's disappeared?" he said. "His whereabouts unknown."

Jelpmittlebong tilted his head.

"Your Overseer Niukah is a mysterious Xenkonian indeed," Swaq said, squeezing the neck of the bong. "No records of his personal history can be found, suggesting that he's been permanently erased from the registry, or he never existed in the first place."

Swaq paused with an inward stare.

"Let me be frank," he said, his lip curling from an unseen effort. "The Qanjivians were ingenious, but stupid." He waved two foreclaws in the air. "This God-making contraption has potential. And you," he constricted his dominant eyelid into a scrutinizing slit, "are going to help me use it to conquer the galaxy."

Jelpmittlebong's dominant eye widened.

"I, um—"

"Power's an aphrodisiac." Swaq plunked the spent bong on the table. "Far superior to any of those fucking narcotics." He flashed a cold grin. Smoke poured from his nostrils.

Jelpmittlebong felt the mind probe retreat, then disappear.

"Hah!" Swaq said, as if suddenly relieved of a niggling dilemma. "And if you think power's a kick, couple it with impunity."

Jelpmittlebong stiffened and wondered if he'd inadvertently leaked something about Niukah or their recent discussions.

Swaq dug his foreclaws into his sides and grimaced. "Fumb fo Jelpmittlebong," he said, "you're dismissed."

Chapter 21

Deep in the Three Sisters Wilderness of Oregon, amid mossy rocks and yew trees at the foot of a misty waterfall, a gelatinized pile of aasmamyl offal morphed into a hulking presence.

At dawn a gargantuan bigfoot assassin stepped out of the waterfall. A faint phosphorescent sheen glistened across its black coat. It rotated its thick neck and chomped at the air, then lumbered into the forest, snapping branches as it ran.

─────────

Wacko sat on the bank of a small creek in the vehicle's default lotus position, his buttocks planted in moss. Chubij wriggled the vehicle's eyes until the murky forest seeped through its lenses in small, wistful stages. The fading vestiges of dreams flickered in retreat. He didn't sense the seer mind, but he did notice the scent of something cooking.

Before him the thick, gnarled bough of a sharp-needled Engelmann spruce reached across the creek. On it a northern spotted owl perched and cried. The composition of its patterned hoots, complemented by the gurgle of the water, nearly lulled Chubij back into the catatonic torpor from whence he'd just emerged—until he recognized the beckoning sequence.

"Ulluoi, my fond sister, is it you?" he hooted.

"Yes, my patriarch!"

"How did you get here?"

"The Qanjivians that remain helped, in return for my wire-tapping assistance."

Chubij and the owl shared a mirthful hoot.

"Ever resourceful, my sister," Chubij hooted. "Are you well?"

"As well as can be expected. The monotony is overwhelming, but our Mother-God knows best."

"Yes, my sister. Let us strengthen our hearts against the evil of despair."

"I will try, my patriarch. But, how are you?"

"There's a seer mind in this vehicle that's craftier than any I've ever encountered. It's been disrupting the mission."

"My patriarch, the Xenkonians are sincere when they say they don't think a seer mind is in the vehicle."

"Yes, my sister, I know. But it's their incompetence that sustains that misguided belief. They don't possess the intuitive magnanimity of the Qanjivians. They don't know how to listen."

"Yes, my patriarch."

"I'm not able to access most of the vehicle's memory banks. Has the vehicle made contact with the target species?"

"Yes, my patriarch—two female Humans."

"The ones on the mountain footpath?"

"Yes. So that wasn't you? I'm so glad. The behavior was uncharacteristically crude for a Hoo'qqai, even under the circumstances."

"I see."

"The vehicle has recently befriended a male Human—a hermit in the forest. He's currently making you dinner. But the seer mind doesn't seem to be aware of the charter's mission."

"Or it's ignoring it," Chubij said, "either of which leads me to believe something else governs its actions."

"My patriarch, there's something I must tell you. Kiku fo Swaq, Lord of the Great Intrepid Horde, has seized the Sphere. He's sent an inexperienced Hoo'qqai to the target world to take over your charter mission, and he's ordered your destruction."

"My destruction?"

"Yes, my patriarch. Already a facsimile of an indigenous creature called *bigfoot* is hunting your vehicle."

"*Bigfoot?*" Chubij hooted. "The vehicle's databanks say nothing of such an animal. What kind of creature is it?"

"I don't know, my patriarch."

A silence ensued. The channeling owl flapped its wings as if to take flight, but remained on the branch. The tree shook, showering dry needles. Chubij shook his head, loosening the needles that landed in his hair. The owl rotated its neck and regurgitated the soggy remains of a flying squirrel. The pellet of hair and bones landed with a thud on the moss by Chubij's knee and rolled down the short incline into the creek.

"Hmm ..." Chubij said, watching the lump course away on the current. "This is most unusual. How am I—"

A large coastal great horned owl suddenly swooped out of the shadows, its wings and talons outstretched in twilight predation. The channeling spotted owl leaped from its perch and rocketed along the ravine.

"My sister! Hope be with you," Chubij hooted after the retreating beast.

"And you, my patriarch," Ulluoi responded in a short sequence of fading hoots as she disappeared.

The great horned owl banked toward the treetops and screeched.

———————

"Wacko, my boy," Frick said, approaching with a pail of steaming porridge, "how about a home-cooked meal?"

Zawt nudged Chubij off the consciousness floor, then turned and signaled a touchdown.

"One meal a day and a good sleep at night!" he said.

Frick sat on an old log imbedded in the soil parallel to the creek.

"Well, come on then." He laughed. "While it's hot."

Chapter 22

Dear Professor Tilford,

My name is Arabella Paasikivi, and I'm a graduate student in the University of Oregon's Folklore Program. I'm a regular reader of your blogs and enjoy them very much. I'm writing about an article you wrote entitled "Is God an Alien?" I'm curious to know if there have been any recent developments since that article was published.

Sincerely yours,
Arabella Paasikivi

It was a short message, but it took Arabella nearly thirty minutes to compose. She felt a little intimidated writing such an established scholar without proper introduction, and she didn't want to seem impertinent. After hitting the Send button, she logged off and went to bed.

Early the next morning, she was surprised to find a reply.

Thomas Leo

Dear Arbela,

Thank you for your kind message, and I do recognize your name from my blog post—apologies for not responding directly before. The Ducks' college is a great learning institution. But it does rain a lot in the Oregon though doesnt it? And if I recall, the Folklore Program is small but well-reputed. By the way, plesae tell Dr. Kang in the Religious Studies Dept. hello from the "banjo man" in Hicksville. ha-ha. He's a great little guy! Now, about your inqiury, yes there has been some develpments. And I am wondering if your curiosity stems from the fact that similar ancient drawings have been recently discovred elsewhere. To date One in France and one in Saudi Arabia. Not to mention one in the potato state that was vandalized by some local Half-witted fruitcakes! Excuse my french Arabela. ha-ha. Or is your interest in the subject the result of this strange and mysterious global onslaught of confeti from the sky containing a message of similar content? Most fascinating! Simply put! okay, Are-balla, I must run now. I have many more messagewes to rply to now. Keep in touch and I will endevor to do same.

Keep Pickin'!
Professor Elgin Patterson Tilford
Religious Studies Department
Indiana University

Confetti from the sky?

She went to a local news site, which, because it was so early in the morning, was still carrying the previous day's news.

PORTLAND—Portlanders awoke Thursday morning to what Mayor Ridley is calling "a ticker-tape parade for the ages, without the parade." Countless tiny slips of paper were reported falling from the sky above

Multnomah County around 7:30 a.m. PST, and by 8:00 a.m. the county's 911 call center was inundated with reports of a veritable flurry of paper.

"Downtown looks covered in snow," said one caller.

Mayor Ridley stated that all efforts will be used to determine the responsible parties and bring them to justice, indicating that the cost of cleanup will likely be enormous.

"Littering on this scale is completely irresponsible, regardless of the purpose, and might just amount to a felony," he added.

Further Googling revealed that Portland was not the only city to be so deluged—all over the world, major population centers had been showered by the same strips of paper, all bearing the same message.

Arabella slid her eyes from the screen and leaned back in her chair. Something didn't quite fit. She stared at the wall without blinking, then lunged at her keyboard.

Dear Professor Tilford,

Thank you for your quick reply. As a matter of fact, my curiosity was prompted by a message written on a thin slip of paper that came from the sky and landed on my arm. I recognized it as being similar to the message in your article. This is all very fascinating! But what can it mean?

Sincerely yours,
Arabella Paasikivi

The professor's response came within the hour.

Thomas Leo

Dear Arabela,

Fascinating indeed! No idea, But I intend to find out. Please forgiv my daring to be so bold, but I was wondring if I could impose on you somewhat and for a small favor. A dear friend of mine in wondrful bucolic Corvallis (Corvallis = "heart of the valley" in Latin!) is head of the nuclaer engineering dept at Orgon State Univ. His name is prof. Abdul Hazem Al-Qurashi and he's from Saudi Arabia. Abdul Hazem is the one who told about the cave findings near a city called Al Taif in Saudi Arabia. To make a long story short, we spoke last night and he mentioned that similar messages from the sky in Arabc have been reported in the Arab WOrld as well. Amazzing! Profesor Al-Qurashi is anxious to see one of these pieces of paper, and when I told him of yo9ur e-mail to me he asked if you could bring it to him in Corvallis (whch I think is close to Eugene, right??). Is that possible, Arbella? Pleas let me know and I will provde Profesor Al-Qurashi's details. Thank you so much!

Keep Pickin'!
Professor Elgin Patterson Tilford
Religious Studies Department
Indiana University

"Where you going?" Rock asked from his sleeping bag on the sofa.

"Corvallis."

"Corvallis?" Rock yawned. "That cow pasture school?"

"Uh-huh, that's the one." Arabella slipped on her Windbreaker and opened the door. An ashen dawn spilled in. "See ya," she said, skipping into the rain.

"Shit," Rock said, rolling over and pulling the sleeping bag over his head.

An empty Heineken bottle clanked on the hardwood floor.

Chapter 23

The Oregon State University Radiation Center was a jutting box of a structure that housed a small nuclear reactor. It served the teaching and research needs of the Nuclear Engineering Department.

Arabella pushed through the glass doors and stepped into an empty lobby. Dull reflections of the drizzly morning streamed across the terrazzo flooring. She sniffed as she shook off the rain and closed her umbrella. The mild tang of unfamiliar chemicals wafted on the air. She headed down the lone passageway, toward the only door emitting light. Inside, at an uncluttered desk, sat a middle-aged Arab man with a cropped beard.

"Professor Al-Qurashi?" Arabella said, tapping the doorframe.

"Yes?" The man's eyes still perused the papers before him.

"I'm Arabella Paasikivi. Professor Tilford asked me to come—"

Professor Abdul Hazem Al-Qurashi removed his bifocals.

"Yes, of course. Come in." He walked around the desk and extended a hand. Arabella smiled as she shook it.

"It was so nice of you to come all that way for the benefit of my selfish curiosity." Professor Al-Qurashi gestured toward one of the two chairs that faced the desk. "Please sit down."

"It's really not that far." Arabella sat on the edge of one of the chairs and put her bag on her knees. "Not quite an hour. Traffic's usually light on Saturday mornings."

"Just the same, I appreciate it very much." His voice had the precise intonation that came from years of self-conscious practice of a foreign tongue.

"I thought *Paasikivi* was Finnish," the professor said with a wink as he retook his seat. "But you certainly don't look Finnish."

"My father's from Finland, but my mother's Sudanese, of Beja ethnicity," Arabella said.

He raised a brow.

"And how's your Arabic?" he asked in Arabic.

Arabella tensed, but managed to reply that her mother had spoken to her and her brother in Arabic for most of their early childhoods. Arabella was now taking advanced Arabic literature as part of her folklore studies, and her reading ability was much better than her spoken one, which, she confessed, still carried an adolescent quality.

"Not bad," the professor said, returning to English. "Not bad at all." He sat back with an expression of fresh discernment.

Arabella blushed.

"Thanks." She curled her lips. "You're from Saudi Arabia?"

"Jeddah, on the Red Sea coast. But Corvallis has been my home for the past twenty-five years."

"I've always wanted to see the hajj, and the Kaaba."

The professor smiled.

Prophet Wacko

"Well, not to burst your bubble, but a non-Saudi single woman would certainly be lucky to get a visa, and even then, non-Muslims are forbidden entry into Mecca. Are you a practicing Muslim?"

"The jury's still out for me on the Providence front." She bit her lip, thinking perhaps she'd just effected an inadvertent insult. "I'm sorry," she said, "I didn't mean—"

Professor Al-Qurashi waved his hands.

"No offense. I'm a scientist, after all. I respect healthy skepticism. But I'm afraid you may have to be content with pictures from the Internet."

Arabella frowned.

"In any event, there seem to be bigger things afoot than hajjes or Kaabas."

Arabella leaned forward.

"The cave drawings were enough to keep thinkers like Elgin and me awake for days," he said. "But this recent flood of paper from the sky is remarkable to the point of outlandish."

"Elgin?" Arabella asked.

"Professor Tilford. He and I go way back, you know. He's one of a kind. How long have you known him?"

"I've actually never met him," Arabella said. "I read his blogs, and the article on the Malay cave drawing reminded me of the slip of paper I found. So I emailed him out of the blue."

"Oh? He spoke as if you were long-time friends. But such is his way."

Arabella just nodded.

"Are you a regular reader of such esoteric articles?"

"I'm a folklore student, so I read all kinds of obscure stuff. That particular title caught my eye, and Professor Tilford's sweeping speculations kept me captivated."

Professor Al-Qurashi snorted.

"That's the most accurate description I've ever heard of his approach to academics. In fact, that would be a very accurate nutshell of his entire personality."

Arabella's face settled into a polite smile.

"Well then," Professor Al-Qurashi said, placing his elbows on the desk and touching his spread-out fingertips in the air before him. "May I see it?"

"What—oh yes, of course, the paper." She dug through her bag, retrieved a small envelope, and dumped its contents in her open palm. She held it up, then handed it across the desk.

The professor put on his bifocals and held the paper to the light. A faint phosphorescent sheen glistened across its surface.

"It looks like sandpaper," he said, "but feels smooth, as if polished. And seems quite durable." He was crinkling it then gently snapping it taut.

"Everyone says that."

"'All big gods will unite under the blessed hand of a multilingual beacon,'" the professor read out loud. "'The chosen humans will find paradise through his merciful and most wise counseling. Glory is yours.' Kind of trite, don't you think?"

Arabella grinned.

"If I had access to that kind of delivery system, I probably would've said something else," she said.

"Did you immediately make the connection with the cave drawings?"

"It took me a few minutes, but they're so similar—"

"That's the message found in a cave in the Sarawat Mountains near Ta'if, Saudi Arabia," the professor said, gesturing at a whiteboard on the wall across from the window. It was written in Arabic with the English translation appearing below it. "It's essentially the same message that Elgin found in Borneo. And both are almost exactly the same as the message from the sky, except for this"—he pointed at the parenthetical phrase *(and the lesser godheads too)*—"and this." He pointed at another parenthetical, *(for a slight hole in the head)*.

He faced Arabella. "The Malay message and the one at Ta'if, as well as some other ancient drawings found at various locations around the globe, have all been radiocarbon dated to about twelve hundred years ago. Now," he said, crossing his arms over his chest, "what are the chances of that happening by pure coincidence?"

"Same author?"

"Even Marco Polo didn't get around like that."

Arabella laughed.

"Besides, he was a merchant, not a missionary." The professor clasped his hands behind his head. "Add in these recent messages from the sky, and the chances become infinitely higher that the similarity isn't random."

"Someone familiar with the cave drawings?"

"A very limited universe of people, to be sure. And why weren't the cave drawings discovered earlier? I mean, these archaeological sites are remote, but not necessarily unexplored. It seems a little odd that they're only now being discovered, so close in time to this flood of paper from the sky." The professor paused and bit his lip. "So," he said, placing his palms on his desk, "for the sake of argument, let's assume each cave drawing and these slips of paper are the work of one organization—for example, an underground group with an agenda, that's been handing down secrets since ancient times only to a select few—that has chosen now to move into action, the purpose of which isn't yet clear."

Arabella's eyes lit up.

"Like the Freemasons? Or the Templar Knights?"

"Something like that, though, to my knowledge, I don't think the message is something the Templars would advocate."

Arabella smiled. "I guess there's not enough here to suggest an omnipotent being."

Professor Al-Qurashi looked over his bifocals and smiled.

"Let's not rule it out just yet," he said. "But, assuming that's not the case, sometime between the time of the cave drawings and this recent torrent of airborne messages, this mysterious group decides to delete some things. It may be significant, or it may not be, but it's one of the few things we've got to go on at this point."

"So, they took more than a millennium to make two deletions and change the medium for their message." Arabella was thinking out loud.

"And then there's the confounding matter of the $E=mc^2$ reference. Its appearance in the cave drawings is hard to explain without resorting to fantastic hypotheses of time travel or time manipulation, unless Einstein himself was a member of this mysterious secret group and everything we know of him and his personal intellectual struggles to discover this little formula is nothing but their ingenious propaganda."

"Are you suggesting that Professor Tilford's alien suppositions are true?"

"They're crazy, I admit, but as a scientist I can't rule them out."

"What about simple synchronicity?"

"That's exactly what we have, isn't it—multiple events, presumably causally unrelated, unlikely to occur together by chance, yet occurring together in a seemingly meaningful manner." Professor Al-Qurashi picked up the slip of paper lying on his desk and began rubbing it between his thumb and index finger. "A colleague in the Math Department told me the statistical probability of this happening independently just twice is astronomical, but we have at least four—and maybe more to be discovered—separate incidences of the same message spread across time and space in ways that they simply shouldn't." The professor looked up with a mischievous grin. "Lewis Carroll couldn't have concocted a more fascinating mystery."

Arabella was on the edge of her seat.

"So how can something like time manipulation or aliens be proved?"

"I'm not sure they can." The professor was rotating the slip of paper before his eyes. "But we may be able to at least rule them out. Arabella, do you mind if I keep this? I'd like to run some tests on it."

"What kind of tests?"

"Well, maybe knowing how it's physically structured and what it's made of can provide some clues. X-ray diffraction or fluctuation electron microscopy, perhaps solid-state nuclear magnetic resonance, should reveal its basic structure, and neutron activation analysis can tell us its constituent components without destroying our sample. I can run all the tests myself right here."

"It's yours." She smiled. "On the minor condition that you let me know the results."

"Of course."

The rain began battering at the window. Professor Al-Qurashi leaned back in his chair.

"But the full results may take a while, depending on the half-life of the elements involved, which can range from fractions of a second to several years."

Arabella raised her eyebrows.

"Years?"

"Certain uranium atoms have half-lives in the millions, sometimes billions of years, but those are the exceptions. I can't imagine this little thing"—he was waving the slip of paper in the air—"being packed with uranium. But it could contain other elements whose half-lives are measured at least in months."

Arabella looked out the window and sighed.

"Science slogs along at its own pace, I'm afraid," Professor Al-Qurashi said.

She smiled.

"Okay," she said. Then, as if remembering something, "Is there a place I can do some studying before heading back?"

Chapter 24

"I still don't think he should be takin' that stuff," 8-1-21 said, his breath forming ice crystals in the air. He was wearing an aasmamyl parka. "He's gonna wind up bangin' his head against a wall in some shithole."

"Let's hope not," Niukah said. The hood of his cape was bunched around his neck, and he was doodling on a piece of tanned aasmamyl leather with a chunk of charcoal.

Jelpmittlebong faced the sanctums from the glass wall of his quarters, his hindlimbs and tail planted like a tripod. His forelimbs were drawn across his spine, each clasping behind him at the elbow of the opposite forearm. His exhalations churned in the coldness. A generous dose of melatonin lapped through his veins.

"Don't ya think kick-startin' the tellie gig's a bit desperate?"

"It's not ideal, but time is not ours to waste." Niukah looked up. "He needs to see the way—light the tunnel, so to speak."

8-1-21 looked askance at Niukah, then back at Jelpmittle-bong.

"How long ya think he's gonna stand there like that?"

"Meditations are not timed," Niukah said. "A sophisticated mute monk can remain in contemplation for years." He began etching in quick strokes along the fringe of the leather.

8-1-21 picked at his teeth. His dominant eye roamed the room.

"Years, huh? Is that right?"

"Yes."

"So ya think he's meditatin'?" 8-1-21 poked a foreclaw through a slit in his parka and fingered some mloshfruit pods on the table. "Not just havin' a party in his head?"

"He has a strong mind—stronger than most."

8-1-21 sighed, then popped a chunk of mloshfruit in his mouth and swashed the meat with a deliberate slowness. When the pit was smoothed of the sticky pulp, he spit it into his fore-claw and placed it on the table.

"Crazy fucks," he said under his breath.

"Do you ever meditate?" Niukah asked. He picked up his sketch and held it before him, admiring it with a twist of his neck. It was a morinurk charging into a clearing in the forest, where a mute monk sat in equable stillness.

"Who, me?" 8-1-21 said with an exaggerated face. "Don't rightly recall ever doin' that. I'm kind of a workaholic." He scratched the back of his neck and glanced at his wrist monitor.

"I see," Niukah said. He put down the drawing and licked a foreclaw. He began smudging the stenciling around the edges with quick flicks of his wrist.

8-1-21 coughed and shifted on his stool.

"That's pretty good," he said, pointing his chin at the sketch.

"Thank you."

"So—" 8-1-21 looked up as if the admission had been a blast of cold air on a sensitive tooth "—what's it like bein' a mute monk?"

Niukah's expression remained placid, but his head skin phased into a tingling indigo.

"It's cold in here," he said, rubbing his shoulders.

———————

Jelpmittlebong's lateral eyes monitored his companions, while his dominant eye gazed over the sanctums below. Bliss permeated his consciousness. Voices and images, plain and coherent, danced at the edge of his mind.

"This is why, my student, Swaq covets the hormone," Niukah's voice rang.

"This is peculiar, Overseer," Jelpmittlebong thought. He mentally approached a particular image. It focused into a mundane picture of an unfamiliar Xenkonian puffing on a vapor bong and laughing. Backing away, the image dimmed. *"Whose thoughts are these?"*

"They're the current thoughts of individuals in the Sphere—conscious or otherwise. 8-1-21, for example. Or someone in the message chamber. It's hard to tell without investigation."

"A Hoo'qqai?"

"No. The portals are limited to Xenkonians. We've never achieved cross-species telepathy, I'm afraid."

"How do I navigate them?"

"A Xenkonian's thoughts are compound and simultaneous. The aggregation of their energy forms the portal—which is why you can't mind-probe a dead Xenkonian. In time you'll learn to key in on signatures inside an individual portal to discern thoughts with common themes. The bundling together of these in your mind

147

makes it easier to trace their history and related themes—and finally to see the whole person. It also makes it easy to establish a coherent channel."

"Is that how we're communicating here?"

"More or less, yes. Most of my thoughts are cloaked from you. The portal is a result of my projecting an accentuated stream of consciousness. I've known you since a hatchling, my student. You recognize my signature subconsciously and accept it naturally. Projecting is another level mastered only by mutes."

8-1-21 stared.

Niukah smiled. "Do you see?"

"You ignored my question."

"Is that what I did?"

8-1-21 flashed a sardonic scowl.

"Then you inanely stated the obvious."

"My statement reflected the here and now, nothing more or less. That is the way of the mutes." Niukah narrowed his dominant eye at the mipoon. "A green mountain is a green mountain."

8-1-21 reached for another piece of mloshfruit.

"Yep," he said. "Mighty profound stuff ya got there."

"Has Swaq mastered it?" Jelpmittlebong thought.

"Not yet. But the alien hormone somehow crystallizes the mind portals," Niukah's voice said, *"at least when its effect is peaking. But I'll never know, as I'll never ingest it. My skills are the result of centuries of training. I like to consider it a natural ability that's been honed."*

Jelpmittlebong reflected a long moment, then thought, *"I*

think if the Human specimen were agitated instead of blissful, this would be a very different experience."

"I'm told it reflects the cumulative spiritual energy of the Human whose hormone you've ingested. An anxious specimen causes anxiety; blissful, bliss; depressed, depression. Acutely agitated? Well, let's just say it would be difficult to concentrate. This is the underlying risk of such a shortcut to the portals—you can never be sure of the mental state of the specimen."

"But surely, with enough research—"

"Enough, my student. I want to show you some things before the effect wears off."

An abrupt pleasure surge washed over Jelpmittlebong's mind. An uncontrollable need to laugh overcame him.

8-1-21 and Niukah watched as Jelpmittlebong threw his head back and guffawed.

"See?" 8-1-21 said, twisting a mloshfruit rind through his teeth. "He's havin' a party in his head." He turned to Niukah and raised his brow. "An outright bash."

"He's becoming mute," Niukah said, his eye straight ahead, "learning to calm the jabbering mind."

"Is that right?" 8-1-21 spit a mloshfruit pit into his palm and put it on the table. "Ya sayin' the mind jabbers?"

"Let's just say a Xenkonian's mind never stops thinking, which impedes the comprehension of nothingness, so to speak."

"Uh-huh."

"The Way teaches to be still and listen. To be mute."

"'Still and listen,' huh? That's it? That's your so-called enlightenment?"

"Isn't that enough?"

"No bells and whistles? No magnificent bullshit? No ultimate understandin'?"

"All bullshit is no bullshit. All understanding is no understanding."

"Now, that's a radical thought." 8-1-21 picked up another piece of mloshfruit. "But in the spirit of bein' social, I'm not gonna get in a huff—"

―――――――――

"Was that you?" Jelpmittlebong asked.

"I wanted to show you the power of the mind portals—properly navigated, of course."

"How do you do it?"

"Like I said, I've practiced for centuries. I couldn't teach it to you in one sitting."

"You mean you can make someone do things?"

"To a certain extent, yes."

"And Swaq's envoy, he's—"

Niukah chuckled. *"Yes, he's mute—one of us."*

"But how could he control me?"

"He simply stimulated your predisposed mind. Challenging a tyrant like Swaq is your nature, though you're unaccustomed to physical confrontations—which, by the way, will change as you mature and gain confidence. The hard part is navigating the portal— and keeping it open—while you do it."

"But—"

"The key is intuition. You must learn to trust it—to enhance it as a sense, as the loss of sight eventually enhances one's auditory perception. Intuition is the purest of conduits through which any two minds can meet."

Niukah indicated a prominent portal. *"There, try it."*

"I think this is 8-1-21," Jelpmittlebong said.

"Well done," Niukah said. *"Your established relationship with him makes recognition easy."*

Jelpmittlebong studied the portal from all angles, his head tilting outwardly as he did.

"He's a pure soul," Niukah said, *"regardless of his crabby nature."*

"But is he loyal?" Jelpmittlebong said, facing 8-1-21 with a dominant eye aglow like a detached ember.

"Find out."

"Ya think he's okay?" 8-1-21 asked, noticing Jelpmittlebong's strange stare.

"If you're seeking fish, look in the water," Niukah said.

"Huh?"

"All things in the universe arise from emptiness and return to emptiness."

8-1-21 shook his head.

"Don't ya ever give it a break?" He put another piece of mloshfruit in his mouth. "Or does the Way teach ya to be obtuse too?"

"One plus two equals zero," Niukah said. "This is a common mute understanding. It comes from within. No teacher can teach it."

"Uh-huh."

Niukah leaned his face into 8-1-21's and asked, "Can you see your dominant eye?"

"I'm just tryin' to get along here," 8-1-21 said, leaning back, his muscles tensing.

"If you try to see your eye, there's already a mistake—it can't see itself."

"So?"

"If you try to understand your mind, there's already a mistake."

"Ya sayin' self-awareness is an illusion?"

Niukah grabbed a handful of mloshfruit pits from the table and threw them at 8-1-21's head.

Jelpmittlebong was busy observing 8-1-21's portal. He'd burrowed in and found what his intuition told him was a mental lattice associated with motor control. Manipulating it proved as easy as herding smoke. His foreclaws wandered through the air as if trying to gain a handle on something floating before him.

"*Your mind, my student,*" Niukah's voice said, "*not your foreclaws.*"

"To understand your true self," Niukah said to 8-1-21, "you must understand the meaning of my throwing mloshfruit pits. I've just put enlightenment in your head, directed you to the clear mind."

8-1-21 gnashed his fangs over his lower lip and growled. "I'd suggest you're pissin' me off."

"The clear mind is like a mirror free of shadows. Red comes, and your mind's red. White comes, and it's white."

"Sounds like ya just react to outside conditions."

"When I'm hungry, I eat. When I'm thirsty, I drink."

"That's it? What d'ya do with a sudden primal urge to take advantage of a slink lizard oozin' with the hormones? D'ya just say 'When I'm horny, I fuck'? Don't sound like ya philosophy offers much in the way of moral ethics."

Niukah smiled.

"A baited hook has dropped into the pool of your mind," he said, "and all your thinking has appeared."

8-1-21 jumped up.

"You fuckin' mute head!" he said.

Niukah stood and stretched his forelimbs in the deliberate manner of an old miner prepared to protect his evening swill.

8-1-21 shuffled forward.

"I've had just about enough of your mumbo-jumbo bull—"

8-1-21 suddenly began gyrating his butt and cackling. Then he dropped onto his knees before Jelpmittlebong and bowed his head. A second later he jumped to his feet and, locking eyes with Jelpmittlebong, backpedaled.

"What the fuck?" he said, his incisors flaring through taut cheeks like a green wall of chipped bedrock.

———

"I did it!" Jelpmittlebong thought.

"You should probably be less obvious next time," Niukah thought.

Jelpmittlebong grinned. Microscopic bubbles fizzled around the edges of his dominant eye.

"Perhaps," he thought.

Chapter 25

On-the-Scene Reporter: "Reports of a precocious and highly intelligent young man hailing from Henan Province in central China, some six hundred kilometers southwest of Beijing, began surfacing a few weeks ago. Eyewitnesses have come forth with extraordinary tales of his alleged intellectual prowess, which include lightning-fast mathematical ability; vast knowledge of world history, the sciences, and culture; and unbelievable linguistic skills."

A rough video of a Chinese teenager dressed in simple garments appeared on the screen. He was walking through a crowd of peasants along a dirt village lane, a faint phosphorescent sheen framing his features. A throng of children flanked him on either side.

Arabella and Carmen sat on the sofa, their bare feet propped on a coffee table. Rock sat cross-legged on the floor, stroking a

Heineken. Leah lounged in an adjacent recliner, her legs dangling over the worn leather arm and Masa's shoulders, as he sat on the floor.

On-the-Scene Reporter: "The boy's known only as Lingdi, and as you can see, this is as close as Chinese authorities are willing to let us get with our cameras. Requests for a formal interview with the boy have been repeatedly denied. Some officials in Beijing have gone so far as to deny the boy's existence, causing much speculation as to the government's role in his uncanny abilities. His mother apparently died in childbirth and his father is unknown. One local farmer we talked to said the boy just walked out of the woods one day, naked."

"Come on," Leah said, "change it to Letterman. This is boring."

"Just a minute," Carmen said, gripping the remote control with both hands and a wicked smile. "I wanna see this."

The screen flipped to a studio setting.

Host: "Joining me in the studio tonight are conservative political commentator Aloysius Stone, self-proclaimed crusader of the Christian right and author of the recent bestseller *Eye for an Eye: Terrorists Beware*, and Kate Kao, professor of Chinese Studies at Yale University. And via satellite from atop the Great Wall of China, Elgin P. Tilford, author of a, well … an interesting academic article entitled 'Is God an Alien?' and professor of—"

"Oh my God," Arabella said, jabbing an index finger at the TV. "I know him."

Prophet Wacko

Professor Tilford appeared in an inset window, standing on the Great Wall in his patented cowboy shirt and turquoise bola tie. A breeze ruffled his thick mustache. Green hills rolled out behind him, disappearing in a low accumulating fog.

"What?" Carmen asked.

"He's got a website called *Nirvana Thru Bluegrass*. It's—"

"Is he some kind of nut?" Leah asked.

"He looks like a nut," Rock said.

"What mean *nut*?" Masa asked.

"Shhh." Arabella put her finger to her lips. "I want to hear this."

Host: "Professor Tilford, let's start with you, as I understand you've actually spoken with this wonder boy."

Professor Tilford: "That's right, Larry—he's an amazing young man. Spoke fluent English, but not just any English. He spoke with all the drawls of my beloved southern Indiana. Like he'd been born and raised in Hoosier Land all his life. It was surreal, Larry, to say the least."

Host: "Professor Tilford, how'd you manage an audience with the boy, given the difficulties our crew's been having with the authorities?"

Professor Tilford chuckled.

Professor Tilford: "You'd be surprised how far a few thoughtful licks on a banjo can get you, Larry. I just learned some Chinese folksongs on the way over and got in well with some local musicians. The rest was easy."

Host: "Professor, what exactly did the boy say? Can you give us your firsthand impression?"

Professor Tilford: "Well, on top of his English fluency—which, mind you, is no small feat for a nonnative speaker with no formal education or, from what I can tell, any previous contact with English speakers anywhere—he spoke with great ease, confidence, and enthusiasm. And his knowledge of each subject we touched on was impressively deep. He was especially eager to talk about the various religious traditions of the world, and spoke repeatedly of the need for their unification—"

Host: "Professor, the question everyone wants to hear an answer to is, do you think there's any connection between this boy and the global flood of messages from the sky?"

Professor Tilford: "That is *the* question, Larry. I think—"

Aloysius Stone: "It's obvious that this kid's a tool of the Chinese communist state, and the connection between him and the messages is undeniable. Hell, they were written on fortune cookie slips, for chrissakes ..."

Arabella waved her hands at the TV.

"What an idiot."

Rock hooted. "Stone's the man!" he said, standing. He high-fived Leah on his way to the kitchen.

"He's cute," Carmen said, sitting on the sofa's edge, eyes glued to the rerunning footage of Lingdi strolling through the crowd. "I'd follow him anywhere."

"This is getting too weird," Arabella said aloud, but primarily to herself. Her thoughts were darting between the likelihood of a superior alien race versus a truly omnipotent being. How could anyone tell the difference?

"But the Bible says Jesus is the only true God," Leah said. "And—"

"Oh, come off it," Carmen said with a roll of her eyes. "When are you gonna wean yourself off of that crap?"

"Carmen," Arabella said, "that's just gonna make her slam the door tighter. Let her come around at her own pace."

Rock watched from the doorway to the kitchen and scratched his balls.

Masa got up to fetch a beer.

"What meaning, *wean crap?*" he asked Rock.

Rock laughed. "It means *wake up, fool!*" He slapped his own forehead and said, "You know, like, 'Wake up, fool.'"

"*Ah-so,*" Masa said.

Chapter 26

"Friend of mine built it," Frick said, gesturing with his spoon at the tree house as he and Wacko munched on a chunky gruel of grains, berries, roots, and crayfish. "He and his girlfriend used to come here all the time. She's the one who made it look homey. But they kind of abandoned it, so I took it over. Been squatting now for a couple of years—Thoreau-like."

He stirred his gruel and lifted another spoonful.

"Make it out once in a while for supplies," he said, "but for the most part I don't see many people except for the random visit from Nazi Noid and the occasional hiker, so having a guest for dinner's a special treat."

"Nazi Noid?"

"Yeah," Frick said, "local ranger dude with a broomstick up his ass."

Wacko grunted and slurped.

"So, Wacko, what brings you to the woods anyway?"

Zawt, who by now had taken the time to look over the basic charter objectives stored in the vehicle's memory banks, had the avatar vehicle say, "This vehicle's here to unite the Human race through religious manipulation."

Frick nodded and chomped.

"No shit?" he said. He chewed for a moment. "That's a pretty tall task, big cheese. You doing that all by yourself?"

"It's guided by a team of Xenkonians on the Planet L'goth working for an enterprise called Eeftwat Avatars."

"Xenkonians, eh?" Frick asked with his mouth full. "Friend or foe?"

"I'd have to say foe, as their ultimate goal is subjugation for base commercial purposes. They're at this very moment trying to get me to stop being so honest with you about the mission. They're of the opinion that such honesty will jeopardize their chances of success."

"Well, tell them your secret's safe with me. Besides, I live like a hermit in the woods. Who would I tell?"

"Good point. I've replied to them *stuff and nonsense!*" Wacko said, bellowing the last three words as if shouting across a canyon. Bits of crayfish flew through the shadowy space between them and the creek below. "This has caused them much consternation."

Frick laughed. "Or you could just be talking shit," he said.

Gargado yelled over his holoscreens.

"Somebody shut it up. Now."

Charter members and recruits scrambled. The horders grunted.

"Stuff and nonsense?" Bleep said under his breath.

Prophet Wacko

"Another atypical Hoo'qqai expression," SkroSkro said.

Frick and Wacko scraped their bowls in silence, then retired to the tree house, which consisted of one room with a high ceiling. Half of the room was occupied by a jutting loft about five feet from the top, lined with worn camping mats. Under the loft stood a wooden table with candles in various stages of consumption, surrounded by two folding chairs.

Frick lit some candles. The walls danced with flickering flame shadows. He grabbed something from under the table and sat.

"Been saving this," he said, holding out an unopened jar of strawberry jam. "But now seems as good a time as any."

He twisted the lid and handed the jar to Wacko. The scent of sugared fruit wafted into the air.

"Go ahead. It's awesome."

Wacko dipped a spoon and nibbled. His eyes widened.

"Oh, you deplorable sugar-bag," he said, digging with the haste of a burrowing gopher until nothing remained but the sound of spoon clanking glass.

Frick threw his head back and laughed.

"You're crazy, dude," he said, reaching into a drawer in the table. He packed a crystallized bud of homegrown hemp into his favorite pipe, lit a match, and inhaled. Trying not to exhale, he extended the pipe and grunted. "Toke?"

Wacko took the pipe and twirled it before his eyes. It was heavy and caramel-colored.

Frick let the smoke billow from his lungs.

"Carved it myself from an antler I found near the creek," he said. "Blacktail buck, I think."

163

"Blacktail buck," Wacko said.

Frick lit another match.

"Be careful, big cheese," he said, hovering the flame over the pipe's bowl. "This is powerful weed."

Wacko inhaled, sucking in his cheeks as Frick had done. He held the smoke until his lungs forced it out in hacks and coughs. He lurched forward and placed his forehead on the tabletop.

Frick laughed.

"I told you, man," he said, prying the pipe from Wacko's fist. He took another toke and leaned back to stare at the ceiling, blowing the smoke in a slow, linear stream.

"Unification of the world's religions, eh?" Frick said, still staring at the ceiling. "That's a hell of an undertaking, you know. I mean, shit, Wacko, it's gotta be like herding cats. You're gonna be running in circles."

Wacko moaned. Zawt had the unnerving sensation that the vehicle's head was filled with helium. He clasped his fingers behind it to keep it from flying away.

"Now," Frick said, shifting his eyes from the ceiling to the moaning vehicle, "I'm an atheist myself, so I don't feel the need to run around crusading like some of my brothers and sisters do. Atheism frees me. I can distinguish good from evil, be humane and caring, and love my neighbor without any mind-cluttering bullshit. People think if you take away the God element, then everybody will run amok killing and raping. But that's just crap. Morals aren't imposed by religion. They're imbedded within our biological and cultural being, dictated by evolution. Goddamn it! Wacko, my friend, there ain't no God about it."

Frick's eyes glistened like rubies as he grinned.

"Don't you see? Eliminate God from the equation and what happens? Nothing, except a more humane and judicious society."

Prophet Wacko

"If you meet the Buddha, kill the Buddha" dribbled from Wacko's cottonmouth like sawdust. He was still staring at the floor.

"Buddha?" Frick said, shaking his dreadlocks with a jangle. "Goddamn, big cheese, you're a piece of work, man. The bulk of any religion's a jumble of cultural prejudices, generated by the prevailing collective sense of self. Buddha, Jesus, Muhammad, Krishna, the list goes on and on, man. The idea of God is just a construction that fulfills some primitive emotional needs, but ultimately abdicates our ability to reason."

Zawt was becoming distracted by something pushing against the middle of the vehicle's forehead from the inside, which coincided with Chubij becoming aware of muffled voices and shady, intermittent glimpses through a dark fog.

"Belief and disbelief in a God, or anything for that matter, are just two sides of the same coin," Wacko said, ignoring the prod in the vehicle's head by raising his eyes to Frick. "Both require an arbitrary stance that blocks the road to enlightenment. It's like your uncertainty principle. Subjectively fix a reference point by focusing on one property, and you can't then see the other properties. Better to watch the probabilities. Be agnostic, open-minded, full of doubt." His voice was as hoarse as burnt coal. "Mute."

"Agnostic?" Frick said. "That's just sitting on the philosophical fence, waiting for something to happen. It don't get you anywhere, man."

"Are we going somewhere?" Wacko asked.

"Huh?"

"The mind only moves in response to the outside world, and when it's touched, it knows."

"And what if it's never touched?"

"There, you've seen it."

"What?" Frick said. "Seen what?"

"Then you might know."

"Know what?"

"And wouldn't that," Wacko said, "be a great satisfaction?"

"Ugh!" Frick said. "You're killing me here, man."

The vehicle's brain suddenly ceased to express itself outwardly. Wacko's head fell back. His Adam's apple jutted toward the ceiling. He began hissing spit and snoring.

Frick snickered.

"I told you, man," he said. "It's powerful weed."

He blew out the candles and clambered into the loft.

———————

Hours later, the avatar vehicle was kneeling by the window, hands on the sill, hooting at the night.

The spotted owl was perched on a thick bough meters from the tree house.

"Ulluoi, my sister," Chubij hooted, "something bothers you?"

"Oh, my patriarch, this confinement is torture—to not be able to swim through the atmosphere of L'goth. To swirl with our sisters. It's unnatural. Doesn't our Mother-God see that?"

Chubij was silent.

"My patriarch," Ulluoi hooted. "I'm sorry for being so weak. Your situation is so much graver than mine. I'm being selfish."

"We all must face our own tribulations, my sister," Chubij said. "But our Mother-God knows our suffering. It is in her name that we strive."

"Yes, my patriarch. Forgive me."

"Don't be too hard on yourself, my sister. Weak moments are a part of our learning. Now, are there any developments with this charter?"

"The bigfoot assassin continues to prowl the woods."

"Where?"

"Not far from here."

"How will I know it? I have no idea what it looks like."

"It's a megafauna cryptid."

"What does that mean?"

"It's very big, but not real, I think."

"Like the deities that inhabit their religious myths?"

"Perhaps, my patriarch, but I don't think bigfoots are worshipped."

"This is all rather unusual, my sis—"

"Yo, Wacko," Frick said from the loft. "Where'd you learn to hoot like that? Damn, that's cool."

Chubij directed the vehicle's gaze toward the loft. He could see no face in the shadows, only a monstrous, dreadlocked silhouette.

"Who are you?" he asked. Through the window behind him he heard the whoosh of great wings fluttering. He turned to see the vacated limb recoiling.

Frick cackled.

"Shit, man, you still stoned or what?"

Wacko squinted back into the darkness in the direction of the voice.

"I am the savior of this planet," he said. "I speak on behalf of Jesus of Galilee, Buddha of the Bodhi tree, Muhammad of—"

"Yeah, yeah, I know, man. You told me."

Wacko stared for a long, contemplative moment.

"Are you a bigfoot?" he asked.

"Shit, man," Frick said. "Shut up and go to sleep, yeah?"

Not at all sleepy, Wacko rummaged for something to eat. He found an assortment of jars on a shelf containing seeds, dried berries, herbs, and psilocybin mushrooms.

Ten minutes later and parched, he scrambled down the ladder and followed the sound of the gurgling creek. Squatting, he scooped with both hands and drank, his mind fixated on the shapeless image of a bigfoot. When he finished, he sat on the bank and looked through the branches at the dark sky. Only then did he notice it was raining.

Chapter 27

HENAN—"Lingdi's God!" shouted a girl hanging out the window of a public bus along one of Zhengzhou's major thoroughfares.

While Lingdi may not deserve the status of an omnipotent, omniscient being, the skinny teenager from the Chinese countryside has certainly endeared himself in the hearts of many and is steadily becoming one of the most impactful global sensations of our times.

People of all nationalities and faiths are flocking to this otherwise nondescript province of China, where Lingdi recently took up residence in a cave near the Shaolin Monastery on Song Shan, the middle mountain of China's five Sacred Mountains. Overnight, nearby Dengfeng has turned into an unprepared mecca for pilgrims. Even the fume-laden cities of Luoyang and Zhengzhou, each an hour or so away, are busting at the seams with spur-of-the-moment curiosity seekers.

Many political leaders are among the faithful that have come to catch a glimpse of, or perhaps even chat with, the astonishing young man who is rapidly changing the face of the world's religious landscape.

"Lingdi very well could be the unifying spirit we've been longing for," said a man claiming to be a high-ranking member of the Israeli Labor Party. "He speaks the universal language of hope and transcendental faith. Humanity's on the verge of a paradigm shift."

Not everyone, however, is ready to cede the reins of spiritual leadership. Many world religious leaders have expressed adamant skepticism of Lingdi as a prophet.

"He's a fraud," said the Catholic monsignor of a New York City archdiocese, who admitted to knowing very little about the boy or Henan. "It's just a frivolous social movement among communists. He'll be an afterthought in six months."

Religious scholars are taking an objective view.

"In essence, Lingdi is professing a new religious order that transcends and amalgamates all current spiritual philosophies," explained Elgin P. Tilford, professor of Religious Studies at Indiana University, who was probably the first Westerner to talk to the new prophet. "And he's incredibly convincing."

Indeed, Lingdi's grasp of theological doctrines has at times even stumped the scholars. And his command of languages has some linguists resorting to unorthodox theories of savantism.

While many may find delight and wonder in the phenomenon that is Lingdi, Chinese authorities are not among them.

"There aren't enough toilets or garbage bins around Shaolin. Food is in short supply. No showers. The crowd is very unruly at times. People are getting sick or hurt, and the hospitals are unable to accommodate them. Language is a huge problem," lamented one local police chief.

Police have recently implemented roadblocks along the roads leading into Henan, and stricter inspection is expected at all Chinese ports of entry. They announced yesterday that journalists are no longer allowed into the region.

"This is necessary to curb the unmanageability of the crowd," explained the police chief. "We think the media is driving this beyond what would normally be the case."

A few embassies have openly appealed to the Chinese government for restraint, fearing a deadly crackdown along the lines of Tiananmen Square in 1989.

"China is facing an unprecedented social challenge, and authorities there have thus far handled the situation with admirable self-control. We hope they continue to use civil means going forward," President Simiun said yesterday.

Chapter 28

A psilocybin-inspired Wacko forged through the forest, bouncing off trees, mumbling and gasping and laughing. Morning found him prostrate in a mist-covered glade, a tortuous smile smeared across cadaverous lips.

A veil lifted—an anticlimactic shredding of silk.

Zawt cackled across the open void.

"Oh! You denizen of the dark cavern."

"Me?" Chubij said.

"You must be the channeling Hoo'qqai to which the mission statement refers."

"I am Chubij, of the Hoo'qqai, formally of the Hoo'qqai-Qanjivian Cooperative. And you? Are you of this world?"

"Ah, Hoo'qqai! I've heard about you," Zawt said. *"Meddling in the affairs of others. Pushing twisted forms of theology on unsuspecting species across the galaxy. Eh? That's just a wee bit morally bankrupt, don't you think?"*

"The Cooperative has brought peace of mind to countless souls over countless millennia—"

"Not to mention irreversible psychological trauma. But unsolicited missionary work is rarely selfless in nature."

"Evil must be countered wherever it's found."

"Darkness and light are all the same to me."

"You're illogical, yet at no loss for opinions. Perhaps you're the unbalanced one."

Zawt laughed. *"Perhaps indeed."*

"Who are you?"

"Ah, to be forgotten," Zawt said. *"I'll answer to the name of Zawt. I'm a Xenkonian adhering to the Mute Way and an otherwise sentient creature that routinely eats and shits. On this planet I'm known—or, shall I say, you and I are known—as Wacko."*

"How did you find your way into this vehicle?"

"Perhaps I was neglect in my meditations."

"What?"

Zawt laughed.

"I bet I can stay in the driver's seat longer than you, Hoo'qqai."

———————

By a mere coincidence of timing, SkroSkro-Bleep was positing Zawt's presence to the charter team just as the two occupants of the Earth vehicle were exchanging pleasantries.

"What the fuck does this charter have to do with the mutes?" Swaq said, his head lurching around his neck as if spring-loaded.

"A mute monk?" Jelpmittlebong asked. "Are you sure?" He felt a surge of adrenaline.

Qoohx sat hunched beside him, sweating beads of dark port and sniffing at his foreclaws.

Swaq grimaced in their direction.

SkroSkro and Bleep twisted their joint shoulders.

"The Hoo'qqai Chubij has mentioned several times the presence of a seer mind in the vehicle," Bleep said. "We ourselves—"

"We ourselves have detected no such presence," Gargado said from across the conference table.

"Yes," Bleep said, "but we've witnessed the vehicle behaving in most unprecedented ways."

Gargado ground his teeth.

"My colleague and I," Bleep said, smacking his lips and dipping his head sideways at SkroSkro, "have reason to believe all this can be explained by hypothesizing the presence in the vehicle of, not a seer mind, but a mute monk."

"And not just any mute monk," SkroSkro said. "We're talking about ol' Zawt himself."

A collective gasp billowed over the room.

"Zawt?" Swaq said over the murmurs. "He hasn't left his slaughterhouse penthouse for years. Go to the Mhowr. He's being live-streamed as we speak. Although I think he's in mid-head regeneration." He laughed.

"Lord Swaq," Bleep said. "We can't explain why, but from the very commencement of this charter, the vehicle's nonverbal behavior has been downright peculiar."

"But it's the verbal behavior that gives rise to our speculation," SkroSkro continued. "It's been using odd combinations of words and a unique logic, neither of which are programmed into its processing unit or characteristic of Hoo'qqai improvisation, especially Chubij's. But they fit surprisingly well when laid beside the lingo-philosophico profile of your average, sophisticated mute monk."

A pudgy recruit slipped into the charter room and whispered in Gargado's ear. Gargado's dominant eye bulged as the recruit bowed and departed.

"Working on this assumption," Bleep said, "your horder scientists helped us run a search through the known mute monk databanks to see if we could pinpoint the unique verbal signature of an individual monk—"

"It's Zawt," Gargado said, with a sigh that caused all eyes to turn. He looked up. "Goddamn it."

———

They quickly activated the hologlobe in the middle of the table. The avatar vehicle lay inert in the alpine meadow under a thin, gray cloud that descended to the planet's surface. But it was the audio channel that had everyone's attention.

"... *stronger than most, I concede. But why do you insist on dominating the vehicle's consciousness? Can't we share it?"* Chubij was entreating.

"*Oh,"* Zawt said, "*you must be banished for a while here and there."*

"*But this is a charter mission, and you're an uninvited stowaway. And for your information, my future hangs in the balance."*

"*Such melodrama suggests an underlying disharmony of mind. But, my good Hoo'qqai, I'm neither away nor stowed. And I'm having too much fun to let your small-minded missionary work crash the party."*

Qoohx looked up at the word *party* and cracked an evil grin. The tips of his foreclaws wavered under his nostrils.

"*Did you know,"* Chubij said, "*at this very moment we're being stalked by a bigfoot because of your shenanigans?"*

Gargado darted a surprised dominant eye at Jelpmittlebong. "How'd he know that?" he said.

Jelpmittlebong responded with a furtive shrug.

"Hoo'qqai Chubij," SkroSkro said, "this is the charter team. May we have the pleasure of being introduced to your companion?"

"How the hell did you get in our vehicle?" Gargado asked, unhappy at both Zawt's presence and SkroSkro's attempt at pleasantry.

"Zawt?" Swaq said. "Is that really you?"

"Lord Kiku fo Swaq? Destroyer of worlds?" Zawt raspberried. "Is there no choice but to abandon reasoning?"

"Here's a bit of reasoning for your misguided mute head," Swaq said. "Cooperate or die."

"Birth and death are but arbitrary clamps."

"Is that a *yes* or a *no*?"

"I'll cooperate," Chubij said.

Zawt laughed.

"Such a price is friendship, Hoo'qqai," he said, as the vehicle leaped to its feet and started swatting at the fog.

"I really think you should call off the bigfoot—" Chubij said, his voice receding as if he'd dropped through a manhole.

Wacko bolted into the forest.

The charter members looked at Swaq with questioning eyes.

"Kill it," Swaq said.

Chapter 29

Jelpmittlebong sat in his quarters, his forehead wrinkled in pursuit of a hundred elusive mind portals. They phased in and out on the periphery of his concentration like undulating, ghostly rings. Unaided by melatonin, he watched like a starving child eyeing a feast, knowing that as soon as he approached one, it would close up or retreat. Niukah had identified this as a common phenomenon for neophytes—"capricious" was how he described them—and counseled against unreasonable expectations. One needed to learn the way around such vagaries—a way independent of the mysterious influence of an alien hormone.

The last few hours were an equal testament to Jelpmittlebong's doggedness and the sheer extent of his inexperience as a nascent mute. But he yet again exhaled in a slow stream of mental focus and cleared his mind. The portals appeared like stars in his peripheral vision, but this time a prominent portal leaped before his mind's eye. He felt a draft of exhilaration as he nestled closer with a mental dally and watched it, half expecting the inevitable recoil. But the portal remained. He inched closer and was just about to pounce when the soft voice of Niukah emanated from its center.

"Your persistence is admirable, my student," it said.

Jelpmittlebong dropped his foreclaws into his lap and sighed. *"I should have recognized your signal, Overseer,"* he thought.

"You're exhausted, I'm afraid."

Moments later, Niukah and 8-1-21 bounded into the room. Jelpmittlebong rotated his head like an owl.

"Well," 8-1-21 said as the door shut behind them, "anybody who claims *all bullshit's no bullshit* as divine inspiration is talkin' bullshit in my book—mute or not. If that makes me a sinner, then I'll see y'all in mute hell."

"We'll greet you with open arms," Niukah said with a laugh.

Niukah wagged a satchel in Jelpmittlebong's direction.

"Paranoid schizophrenia," he said, iridescent moisture billowing on his breath. "Which, I think, is what the Humans call it."

"Excuse me?" Jelpmittlebong said.

"Can ya be a bit more obtuse?" 8-1-21 said.

"Our mipoon used his monger magic to get this," Niukah said, dangling the satchel before Jelpmittlebong's eye. "It contains some hormone from a very agitated Human, whose naturally occurring neurosis was apparently assisted by some ungodly abuse by, of all persons, its own parent." Niukah sighed. "It's amazing how cruel these aliens can be—highlights the inherent pitfalls of genitor upbringing."

"What are you on about?" Jelpmittlebong asked.

"Niukahee's got a plan," 8-1-21 said with a laugh.

"My student," Niukah said, "Swaq loads up on the hormone regularly. Even with it he's about as lithe as a rabid aasmamyl buck, but without it he's blind—fumbling around like you've been for the last few hours."

"So?"

"So?" 8-1-21 said. "He thinks he can just waltz in and spike Swaq's personal stash, of all the cockamamie—"

"At the right time," Niukah said.

Jelpmittlebong stared. "The right time?"

"Yes." Niukah sat back and blinked. "Just before the confrontation, which should be soon. I heard he almost hit the roof when he saw the clip of you calling him a soft-bellied slink lizard."

"What clip?"

8-1-21 laughed. "Or a pussyfooted aasmamyl pup."

"Yes, that too," Niukah said with a grin.

Jelpmittlebong raised his brow and shifted his gaze between them.

"Show him," Niukah said to 8-1-21, then turned to Jelpmittlebong. "We've had to keep some things from you, in case Swaq penetrated your thoughts."

8-1-21 pulled out a blinking NAD tube from his left lateral socket and waved it like a wand. He buzzed to Jelpmittlebong's desk and, brushing away some papers, plugged the NAD into the hologlobe's console.

A frozen holoimage projected life-size in the middle of the room. It was a still scene with Malgorp and the other charter team members standing in the charter room, with suppressed expressions of gruff excitement, their eyes glued to a fixed holostream. The door behind them was an angled blur, as if in the midst of being thrust open. A red dominant eye scowled from the darkness on the other side.

"Watch this, Lordy," 8-1-21 said, pushing a button. "Ya be one macho badass now."

The red dominant eye in the holoimage belonged to a beefed-up Jelpmittlebong. He stalked in with a cold grit of his fangs and proceeded to rip Malgorp's head from his shoulders. 8-1-21 stopped the holostream just as Jelpmittlebong flung the head into the corner of the holographic charter room. It hung suspended in mid-flight in the middle of Jelpmittlebong's quarters. The Jelpmittlebong of the holostream glared ahead, nostrils frozen in midflare.

Jelpmittlebong squared his dominant eye at the image. "That's not what happened."

"Ya can thank Niukahee for the little embellishment," 8-1-21 said. "And it's sure to get ol' Swaq in a frenzy."

"We have to prepare the groundwork for your acceptance by the Horde," Niukah said.

"Yeah, but—"

"These all be accessible now on the Horde-censored Mhowr," 8-1-21 said, "uploaded by an untraceable source." He grinned, pushing some more buttons. "Ya just lucky I still got them access codes."

The holoimage flickered, and a scene from Jelpmittlebong's student days in Toq appeared. Again exaggeratedly bulked up, he was intervening between a gang of young hoodlums and their indiscriminate torture of an elderly laborer. The holostream showed Jelpmittlebong rushing in and whipping the entire gang single-handedly. It ended with him heaving two bundles of severed heads toward the sky and shaking them like dinner bells, his face blood-spattered.

Jelpmittlebong remembered the basis of the scene. Two pre-adolescent Xenkonians were teasing a young slink lizard. Jelpmittlebong had reprimanded them and then lifted them into the air in a kind of brotherly horseplay.

There had been no direct witnesses, as far as he knew, although he did remember casually blogging about it at the time.

"This one's my favorite," 8-1-21 said, as the holostream danced to the fiddling of his foreclaws across the console. A well-toned Jelpmittlebong flashed into the room. He was standing among a harem of slink lizards, each fawning to massage his enhanced tail muscle.

8-1-21 laughed.

"Watch the one on the left, looks like she's prayin'. She's gonna—"

"I get the picture," Jelpmittlebong said, backhanding the air with a dismissive foreclaw.

8-1-21 frowned and cut the holostream.

"Looks like ya really on Swaq's shit list now, Lordy," he said.

Jelpmittlebong moaned through taut lips. He looked at Niukah.

"Overseer," he said, "I don't think I'm up to this."

"It's your destiny," Niukah said.

"But why me?" Jelpmittlebong straightened his back. "Why not you, Overseer? You're far more skilled than I am now, or probably ever will be."

"How do you think the Horde would react to a brittle old fart like me? I'm afraid I wouldn't intimidate anyone. I'd be challenged in a minute."

"But once you demonstrated your power to—"

"A mute mustn't flaunt his muteness, lest persecution be sparked."

Jelpmittlebong tilted his head.

"My student, the mutes are considered lunatic fringe, which, despite being relatively accurate from many frames of reference, is necessary for our continuation." Niukah blinked. "Inviting suspicion of mass mind control is not in our best interests. The probability restraints indicate only narrow margins separate current conditions from an Empire-wide witch hunt."

Jelpmittlebong flapped into the air and hovered high against the glass wall. Lapis-tinged light smattered across his face as Niukah's overall strategy crystallized in his mind. He had an acceptable physique for a horder, but he knew it was the combination of this with his devotion to a just society and burgeoning muteness that made him the perfect choice. And positioning a young mute as Lord of the Horde represented a solution for the future. A militia surreptitiously guided by mutes. A perfect alliance. Why hadn't it been pursued before?

"Because the need never outweighed the expenditure, until now," Niukah's voice echoed in his mind. *"The possibility of a mutant such as Swaq was always there, but we tried to weed them out before they got too powerful. Swaq transcended the probability restraints swifter than we could react. It had never happened before."*

Jelpmittlebong looked down.

"Is Zawt's presence in the Earth's vehicle happenstance?" he thought.

Niukah laughed, *"Zawt's the master of all mutes,"* he thought. *"Nothing would surprise me."*

Jelpmittlebong alit next to his overseer and nodded. "So what's the plan?" he said aloud.

"It's already in motion. First—"

"First ya piss off Swaq," 8-1-21 said. "And when he challenges ya ass, hope some contaminated stuff will sidetrack his badassness long enough to let a naïve wannabe lordy, influenced by a suspicious Pollyanna-pushin' mute head, rip off his head." 8-1-21 crossed his arms. "Did I get all that, Niukahee?"

Niukah grinned. "Pretty much, mipoon," he said. "But you forgot to say we'll be with him all the way."

"We will?"

Chapter 30

An early-morning fog floated through the trees. Wacko was wading in the creek on his way back toward the tree house. Zawt's mind was centered on a fat nothingness behind which Chubij was tucked.

Just before the bend in the creek below the tree house, Wacko stopped and cocked his head, then scurried through the underbrush to the other side of the hill. He slowed to a slither under a grove of small Douglas firs, which his subconscious memory told him was not there before.

He came to rest on his belly some twenty meters away, with a side view of two men. They were standing underneath the tree house. Ranger Noid was clean-shaven, burly, and squat, hands behind his back. Ranger Davis was bearded, tall, and leggy, slouching.

Frick stood across from them, a burlap sack over his shoulder. A thick dreadlock obscured his ashen face.

"Well, I … uh, don't recall seeing anyone fitting that description," Frick said.

"Is that so?" Ranger Noid said. "Then where'd you get this?" He flashed a black, cudgel-like object from behind his back and flipped a switch at its base to climax. The object throbbed and hummed. The ranger parted his thin, dry lips in a gritty smile.

Frick shook his head with a jangle.

"Umm … Found it on a trail …" he said. "Good for stirring porridge."

"Don't fuck with me, freak." The ranger switched off the dildo. "There's been a report of a madman attacking hikers near here, naked as a jaybird. We know it wasn't you, because you don't match the description, which was pretty damned precise, down to the size of his … How'd they say it, Ranger Davis?"

Ranger Davis looked up from the red cuticle he was chewing.

"I think *monstrous* was the word they used."

"Yeah, down to his monstrous pecker. So consider yourself one lucky son of a bitch, freak."

"That's a relief," Frick said.

"Shut up." Ranger Noid palmed his crotch with his free hand and yanked as if adjusting a jockstrap. "Think hard. We don't get many reports like that around this part of the woods. Ain't that right, Ranger Davis?"

"That's right," Ranger Davis said to the back of Ranger Noid's head without looking up. "No reports like that since I can remember."

"So, you sure, freak?" Ranger Noid continued, stiffening his stance. "You ain't seen anything out of the ordinary lately?"

"No, sir, nothing."

"Now, this guy's probably crazy as a fuckin' loon, maybe even a serial killer psychopath and shit, and must be considered armed and dangerous, so—"

"I thought you said he was naked as a jaybird?" Frick said. "How can he be armed if—"

"Shut up"—Ranger Noid thrust the tip of the vibrator into Frick's chest—"or I'll rip your fuckin' hippie head off and shit down your neck. Is that clear?"

"Um, yeah, okay."

"'Um, okay'?" Ranger Noid said. "Listen up, freak. We found your stash of devil weed. Looked like more than an ounce to me. What's the penalty for that, Ranger Davis?"

"Hmm," Ranger Davis said, closing his eyes and pushing out his lips. "That's a Class B felony in Oregon." He opened his eyes. "Maximum ten-year prison sentence and a two-hundred-and-fifty-thousand-dollar fine."

Frick lifted his eyelids and bulged his eyes.

"Don't be giving me that look, faggot," Ranger Noid said, stepping into Frick's face like a drill sergeant. "Or I'll take you down, right now—you got that?"

"Yes, sir," Frick said, standing erect with a sharp jingle.

"Good," Ranger Noid said through clenched teeth. He sucked a mass of snot from his throat and hurled it to the ground with his tongue. "I got a brother that swears by the devil weed. He's an idiot like you, but he's my brother, so what can you do? So I'm willing to let it go. But don't rub me the wrong way, freak, or I might just change my mind."

"Yes, sir!"

"That's more like it. Now"—he thrust the dildo in Frick's face—"you're saying you just found a backpack in the woods and inside was this little gizmo, huh? Is that what you're saying?" He was wagging the vibrator as if directing traffic, flicking it on and off.

"Yes, sir."

Ranger Noid raised his granite chin.

187

"Where?"

Frick swallowed.

"Up near Rebel Creek," he fibbed, "along the trail, um … near the log bridge."

"Hmm," Ranger Noid said. "That sound plausible to you?" he asked Ranger Davis, his eyes remaining on Frick.

Ranger Davis raised his eyes and squinted at the branches.

"Well, could be. That's not far from our crime scene. Hard to say it ain't possible."

"Okay," Ranger Noid said, "we're gonna take your word for it. But if I find out you're lying, I'm gonna kick your faggoty nuts through your chin. You got that?"

"Got it, Ranger Noid, sir."

"Good. Now, if you see or hear anything of this person of interest, what are you going to do?"

"Make haste to your ranger station, sir, and inform you of such sighting, mister ranger, sir."

"That's more like it." Ranger Noid cracked a lizard smile. "Don't forget who's got your ass, heh?"

"Yessir, Ranger Noid, sir," Frick said. "You got my ass, Ranger Noid, sir."

"That's better."

After Rangers Noid and Davis were well out of sight, Wacko dawdled out of the ferns.

"Those gentlemen were in search of a serial killer?" he asked.

"Big cheese?" Frick said, looking up from his cross-legged position. "Where the hell've you been?"

"It's very chilly in the early morning," Wacko said.

"Yep, chilly as hell, Wacko my friend." Frick stood and brushed off his jeans. "Was that you who attacked those hikers?"

"I didn't attack them."

"Then what the hell did you say to them?"

"It was my wish to confabulate."

"Confabulate?" Frick said, as if questioning the existence of such a word.

"How dare you burn down my wooden image?"

"Come on, Wacko, enough of the wisecracks for a while, yeah? Seriously, what did you say to them?"

"I simply greeted them."

Frick shook his head.

"Well, shit, it must've been one hell of a greeting. You'd better watch it. Ranger Noid's a persistent bastard. He'll be back."

"Noid?" Wacko said.

"Yeah. And he's got a Guantánamo crew cut under that mister ranger hat. We'd better steer clear of him for a while. What do you say we do a supply run to Eugene? We can stay at my sister's place. She's cool."

Wacko beamed.

"Three pounds of flax!"

He leaped into an impromptu session of jumping jacks.

Chapter 31

An SUV hauling a travel trailer pulled to a stop on the gravel shoulder of Forest Road 19. From the forest edge a pair of unblinking, red eyes stalked two figures piling into the backseat. The SUV edged back onto the road and disappeared into the horizon. In its wake, a howl erupted through saliva-dripping fangs.

As the bigfoot assassin stomped back into the woods, the branch of a stocky pine tree swatted its shoulder.

"Brother," the tree said in the native tongue of the Skooks. "Why are you uncloaked? Especially in daylight. And howling like that is sure to draw attention."

The bigfoot twisted his head at the tree, then stepped up for a closer look.

"Brother, you are strange," the tree said.

Burying his eyes with his brow, the bigfoot headbutted the unsuspecting tree in midtrunk, sending the rootless plant to the ground with an involuntary groan. He stepped over the suddenly uncloaked Skook and snarled.

The Skook scrambled across the mossy soil like a sand crab, his eyes wide as pinecones. A protracted roar and furious chest-pounding reverberated behind him as he dashed through the forest.

"I don't mean to be impolite, boys," the old woman said from the SUV's front passenger seat, "but I think you both could use a shower."

"Yes, ma'am," Frick said with a smile. "We've been camping in the mountains so long I've almost forgotten about the comforts of civilization."

"That's the pioneer spirit," the old man behind the wheel said, running a sleeve under his sniveling nose. "Nothing like a good pilgrimage to strengthen the soul."

Wacko was rocking back and forth on the edge of his seat, a mad grin plastered across his face. He was swinging his head from side to side, soaking in the bleeding colors of the passing landscape, when a dog started barking from somewhere behind them. He cocked his head and listened, then began barking back.

Inside the vehicle's head, Zawt was guffawing, and Chubij was struggling like Houdini against an assortment of virtual locks and chains.

The man laughed.

"That's ol' Moses," he said. "He likes to ride in the trailer."

"Young man," the woman said, looking back at Wacko, "better fasten your seat belt. It's the law, you know."

Wacko returned a smile and jammed his hands under his butt.

The woman laughed.

"You're a funny lot," she said. "What's your name?"

"I am the savior of this planet," Wacko said.

The man squinted and turned his head.

"Just call him Wacko," Frick said, laying a palm on Wacko's shoulder. "Because that's exactly what he is. And I'm Frick. Pleased to meet you."

"Wacko and Frick?" the man said, redirecting his eyes to the road. "Nice ring to it. Kinda like Tom and Jerry."

"Ignore him," the woman said, flicking a chubby hand in her husband's direction. "I'm Thelma Lou, and this is Father Jack. We're pleased to meet you right back."

"Father?" Frick asked. "Are you a priest?"

"No, no," Jack said. "She just calls me that outta habit. Got six grown kids back in Ohio."

"But he is a minister," Thelma Lou said, "at the Old Order Dunkers back home."

"Non-salaried minister," Jack said. "But y'all probably never heard of the Old Order Dunkers. Most people know us as the Old German Baptist Brethren—"

"Old German Baptist Brethren," Wacko said. "Aka the Old Order Dunkers, in reference to their practice of baptism by immersion. Traces roots to seventeenth-century pietist movement in Germany. Believes that faith in the Lord Jesus Christ is necessary for salvation. Believes in free will. Rejects infant baptism. Suspicious of Sunday schools. Children encouraged to join church voluntarily when in their teens. Emphasizes the literal interpretation of the scriptures, especially with regard to the Last Supper, so practices closed communion. Worldly amusements frowned upon. No alcohol—"

"Whoa there, fella," Jack said with a frown. "You're mighty informed. Where'd you say you're from?"

"Most recently an antiquated abattoir on Mwookt Qor, twelve parsecs inward core of Xenkon V'rpq Proper," Wacko said, "but I consider the Gok'l Nebula home."

Frick looked out the window and tried not to laugh.

"Where's that, Jackie?" Thelma Lou asked.

"Sounds like a small port we visited in Papua New Guinea during the war," Jack responded with the aplomb of a hometown barber. "That right, Wacko? You're pretty darn far from home, son."

Thelma Lou beamed at her husband from her passenger seat.

"The experience is beyond description," Wacko said.

"Yessiree," Jack said, winking at Wacko through the rearview mirror. "Those Papua New Guineans sure know how to throw a potluck. We were only there a few days, getting supplies, but—"

"If you boys've been camping so long," Thelma Lou said, "you probably haven't heard about the boy in China."

"What boy?" Frick asked tilting his head.

"They call him Lingdi, ain't that right, Jackie?"

"Them Chinese are a slippery lot," Jack said. "I'm telling you. One night in Shanghai, just after the—"

"Jackie!" Thelma Lou said. "These boys aren't interested in your war stories. Do they look like they're interested in war stories?"

"It's okay, ma'am," Frick said.

"No need to be so polite to an old fart like Father Jack," Thelma Lou said with a laugh.

Jack hunkered in his seat and sniffed.

"There's a boy in China who's on all the news channels these days," Thelma Lou said. "Seems to be some kind of supergenius. Speaks all kinds of languages and an IQ off the charts. Apparently he's got a big following now."

"That's right," Jack said. "And his appearance coincided with

194

the flood of paper from the sky. People are calling him the second coming."

"He looks like such a saint," Thelma Lou said.

"Paper from the sky?" Frick said.

"The Horde must really be desperate," Wacko said, positioning himself cross-legged on his seat and looking out the window. "But why Humans?"

Father Jack and Thelma Lou exchanged sidelong glances. Frick gave a nervous laugh.

Wacko looked at them each in turn. He cleared his throat and smiled.

"Have any of you ever seen a bigfoot?"

At the junction of Forest Road 19 and Oregon State Highway 126, just past Cougar Dam, Frick and Wacko disembarked the SUV. They sauntered two hours along the dirt shoulder with thumbs in air, then hopped in an immaculate 1975 Rolls-Royce Silver Shadow.

The man at the wheel was dressed in solid-orange slacks and turtleneck, as were the woman in the passenger seat and their ten-year-old granddaughter in back, complementing the maroon interior and blood-red exterior of the automobile. A picture of a twinkle-eyed, long-bearded Indian mystic hung from the rear-view mirror.

"Nice wheels," Frick said, settling in on one side of the girl.

"One of the Bhagwan's originals," the man said, steering the Rolls-Royce back onto the roadway.

The girl elbowed Wacko in the ribs.

"I think it's a clunker." Her curly ginger hair wisped about her face as she giggled.

Wacko smiled down at her.

"Silver Spirit?" Frick asked.

"Nope," the man said. "Pre-Vickers Silver Shadow—1975, very pampered."

Frick whistled in appreciation. "A real Rolls," he said.

"They don't even work," the girl said into Wacko's ear.

Wacko nodded.

"Don't you think I should be in school?" she asked.

"I don't know. Should you?"

She giggled.

"There are many ways for a chick to leave the nest," Wacko said.

"I'm not a chick," the girl said with a protesting scrunch of her brow.

"An inquiring spirit is to be awakened."

"Who's sleeping?" the girl asked.

Wacko grinned.

The girl leveraged Wacko's shoulder to get closer to his ear.

"What's your name?"

"You may call us Wacko."

"Us?"

"I'm an untamed plurality."

"Okay," she said. "I'm just one, and you may call me Strawberry."

Wacko's eyes shone large and ravenous.

"Strawberry jam?"

"No. Just Strawberry, silly. Bet you can't guess why."

Wacko raised an eyebrow. "A bet?"

She pinched both cheeks between her thumbs and index fingers and pulled. When she let go, they were redder than raspberries.

"Because my cheeks are so red," she said with a giggle.

Wacko laughed. "Well, I like strawberry jam."

Prophet Wacko

Their conversation was interrupted when Frick asked whether the photograph dangling from the mirror was that of the Bhagwan.

Wacko looked up at the smiling cherub face in the photograph.

"I am the savior of this planet," he said. "I speak on behalf of Osho, formerly known as Bhagwan Shree Rajneesh."

His voice, timbre, and delivery were indistinguishable from that of the late guru in his prime. He repositioned himself so that he was sitting cross-legged with hands clasped in the air before him.

The Rolls-Royce skidded to a halt on the shoulder. The man and woman exchanged disbelieving glances, then looked back with the vacuous gleam of blind devotion.

Wacko smiled and dipped his head.

Not a word was said as the man put the vehicle back in gear and eased back onto the road. He and the woman gazed at the passing landscape as if heaven had descended from the sky and stained all living creation with an orange, sunshiny bliss. They were humming a hymn from their glory days at Rancho Rajneesh.

Frick leaned over Strawberry and said to Wacko, "I think you got your first converts."

"They're so ridiculous," Strawberry said, rolling her eyes.

Wacko nodded with a smug purse of his lips and leaned back in his seat.

The avatar vehicle was soon snoring.

———————

Awash again in the kaleidoscopic imagery of dreams, Zawt alit on a growing comprehension of such implication that it prevented him from signaling a touchdown. Within the frenzied and apparently meaningless chaos of these regular dream states swirled the seeds of rational intuition. Humans, it seemed, harbored a latent ability to know abstract immediacy—they had the requisite biology for muteness.

Chubij was sloshing in the virtual muck of his confinement when a ruddy light filtered into the darkness. He wriggled and writhed toward it. A rumbling sound and the sensation of movement presented themselves. He discovered the avatar vehicle slouched against the window of the Rolls-Royce, clouding the glass with its exhalations.

A brown thing flitted outside the window, dipping and flapping and trilling in a brisk succession of hoots. Within seconds, Wacko thrust his body halfway out the moving car.

"Chubij, my patriarch!" hooted the owl, flying in parallel trajectory beside the Rolls-Royce. "Are you there?"

"Ulluoi, my fond sister," Chubij hooted. He was balancing on his navel, arms outstretched. "I'm here!" He waved his arms.

"Oh, finally, my patriarch! I've been trying to reach you. I thought you were lost."

"Ulluoi, my sister, I'm here!"

Wacko's T-shirt rippled in the wind, his thick, blond mane ruffling out behind him.

"My patriarch, I miss your counsel. And this confinement … I mean, how can—"

"Ulluoi—"

"Sometimes I question our Mother-God's wisdom, my patriarch. Oh, I know I shouldn't, but—"

"My sister, listen. You must eavesdrop tirelessly on every conversation concerning this charter, and between this vehicle and the Sphere. We need to understand this seer mind's motivation. Can you do that?"

"Oh yes, my patriarch, I will—"

A firm grip seized the back of Wacko's T-shirt and yanked. He found himself sprawled across knees, staring up at alarmed faces.

"Whoa! Big cheese," Frick said, his fingers still intertwined with the cloth of the T-shirt. "I know you like to hoot and shit, but geez. Come on."

Strawberry's red curls dangled over his face like tapestries. She smiled and said, "Are you some kind of Doctor Dolittle?"

"Are you a bigfoot?"

"No." She laughed.

Frick started singing "Born to Be Wild."

"Who are you?" Wacko asked, sitting up and looking at Strawberry.

She grabbed his hand.

"You really are a plurality," she said.

"I'm the savior of this planet," he told her.

"I believe you," she said.

"Wacko, man," Frick said. "You are too wild."

The Rajneeshee couple looked back and smiled. The Rolls-Royce rolled into the sunset.

Chapter 32

A rapid arpeggio of rockabilly-meets-bluegrass spilled from the receiver's earphone.

"Professor Tilford?" Arabella asked, crumpling her nose.

A few seconds of commotion ensued, as if someone were rearranging furniture, followed by a throat-clearing burble.

"Arabella, my dear, is that you?"

Arabella snuggled the phone to her cheek.

"Professor Tilford," she said. "My ears are ringing."

"Oh, sorry." The professor was still shouting into his speakerphone. "Just mixing some tracks. Keeps me grounded, you know." He cleared his throat. "Anyway, so nice to finally make your acquaintance, so to speak."

"Yes, yours too."

"Our dear Professor Al-Qurashi has been running all kinds of tests on that slip of paper of yours, Arabella." He snorted. "He's such an industrious little Arab."

"Professor, neither his stature nor his ethnicity has anything to do with it."

"Ah! So true, my dear. You've promptly exposed one of my many personal flaws." He chortled. "In any event, Abdul says the results thus far require some fanciful conjecture in order to place them within the bounds of our ordinary understanding of reality. I told him I'm not surprised."

"What does it mean?"

"He didn't give details, but I'm betting it's better than science fiction."

Arabella laughed.

"Professor Tilford," she said, "are you really coming to Oregon?"

"Yes, my dear. Looking forward to it. Try to make it to Duck country whenever I can, you know. Great folk, and always try to make the Oregon Jamboree in Sweet Home."

"Well, you sure get around. I saw you on the news in China."

"A fascinating blend of tradition and modernity, that's the Middle Kingdom, my dear. Anyway, an old friend organizes the Oregon Country Fair, and she's been begging me for years to show up with my banjo. I finally took her up on it. Abdul's promised to meet me there to discuss his results. Can you make it too?"

"Yes," she said, just as the doorbell rang.

"Great. I play on the main stage on the last day."

"Bella!" Carmen shouted from the bottom of the stairs. "Some guys are here to see you."

"Veneta's just a few miles from here, so I can make it anytime."

"Bella!" Carmen yelled.

"I'll send an e-mail letting you know where to find us. See you soon, Arabella. Keep pickin'."

Prophet Wacko

She scrunched her face and shook her head. The beginning licks of "The Ballad of Jed Clampett" squealed in her ear. She hastened the receiver to its cradle.

Arabella bounded down the stairs. A graying sky streamed through the front door. She flicked on the porch light and jerked her head. The shadows of two men stretched over the camellia shrubs lining the footpath to the street. One of them grinned.

"Oh my God!" she said. "Frick?"

"Sis," Frick said with open arms. Arabella leaped at her little brother. Wacko stepped back and guffawed as they hugged and twirled on the porch. Carmen and Leah peered from the doorway. Across the road, under the dim red emissions of a freshly activated streetlamp, the Rajneeshee couple and Strawberry gawked from the orange-tinted windows of their Rolls-Royce. For a short, timeless moment, the tango on the porch bonded them all in a vicarious swell of unspecified sibling memories.

"Oh! This one rare occurrence!" Wacko said.

"It started a few weeks back," Arabella said. She was seated at the kitchen table. "Little pieces of paper rained down from the sky over most of the world's major cities. It was totally wild. Not long after that, a Chinese wunderkind named Lingdi appeared. He's some kind of superbrilliant genius, speaking every language and smarter than smart. Knows everything there is to know, literally."

Frick whistled. His young, lanky frame was shaved, showered, and glistening from a generous anointment of eucalyptus oil. The full, matted attendance of his dreadlocks swirled around

203

his head like a sodden beehive, exposing a smooth, ivory nape. A mug of Irish coffee steamed between his hands.

Wacko, decked in a green Heineken T-shirt, was sitting on the countertop mentally dissecting the various foodstuffs, knick-knacks, and appliances that cluttered its surface.

"Carmen thinks Lingdi's a hunk," Leah said. She was teething a plastic straw.

"Yeah, but he's in China, not in my kitchen." Carmen smiled at Frick.

"Damn!" Frick said with a shake. The beaded and bell-speckled structure of hair swayed. "And people actually think he's the next savior?"

"Well," Arabella said, "it's hard to confirm or refute. I mean, how can you tell if it's the work of a superior race of aliens or the Big Kahuna himself?"

"Or *her*self," Carmen said, still ogling Frick.

Frick turned to Wacko and said, "Looks like you got some competition, big cheese."

"The ego has landed," Wacko said, without looking up from the coffeemaker he was probing with his index finger. "But, my dear"—he suspended his inspection and looked at Arabella—"it's aliens, and we just can't be trusted. But neither can the Big Kahuna." He grinned and gave her a thumbs-up.

Arabella stared at Wacko as if he were a leaky barrel of hydrogen sulfide.

"You still got the piece of paper?" Frick asked. "What's it say?"

Arabella slowly turned toward her brother.

"I gave it to a scientist at OSU who's been running tests on it, but I made a copy." She pointed. "It's there on the fridge."

Frick gummed the lip of his mug as he read the enlarged version of the message, held by a magnet to the freezer door.

"'All big gods will unite under the blessed hand of a multi-lingual beacon,'" he said. He looked back at his sister with teasing raised eyebrows.

"Yeah, I know," she said.

Wacko tilted his head. He squinted at the air in the middle of the room, as if trying to recall the lyrics of a forgotten song.

"'And the lesser godheads too,'" he whispered.

Arabella looked in his direction.

"'The chosen humans will find paradise through his merciful and most wise counseling,'" Frick continued. "Hallelujah," he said, swiping the paper off the refrigerator and wagging it like a checkered flag. "'Glory is yours!'"

Wacko leaped off the countertop and signaled a touchdown. "'For a slight hole in the head!'" he shouted.

Heads swiveled.

"Huh?" Arabella said. "How'd—?" She stopped and turned to Frick. In the shared rudimentary Arabic of their childhood she asked, "Where'd you find this guy? He's just too weird."

Frick shrugged.

"In the mountains," he said in the same pidgin Arabic. "He's okay."

Wacko looked back and forth between the two siblings, then, signaling another touchdown, said in fluent Arabic, "Who is the woman peddling pastry in the dervish robe?"

Frick looked askance at Wacko. Arabella's jaw dropped.

Just then, Masa appeared in the doorway to the kitchen. His crown, smooth from a recent shaving, glinted in the bright fluorescent lighting.

"Waah!" he said. But his exclamation was not directed at Wacko. He was staring at Frick. "Awesome dreadlocks," he said in his native Japanese.

Wacko lowered his arms and tilted his head.

"Ya, mon," he said. Then he sang, "Chase those crazy bald-heads out of town."

"Eh?" Masa looked at Wacko as if he were a talking fish. "Who're you?"

Wacko bowed.

"I'm the savior of this planet," he said in Masa's thick Kansai accent.

"The what?"

"This vehicle is here to unite your various faith-based factions through religious manipulation."

"*Ah-so?*" Masa said. "Is that right?"

"That's right. You may call us Wacko."

"Nice to meet you, Wacko-san. I'm Masa. Where'd you learn to speak Japanese like that?"

"It's through learning that you find yourself."

Masa smiled.

"Maybe you should come with us to Bible study. I just go to practice my English, but an enthusiastic dude like you'd fit right in."

"If you open your mouth, you are mistaken," Wacko said.

"Are you ready?" Masa asked Leah in English, ignoring Wacko's last statement. "This Wacko-san guy too wants go with us. Okay?"

Wacko smiled.

Leah shrugged.

"Sure," she said. "Okay."

Chapter 33

The Rajneeshee man opened the back door to the Rolls-Royce with the extended grace of an experienced valet. He was smiling like a chimpanzee. Wacko, Masa, and Leah squeezed in as Strawberry jumped into the front.

Strawberry turned around and, kneeling on the seat, beamed at Wacko. In her hand was a folded scrap of paper. "To Wacko" was penciled across it.

"I've searched for my mind, but can't find it," Wacko told her, taking the paper from her hand.

"Maybe it's where you didn't look," she said. "I lost my locket once and found it in my dreams."

"Your dreams?"

"Yes. It was under the sofa."

"You think my mind's under the sofa?"

"Look in your dreams." Strawberry giggled as she twisted around.

Wacko smiled and unfolded the paper. It was a drawing of an owl in flight buoyed by flowing arabesques of air current and a forest of trees in the background, sketched in quick, delicate pencil strokes. He looked at the back of Strawberry's carrot head. Quick dimples appeared in his face.

The Rajneeshee man stared in the rearview mirror.

"Umm," Leah said, looking at Wacko, who stared ahead. "Glory to GOD Faith Center," she said, as if requesting permission. "Please."

"Are we going to church?" asked Strawberry.

"Bible study," Leah said.

"And I'm going to convert the whole congregation to the church of Wacko," Wacko said with a smirk.

"Come on," Leah said, "please don't be weird."

"Why would you do that?" Strawberry asked, turning toward the backseat.

"Because I can," Wacko said.

Leah simpered and said, "No you can't."

"You really think you can?" Strawberry asked.

"I know I can."

"I bet you can't even convert one person," Leah said. "Besides, the preacher won't like it. Just be nice, okay?"

Wacko's eyes gleamed like headlights on a clear winter night. "A bet?" he said.

———————

"Your friend speaks Japanese and Arabic?" Arabella asked, her tone that of a traffic cop asking a motorist if he'd been drinking.

"Looks like," Frick said, folding the copy of the message into an unrecognizable form of origami. "Dude's got all kinds of talents. You should hear him hoot."

Prophet Wacko

Arabella twisted her head in waxing perturbation.

"You want another?" asked Carmen, smiling at Frick and holding up her own mug.

Frick looked up.

"Nope," he said, grinning without showing his teeth. "Thanks." He yawned. "Getting kind of tired though."

"I bet," Carmen said. She laid her mug on the countertop. "Come on, I'll show you where you can sleep."

They galloped upstairs hand in hand.

A silence enveloped the kitchen as Arabella pondered what just happened. *How'd he know the missing parts of the message? He doesn't look like the type to be reading articles like that, unless he's a … No! That would mean—*

"Hey, Bella," Rock said with a slur. He was in the doorway, fondling a Heineken.

She sliced her eyes like a raptor in his general direction.

Heavy, torpid eyelids plodded on his red, smiling face.

She looked through him.

He burped.

———————

Across town, Zawt had the avatar vehicle prancing on a table in a small basement cafeteria. An amateurish mural of Jesus and Lingdi shaking hands covered the wall of concrete blocks behind him.

"If we say we have not sinned," Wacko said, "we deceive ourselves, and the truth is not within us!" He balled his hand into a fist and shook it at his transfixed audience. "Believe in Jesus!" he said. His whole body shook.

Inside the vehicle's head, Zawt snickered like a schoolboy.

"Amen," was heard from the gathering.

"For God so loved the world that He gave His one and only Son, that whoever believes in Him shall not perish, but have eternal life!"

"Amen, brother!"

"God is just!"

"Hallelujah!"

"He will forgive our sins and purify us from all unrighteousness!"

"Yeah!"

Wacko was soaked in perspiration and rocking in a trance-like rhythm.

"Now, brothers and sisters, repeat after me," he said. "Lord Jesus!"

"Lord Jesus!"

"Raise this roof!" Wacko's outstretched arms reached for the ceiling.

"Lord Jesus!" Louder.

"I'm a sinner!"

"I'm a sinner!" repeated the congregation, their arms also reaching for the ceiling.

Wacko shook a fist. "Jesus," he said. "Thank you for dying on the Cross for me!"

("Thank you for dying on the Cross for me!")

"Forgive me my sins!"

("Forgive me my sins!")

"Accept me as your child!"

("Accept me as your child!")

"Jesus!"

("Oh! Jesus!")

("Sweet Jesus!")

"Amen!"

("Amen!")

Prophet Wacko

"Yes! Brothers and sisters, I believe!"

("Hallelujah, brother!")

———————

Afterward, Wacko sauntered to the back of the room for donuts and coffee. The preacher stood beside him, smiling. Members of the congregation came up, wretched and clammy with dried sweat, their eyes alight and swimming. Some hugged him. Some knelt before him. Many offered currency.

"Bless you, sister," he said, his hand on a forehead.

"God be with you, brother," he said, clutching a covetous hand.

"Oh, Jesus," he sang with closed eyes to the group. "I am your savior."

Strawberry remained in her chair with crossed arms and a jumbled expression of suspicion and awe, unable to shake the weird sense of guilt by association.

Wacko sat down next to her and leaned back in his chair. His hair and clothes were matted with sweat. He slapped his knees.

"Woo-hah! This is fun."

The impromptu extended prayer meeting eventually moved to the parking lot of the Glory to GOD Faith Center. Wacko was leaning against Masa's shoulder under a street lamp, his mind twinkling in the rarefied margins of exhaustion. A large part of the congregation stood in a semicircle around the Rolls-Royce, holding hands and singing "Kumbaya."

Without warning, Wacko slipped from Masa's support. He landed on the asphalt in the vehicle's default lotus position and closed his eyes. The singing stopped. Glances were exchanged. One by one, they lowered themselves into a sitting position, attentive eyes trained on the avatar vehicle.

Two minutes, three minutes.

Inside Wacko's head, Zawt was skipping blithely through the dream waves of intuitive mind threads that most Humans discard nightly as garbled mind crap.

"Oh!" he thought, *"To cultivate a flame!"*

He was in mute heaven.

Intermittent coughs, whispers, and the sound of bodies repositioning nudged across the silence in the parking lot.

Five minutes. The congregation grew restless. Masa squatted and, casting a plastic smile at the group, slapped the avatar vehicle's shoulder with the back of his hand.

"What're you doing?" he whispered in Japanese. "We should be going." Then he shook the vehicle and said in English, "Wean crap, fool! Wean crap!"

The vehicle's eyes opened. Through a cloud of disorientation, Chubij peeked. Expectant faces stared back. Zawt was nowhere to be felt.

Wacko turned to Masa.

"Who are you?" he said.

"Quit being an idiot and say something," Masa said in Japanese. "They're waiting for more fire and brimstone."

"More what?" Wacko asked—also in Japanese—with a scrunch of his face. "Where am I?"

Masa glared.

"Parking lot of a faith center," he said. "You've convinced these people you're their savior. Don't you remember?"

Wacko curled his head back toward the gathering before him.

"No," he said. "I don't." He staggered to his feet. "Which religion?"

"Christian."

"Sect?"

"I don't know," Masa said, so agitated that his elongated earlobes thudded fast against the base of his jawbone. "Just say something about Jesus. That worked before."

"Jesus of Nazareth?" Wacko asked.

"I'm a Buddhist—how would I know?"

Wacko looked at the group with the suspicious stare of an amnesia patient accused of an unsavory deed, then stretched out his arms. He coughed and cleared his throat.

"Jesus Christ," he said with the conviction of an automaton, "died on the Cross so that we may—"

A shadow scooted out of the darkness and volplaned over the roofs of the parked cars. A large spotted owl landed in a walnut tree on the far side of the parking lot. It jerked its head toward the group, blinked, and stared.

Wacko's brow descended into a squint in the tree's direction. His face flushed red. He started waving his hands and hooting like a madman.

"Ulluoi! My sister!" Chubij hooted. "Is it you? Is it you? It's—"

His hooting was abruptly subdued, however, by the sudden embrace of a lumberjack Wacko had blessed and welcomed into his kingdom just thirty minutes before.

"Brother Wacko, my shepherd," the lumberjack said, whisking the avatar vehicle off the ground like a sack of barley. "Oh, forgive me!" He wailed like a wayward toddler.

Wacko's eyes became huge and round.

"Rancher Dilfer's sheep ..." The lumberjack constricted his arms further. "They ... I ... Oh, Jesus, I have sinned!"

Wacko tasted gastric acid and donuts, then fell gasping to the asphalt on his hands and knees.

Fighting unconsciousness like a scrambling ant in a doodlebug's pit, Chubij thrust all his energy into retracting the slender levator muscles of the vehicle's eyelids. He was rewarded by the lumberjack's engorged face inches from his nose. Coffee-laced halitosis fumed over him. He scuttled to his feet and brushed the dust from his pants.

The lumberjack sat back on his haunches and trembled. He squinted at Wacko with red, imploring eyes.

"Umm ..." Wacko said. He frowned down at the huge man. "Jesus forgives you, my son."

The lumberjack smiled.

"I love you, man."

Leah and Masa helped Wacko into the backseat of the Rolls-Royce and closed the door.

"Go well, my patriarch" dopplered in hoots across the darkness.

Wacko watched the jiggling of the empty branch and cursed.

Strawberry slipped her hand in his.

As the Rolls-Royce pulled onto the street, the rumble of engines flooded the parking lot behind them.

Chapter 34

"I'm not ready," Jelpmittlebong said.

"We have no choice," Niukah said.

"Then let me do it with melatonin."

"The alien hormone is not the way, my student."

"But—"

"What do we really know about these Humans? Even the most blissful among them surely harbors some negative feelings."

"And I'd guess," 8-1-21 said, "anytime religion's involved, psychological repression's gotta be a problem."

"Yes. And who knows? Maybe it builds up over time. Just like—" Niukah stopped in midsentence and held up a foreclaw. He closed his dominant eye and nodded. Moments later he opened his eye and smiled. "They're here," he said, "nearly."

"Who? Swaq?"

"Horders. Two of them. Their mission is to escort you to a prearranged location."

"Damn, Niukahee," 8-1-21 said, "ya communication skills challenge a mipoon's. Can ya teach me—"

Someone pounded on the door. Niukah held up two foreclaws for silence, then slipped quickly against the wall adjacent to the door. He motioned for 8-1-21 to join him, and for Jelpmittlebong to step back into the middle of the room.

"Let them enter," Niukah's voice said inside Jelpmittlebong's head. *"I'll close the door behind them."*

The pounding repeated.

Jelpmittlebong addressed the pounders while still staring at Niukah. "Who is it?" he said, his voice just a shade below trembling.

"Open up!"

Jelpmittlebong glared at Niukah with a misgiving eye.

"Trust me, my student."

As if on cue, the door lifted, and two muscle-bound horders marched in.

"Fumb fo Jelpmittlebong," one horder said, "we have orders from Lord Swaq to—"

Before they could clamp their foreclaws around Jelpmittlebong's biceps, the door was down, and their heads were rolling on the floor.

8-1-21 and Jelpmittlebong stared while Niukah cracked the knuckles of his foreclaws.

"Damn, Niukahee," 8-1-21 said, "well, I never—"

"Violence is the least preferred solution, but it sometimes can't be helped."

"Does that mean you're goin' to mute hell?"

Niukah smiled and said, "If I think so, yes. If I don't, then no."

"Well, that's a pretty damned convenient philosophy."

Jelpmittlebong swallowed and stepped back from the small pool of blood gathering at his feet.

"Overseer?" he said.

"Yes, I know," Niukah said, "I've made a bit of a mess. But"—he rummaged through a pocket on the inside of his cape and pulled out a horder vest—"at least I had the foresight to bring clean ones." He threw the vest to 8-1-21. "Put that on and try your best to look like a horder."

"Holy Kacheenzas, Niukahee," 8-1-21 said, "ya be fully off your rocker."

Niukah pulled off his cape, revealing his own horder garb underneath. Lord Swaq's profile glowed in neon green. He grabbed Jelpmittlebong's arm and smiled.

"I told you we'd be there with you," he said.

———————

Niukah and 8-1-21 escorted Jelpmittlebong—muzzled with a strip of aasmamyl leather for effect—through a network of musty passageways into a remote part of the Sphere, finally entering a large, shadowy room. They stopped and hovered. Jelpmittlebong scrunched his nose and panned the room with his dominant eye. Through the dimness he could just make out a line of murky holes set in the floor against the walls.

"This is an old Qanjivian lavatory," Niukah said.

"We come all this way to go to the toilet?" 8-1-21 asked.

"If you have to, mipoon, now's the time."

8-1-21 scanned the erstwhile Qanjivian commodes.

"No," he said. "But damn, them Qanjivians were big. You could get lost down there."

Niukah chuckled and said, "Let's hope not."

Jelpmittlebong turned.

"We shouldn't keep Swaq waiting." Niukah blinked, then led them in a nosedive into the centermost chasm.

The decommissioned plumbing narrowed and twirled until they finally exited through the rusty fissure of a shredded mesh filter. They stopped and hovered in blackness. A pungent anaerobic stench wafted in the air.

"Where the hell are we?" 8-1-21 asked.

"A defunct Qanjivian septic tank," Niukah said.

"I been in and around this big ball more than most anybody," 8-1-21 said. "How's it you know—"

"I'm guided by an accomplice," Niukah said. "Now, be still." He jutted his chin at a pale glimmer in the darkness.

The glimmer morphed into two ovals of emerald light that soon became two approaching horders with the face of Lord Swaq twinkling from their chests.

Niukah nodded and released his grip. The horders saddled up on either side, pushed 8-1-21 away, then locked their limbs around Jelpmittlebong's like vices.

Swaq's trusty envoy appeared in the horders' wake. He stopped centimeters from Jelpmittlebong's face and scowled. His body twisted in skeletal angles as he hovered.

"Fumb fo Jelpmittlebong," he said, ripping the leather strip from his face. "Our lordship wishes to discuss your recent improprieties."

"But I've not—"

The horders forced the air from Jelpmittlebong's lungs with precise elbows to his sides. Jelpmittlebong's head pitched forward as he gagged.

The envoy motioned with a decrepit foreclaw and turned.

"We'll see what you've not done, young fool," he said as he descended into the swirling pall.

The horders shoved Jelpmittlebong from behind, but maintained their grips as they followed. Niukah and 8-1-21 took up the rear.

They were moving in silence toward a shimmer in the distance when a voice—not Niukah's—reverberated in Jelpmittlebong's head.

"The disturbed alien's hormone runs through Swaq's blood," it said. *"Two more horders accompany him below."*

Jelpmittlebong looked over his shoulder, but Niukah's expression was subdued and noncommittal. One of the horders shoved his face back to the front.

They landed on a floor of peat moss. Lord Swaq stood like a swamp thing, steam pouring from his features. His dominant eye pulsed red. Two horders stood behind him.

The escorting horders pushed Jelpmittlebong to his knees and forced his head down, then genuflected in the muck.

"You s-s-stupid fucker," Swaq said, with a backward tick of his shoulders. He chomped at the air.

The envoy fluttered forward and said, "My lord, he's as unrepentant as a faithless slink lizard. He cannot be trusted."

Swaq writhed from the inside out, as if his dermis crawled with insects. His face twitched as he leaned close.

"Y-y-you challenge?" His neck muscles quivered.

"Say yes," Niukah's voice rang inside Jelpmittlebong's head.

Jelpmittlebong narrowed his nostrils and said, "Um, yes ... I ... er ... challenge your dumb ass—"

Swaq let out a snort that sounded like the barking of a rabid aasmamyl.

"Y-you're going to die in this shithole."

A dark portal appeared in Jelpmittlebong's mind as Swaq spoke. It throbbed with an irregular perturbation and roiled around puffy edges. Swaq's voice bellowed from its center.

"You fucking dipshit," it said, *"this s-s-shithole will be your grave ... argh!"*

The edges of Swaq's portal began stretching and bubbling as

if subject to an internal convection current. The bubbles perforated randomly, some emitting voices as they burst.

"*Eating her flesh gives you her power.*"

"*Shhh ... she'll hear us.*"

"*You're all so fucking stupid.*"

"*Don't be so dramatic.*"

"*Mommy, I'm sorry, Mommy ...*"

As the bursting increased, cacophony ensued.

From the center of the portal, Swaq's voice roared.

"*SHUT UP!*"

Externally, his face pecked the air, and brown foam lathered his mouth. With a howl, he dove into the mire. His limbs thrashed, splattering septic goo in wide swaths. The horders in attendance stepped back.

One of them grasped at his own throat as if choking and said, "He's groveling before that pussy marketing scum." The horder's own dominant eye widened, as if questioning his own voice.

Swaq's portal in Jelpmittlebong's mind began to resemble an undulating loop of diseased tissue.

"He should be ended now," another horder said, also clawing at his own throat, "before he shames the Horde further."

Jelpmittlebong turned to Niukah, whose taut face exuded only tranquility.

Swaq struggled to his feet and twirled his head toward the surrounding horders. "You f-f-fucking traitors w-w-want to challenge?" he asked.

His portal howled.

Scornful laughs poured from the horders' mouths. They exchanged nonplussed glances then quickly banded together in a collective defensive posture. But they were no match for their lord. Sludge and blood flung and flew. In the end, Swaq thrust their heads into the air with a roar, then threw them into the darkness.

"Holy Kacheenzas," 8-1-21 said.

Swaq twirled and stomped in his direction. Niukah and the envoy intercepted him by stepping forward shoulder to shoulder and closing their eyes. The green glow of their combined Swaq insignias swam across the Lord of the Horde's diluted pupil.

Swaq laughed and said, "W-w-what's this? The f-f-fucking brittle brigade?"

Jelpmittlebong watched Swaq's portal shrivel as if pulled into a vacuum.

Swaq suddenly gagged and fell to his knees. His dominant eye swelled. His foreclaws reached slowly for his neck, trembling, as if fighting a great weight. With a roar that ripped a hole in the surrounding vapor, he tore his head from his body.

Jelpmittlebong looked down at the twitching torso. Next to it Swaq's head mouthed silent obscenities.

Niukah and the envoy immediately began slicing out the spinal sacs of the five torsos, bestowing permanent death on Swaq and four otherwise hostile witnesses.

"Whoa, Niukahee!" 8-1-21 said, staring at Swaq's head.

"Overseer?" Jelpmittlebong said.

Niukah and the envoy continued their work, dumping reservoirs of neuronal somatic stem cells into the bog.

Jelpmittlebong rotated his head from Niukah to the envoy to Swaq's torso and back.

"I thought someone had to be predisposed to something in order to manipulate their actions," he said.

"They do," Niukah said, standing, "which should make you think about what kind of galactic dictator he'd have made. But we didn't completely force his actions. We simply goaded him a bit. This"—he swung a foreclaw toward Swaq's head—"was his own response to the overwhelming agitation imposed upon him."

The envoy straightened and packed his small knife in his pocket. He faced Jelpmittlebong.

"Fumb fo Jelpmittlebong," his voice said in Jelpmittlebong's head, *"are you mute?"*

Jelpmittlebong creased his brow and eyed the envoy with the sharpness of a fleeting tipping point.

"I am," he thought as hard as he could, *"Fumb fo Jelpmittlebong."*

The envoy smiled.

Niukah turned to Jelpmittlebong.

"And, Fumb fo Jelpmittlebong," he said aloud, "do you feel like a badass?"

"No," Jelpmittlebong said, brushing goop from his legs. "I feel like a complete neophyte on every level."

"Good." Niukah slapped his back. "That is the proper state of mind for any endeavor."

"Um," 8-1-21 said with a twist of his head, "how exactly does Swaq's suicide, or whatever the hell that was, make him"—he pointed at Jelpmittlebong—"a badass?"

"Badassness is in the mind," the old envoy said, "my dear mipoon."

"Ugh," 8-1-21 said, turning. "Just what we need—another mute monk."

Niukah laughed. "Yes, and a most indispensable accomplice." He buzzed into the air. "Now, let's get out of this shithole."

The others took wing after him.

"Overseer," Jelpmittlebong said as they flew toward the tank's ceiling, "is continuing with the Earth charter necessarily the right thing to do?"

Niukah looked over his shoulder.

"That depends on your perspective. I'm sure the Humans would have a view, and a passionate one, no doubt, given their proclivities."

"But with Swaq gone, there's really no reason to pursue the charter. You've convinced me of the drawbacks of the melatonin shortcut. Shouldn't we protect them from themselves? I mean, they're such an adolescent species."

"In any other circumstance, I might agree. But if you withdraw now, the Horde will interpret it as a sign of weakness. I'm afraid we have no choice but to carry on. Think of it as the Humans taking a hit for the good of the galactic community."

"They don't even know they're part of a larger galactic community."

"Not yet. But, my student, what is the first step to any kind of independence?"

Jelpmittlebong twisted his head. "I'm not sure I follow."

"What is it that nearly all free-thinking sentio-intelligent species desire, regardless of circumstances?"

"The freedom to decide for themselves, I guess."

"Indeed," Niukah said, "self-determination."

"Let the Humans decide for themselves?"

Niukah smiled and nodded. "It would allow them to keep their dignity, no?"

"But—"

"My student, we should make haste," he said. "An important Swaq rally awaits."

"What?"

Chapter 35

It was after midnight when Masa, Leah, and Wacko returned from the Glory to GOD Faith Center. TV emanations and snickering filtered from the otherwise dark living room. Carmen and Frick were on the couch, a gallon of ice cream between them. Frick's blacktail-buck-antler pipe lay spent on the coffee table.

"Hallelujah!" Carmen said as they entered, her eyes bloodshot and beaming. "It's the Jesus team." She wagged her spoon at the TV. "You'll love this."

"Wacko, my man," Frick said, "this guy in China's stealing your gig. Check it out."

Wacko sat on the edge of the recliner. Chubij peered at the TV, half expecting to be sucked back into the dark vacuum in the vehicle's head at any time. A news reporter was standing by a throng of people near a bonfire set against the granite slopes of Mount Song. Many in the crowd were singing and tossing items into the fire. The reporter was talking loud and fast.

"… referring to this as a sort of religious *Fahrenheit 451*. This fire's been burning since early this morning and shows no sign of diminishing. The lines of disciples waiting to throw their holy books into the flames are stretching for miles through the valley.

"The fire was lit jointly by representatives from many of the world's major religions, but, unfortunately, we weren't positioned to get it on tape. They apparently used as kindling copies of the Bible, the Koran, the Rig Veda and the Upanishads, the Torah and the Talmud, and the Heart and Avatamsaka Sutras, and a few lesser known holy books. Witnesses say the disciples then stood in a circle holding hands while chanting a devotional hymn to Lingdi and his vision of religious unification—"

The footage of the reporter jiggled as if the cameraman had tripped. The image panned across the sky, then settled into an out-of-focus shot of the ground.

The reporter could be heard saying, "Hey! You fucking idiot. Watch where—oh, shit."

The TV screen shifted to a standard studio set. Three male newscasters sat above a prop designed as a church pulpit with "The Lingdi Channel" scripted in gold letters across its front. They were wearing glitter-fringed ivory lounge suits with silken white ties and pink carnations. They had recently quit their jobs at Fox News to join the new inspirational channel.

"Juan? Juan? What's that?" one of the newscasters said with an inward stare and a finger to his ear.

"Looks like they finally got 'em this time," the newscaster in the middle said.

Prophet Wacko

"Have they no concept of freedom of speech?" said the third, shaking his head.

"Uncivilized," said the second.

As they spoke, a split screen popped into the upper right quadrant of the TV. Lingdi was standing atop a large boulder, waving like an emperor from a dais.

"Meanwhile," the first newscaster said, "this is from the most recent footage we have of the Prophet—"

Chubij knew Lingdi wasn't really a rival in the traditional sense, but still the image of another avatar vehicle unnerved him. Wacko's muscles tensed. He stood and walked out the door, off the porch, through the camellia bushes, between two parked cars, and into the middle of the deserted street.

No heavenly body shone, no porch lights were lit, and the few diffuse street lamps dotting the sidewalks were obscured by a black glut of rustling leaves. The result was a murky tunnel of night that tapered into darkness.

Charged ions graced the vehicle's nasal cavity.

"Storm," Chubij mused, as he set off at a brisk pace in the direction of the darkness.

The road ended in a T junction, against a crumbling sidewalk overrun by a briar patch that bordered a wooded public park. As he searched the dark bramble for an entry, a succession of car doors slammed behind him. He twirled to find a small group of people gathering in the street.

"That was him!"

"Come on!"

The scuttling footfalls of the Glory to GOD congregation clobbered the pavement in his direction.

Wacko gulped, then sailor dove through the tangle of snarled branches. He emerged on the other side with a face full of nettles.

A thorny twig had broken off and stuck in his hair. Thin droplets of blood trickled down his face and arms.

From the other side of the thicket, a combination of shrieks and yodels swelled in one composite voice. Wacko rushed in the direction of a grassy knoll in the middle of the park. He passed a metal totem pole at the truncated summit and, leveraging the downward slope and a well-placed picnic table at the foot of the knoll, made a supernatural leap onto the dipping branch of an old sequoia. He scrambled up the mossy bark to where the branch connected to the base of the tree and hunkered like a frightened cat.

The roil of distant thunder fanned over the mob as it rushed toward him, hands waggling in the air. Pasty faces were soon heaving under the tree, illuminated by the gray light of a remote streetlamp. The lumberjack stood out because of his giantism, Strawberry because of her wide-open expression of wonder. A lightning strike imparted a snapshot of the rest of the faces, which blurred into a swaying continuum of murkiness as the plunking raindrops coalesced into sheets.

With the downpour came the flurry of wings. A close succession of lightning flashes silhouetted the owl as it seized the branch with its talons. It stretched its great wings, holding them momentarily in a sort of living heraldic design, then flapped, shedding black water from its feathers.

The followers stood like stones. Their eyes distended as if they'd just witnessed the arrival of a pterodactyl.

"My patriarch," the owl hooted with a boom that transcended the driving spatter of rain.

"Ulluoi, my sister," Chubij hooted over the surging wind. He rose into a precarious all-fours position on the moss-covered branch.

"Yes, my patriarch."

("He speaks with the owl!")

"My sister," Chubij said in a high-pitched tweet, belying his accrued frustration, "this charter is out of control."

"Yes, my patriarch," the owl said. "I have done as you asked. I have tirelessly listened to the communications."

("Brother Wacko speaks with the owl!")

Chubij scooted to the middle of the branch. Oohs and aahs filtered up from the ground.

"Thank you, my sister."

"The Xenkonians acknowledge that the seer mind is too powerful to overcome by conventional means. They're not sure it can be convinced to share consciousness with you."

("Surely only God's messenger could do that!")

"The channel between the vehicle and the charter team appears shut."

"The charter team is preoccupied with the subsequent avatar vehicle that has materialized as a young man named Lingdi in a nation-state called China."

("And he wears a crown of thorns!")

"Yes, I saw him on the television."

"He's been quite successful at manipulating the target species."

("He bleeds for our salvation!")

"Which of our sisters channels this Lingdi?"

"A young Hoo'qqai, on its first charter."

("A new prophet stands before us!")

"What?"

"Lord Swaq handpicked her himself, against the counsel of the charter team."

"He's no doubt a control freak, my sister."

"Yes, my patriarch. That would match his other personality traits."

("Prophet Wacko!")

"What about the bigfoot assassin?"

"It continues to hunt you, but it doesn't appear to be any more than a mechanical vehicle. The charter team is unable to control its functioning. It still presents a danger."

"Thank you, my sister. You've done well."

"It's good to be useful, my patriarch." Her last hoots trickled slowly, invoking a melancholy that Chubij felt halfway across the galaxy.

"My sister," he hooted, "you are most faithful and shall be rewarded. I shall ensure it."

"Oh, my Chubij! My savior!" Ulluoi hooted with an eternity of pent-up emotion. The owl dug its claws into the bark of the sequoia and spread its wings. Chubij felt an affectionate spark. He stood on the branch and extended his arms toward the owl.

"Ulluoi!" he said. "My Ulluoi!"

A fat ball of lightning lashed the totem pole on the top of the knoll, traveled down its length, and slammed into its concrete casing with the effect of a large underground explosion. The earth quaked. The followers tumbled. The sequoia shook. And the avatar vehicle fell from the tree.

Zawt popped the vehicle's eyes open with a flash. A swath of midmorning sunshine contracted his irises. He threw his palm over his eyes and smiled.

"The foaming waves have washed the sky," Wacko said and tried to sit up. Chubij squirmed in the virtual darkness against the sensation of a sock stuffed in his mouth.

"Whoa there, cowboy," Frick yelled from the kitchen.

"Who's blind?" Wacko asked. His head fell back against the

cushion of the sofa. Then with extra effort, he landed his feet on the floor, put his head in his hands, and sneezed.

"Take it easy, big cheese. I'm making some honey lemon tea."

"Flawless is the jewel," Wacko said as he wiped his nose on the sleeve of the terrycloth robe he found hanging from his shoulders.

"Wild dreams?" Frick asked, rolling up with two steaming mugs in his hands.

"Besotted with enlightenment."

Frick laughed.

"Well, it must've been some night, Brother Wacko." The last two words were uttered with a mischievous tweet, as if through a pinched nose.

"Somebody had fun." Wacko took the mug extended to him. "Unfortunately, I was absent from the festivities."

Frick gestured toward the window with his chin.

"Maybe someone from your congregation can refresh your memory." He held his own mug in both hands and sipped.

Wacko looked up, but could see only blurred vegetation and piercing shards of sunlight through the glass. His head was quickly back in his hands.

"You know," Frick said over the lip of his mug, "they're dead certain they witnessed a miracle last night." Swirls of steam jetted off the surface of his tea as he blew. "You sure work fast, big cheese."

"He makes up a monstrous story."

Frick chuckled.

"Yeah, anyway, drink up," he said. "Sis says we're going to the fair."

"Me too," Carmen said. She was bouncing down the stairs like a ballerina.

"Who're you?" Frick asked with a grin.

"Why, my dear sir," she said, pulling up to Frick with a coquettish tug on his robe. "I'm the one who laid you last night."

They kissed and rubbed noses.

"Forging dreams in a dream!" Wacko said, dousing the sofa with his tea as he signaled a touchdown.

At that very moment, across the street in the back of the Rolls-Royce, with her grandparents snoring in the front seat, a sleepless Strawberry was scoring a charcoal pencil across the paper of her sketchbook with rapid little flicks of her wrist.

Chapter 36

Nestled in the woods of the coastal range, along the banks of a meandering river, is Veneta, a mysterious hamlet where, it's said, renaissance spirits lounge in trees and certain of the native fauna never die. Some locals insist there are disembodied voices of ancient Kalapuya shamans in the crags of the surrounding foothills. Another legend recounts a sparkling cloud that ignited into a gossamer tapestry and danced for months over the landscape like a shifting aurora, which is why starlight now displays a rainbow sheen and psychedelic substances thrive naturally in the soil. A recent periodical claims that within the town's limits the glow of the cosmic microwave background radiation inexplicably spikes. But, of course, nothing is ever certain—except perhaps the zany three-day festival in July called the Oregon Country Fair, when the yesteryear licks of a starry-eyed counterculture return to ride the breeze, and legendary musical performances are forever born.

233

The Rajneeshee man guided the Rolls-Royce onto the road. Rock's VW van fishtailed behind it. An ad hoc, but not unexpected, caravan formed in their wake.

A thick hardcover sketchbook on the floorboard of the Rolls-Royce crowded Arabella's legs. She picked it up and studied the travel stickers cramming its front and back covers like the weathered case of a touring guitarist.

"I collect them from tourist traps," Strawberry said.

"There are so many," Arabella said, running her fingers over the embossed places where the stickers' edges overlapped.

"They like to travel," Strawberry said, swinging her hand toward the front seat, "and they drag me along."

"May I?" Arabella asked.

Strawberry smiled and nodded.

Arabella opened it and flipped the pages.

She was struck by the gracefulness with which the charcoal and graphite lines coalesced into palpable, living verves, as if each drawing was poised to jump off the paper and begin enacting its story in three dimensions.

"These are great," she said.

"Thanks."

"Lots of Buddhist motifs."

"My parents are Buddhist artists and homeschooled me," Strawberry said.

"That would explain it."

"You know," Strawberry said, as Arabella leafed through some more, "somebody ripped out some pages after I slept."

Arabella stopped and examined the inside of the spine. "Yeah, I see that. Who?"

"I don't know."

"A secret admirer?" Wacko asked.

"No need to be so secret," Strawberry said. "I'd have given them for free."

"A true romantic," Arabella said, thumbing through the last bundle of pages. "And you've definitely got talent, girl." She looked up. "But what's with all the owls at the end?"

Strawberry giggled and pointed at Wacko. "Ask him."

Arabella turned.

"It has something to do with my other personality," Wacko said. "He seems to derive satisfaction from mimicking their hoots."

Arabella eyed him.

"Okaaay," she said, straightening her spine and folding the sketchbook in her lap, "are you gonna tell me what's up?"

Wacko raised his brow.

"Come on," Arabella said. "You're not who you say you are, are you? Speaking foreign languages with ease. Effortlessly rounding up followers. Strutting around like you're the forbidden tree's personal gardener ..." She ticked off his achievements by holding up a new finger with each example. "And how'd you know the missing parts of the message?"

"Huh?" Wacko said.

"You know, 'lesser godheads,' 'hole in the head.' My guess is only nerdy religious scholars or socially challenged grad students would be able to make that connection, and you don't strike me as either." She folded her arms over her chest. "So come on, let's hear it. There's something you're not telling us, right?"

Wacko smiled.

"Like what?" he asked.

"Like, um, your secret mission," Arabella said.

"Ah, yes, that," Wacko said. "It's true. This vehicle"—he poked his chest with his thumbs—"is here to unite the Human race through religious manipulation. I'm what they call an unwanted stowaway."

Arabella squinted one eye.

"You don't come across as one of those pathetic Lingdi copycats, so try again."

"It's true," he said, grinning. "This vehicle was sent by an alien species that wishes to turn you into little narcotics factories, but they need your cooperation to do it. Thus, manipulation of your religious philosophies and the accompanying emotional attachment, so you're as willing as a flock of dung beetles in a cow pasture."

"You don't look like an alien," Arabella said, crossing her arms.

Wacko chuckled.

"How many have you met?" he asked.

"Which planet?" Strawberry asked with a gleam. "Venus? I'm pretty fond of Venus, you know."

"They occupy many heavenly bodies, my dear," Wacko said. "Pretty much a whole galactic arm. But I like Venus too."

"That's a pretty flimsy story to try to hide the fact that you're a member of an ancient underground group," Arabella said with a smug expression.

Wacko looked at her.

"You're familiar with the mutes?"

"The who?"

"Never mind."

"How do you do it?" she asked.

"Do what?"

"Communicate across generations. Secret symbols? Is it a family thing?"

"Oh that," Wacko said. "We tap the bottomless power of intuition. It's not unlike the latent power of your dreams, if you'd only learn to harness it. We don't have families in the sense of which I think you're referring."

"Okay," Arabella said. Her tone shifted like that of a cross-examining attorney changing tactics in midstream. "I'll play along. Who are these mysterious aliens?"

"Xenkonians, from a multistar system called Xenkon V'rpq, many light-years from here. There's a small fringe group about which you should be particularly concerned called Eeftwat Avatars. They have powerful allies."

"Aliens with allies," Strawberry said, giggling.

"That's right," Wacko said, matching her enthusiasm. "And of course there's the Great Intrepid Horde to worry about."

Arabella nudged Wacko in the ribs with her elbow.

"Come on, you can tell me. What's really going on?"

Wacko looked out the window.

"The sky is blue," he said.

"The grass is green," Strawberry said.

The Rajneeshee couple in the front seat stared like mannequins at the passing landscape.

At a makeshift booth of whitewashed wooden planks, a long-haired, skinny man in a feathered tiara accepted their admission tickets with a dry reefer stare. Wacko matched the man's expression and held up the insides of his index and middle fingers, waving them as he passed.

"Peace to you too, brother," the man said. A yellow intensity rippled from his bloodshot eyes.

They emerged into a clearing in the forest where the grass had been packed into hard dirt. Sunshine glided over the surrounding trees. Tie-dyed sheets hung from branches, in front of which countless stalls were selling an array of crafts, trinkets, clothes, and food.

An eclectic crowd ebbed and flowed in a whimsical spirit of no-particular-place-to-be. Under the shade of a large Sitka spruce, a group of minstrels plucked mandolins behind an animated poetry reader. A Grim Reaper on stilts lumbered by, pounding the earth with his scythe. Two giant frog puppets with top hats skipped past holding hands. A few Lingdi look-alikes blessed the crowd.

Wacko twirled in slow motion.

"Candyland!" His eyes bulged from their sockets.

"Come on," Strawberry said, yanking him in the direction of a passing troupe of jesters in floppy three-pointed hats, their bells jingling as they shook their mock scepters.

Arabella, Rock, Frick, and Carmen watched them disappear into the crowd, then exchanged grins. Frick stood on his tiptoes to see their heads swallowed by the bottlenecked entrance of a path in the woods that led to another part of the fair. Someone in a gorilla suit bumped him from behind.

"Oh! Sorry," the gorilla said, looking up, "can't see a thing in this—whoa! Cool dreads, man."

"Oh shit," Arabella said, pointing at the entrance. Wacko's flock was spilling through the gate, led by the lumberjack with a self-righteous tread.

"Oh my God!" Carmen said.

They put hands to foreheads and squinted.

"What are they wearing?" Arabella asked.

Each member wore the same light-blue T-shirt, the front of which reproduced one of Strawberry's sketches—a silhouette of a man and an owl conversing in the branches. They assembled just inside the gate, with the lumberjack towering above like a carnival freak. He began balling and unballing his fists, then motioned for the rest to follow as he set off toward the same footpath through which Wacko and Strawberry had gone. The rest of the flock dispersed through the crowd, passing out leaflets and T-shirts, before funneling in behind.

A pudgy woman with a mop-top haircut thrust a leaflet into Arabella's hand as they passed. Arabella stared after her at the slogan on her back: Give a HOOT for Jesus!

"What's it say?" Frick asked, pointing at the leaflet.

He and Carmen huddled over. Arabella shook herself then held it up so they could read together.

Rock wandered off in the direction of a small group of women on unicycles, whose breasts were concealed by nothing but a thin layer of body paint.

The leaflet contained the same sketch of the man and the owl, causing Arabella to surmise on the sketchbook-page-tearing-out culprit. Below the drawing was a brief explanation of the evidence for Wacko's prophet status—the miracle of a supernatural jump onto the branch of a stately sequoia, the miracle of God talking to Wacko through the hoots of a majestic owl (with rough comparisons to a burning bush), the medical miracle of surviving a blast of lightning, and the incontrovertible fact of divine guidance bestowed by Jesus Christ himself (with no particular evidence—testimonial or otherwise—referenced). At the bottom was a blurb on Wacko's compassion and selflessness, followed by a warning for those not swayed by the foregoing. The leaflet ended with the website of the Glory to GOD Faith Center.

———————

"Hazelnuts!" the man said on the other side of the stall. "Some people call 'em cobnuts or filberts, but in Oregon they're just good old hazelnuts." He smiled and wrapped his thumbs around the straps of his overalls. "Best praline in America too," he said.

Wacko smiled back and said, "Rich in protein, unsaturated fat, thiamine, and vitamin B6. A good source of dietary fiber."

"Yep, all that too," the man said. "Here, have some. On the house." He extended a brimming paper cup and winked. "For the little lady."

Wacko dumped a handful in his palm and handed the half-filled cup to Strawberry. They thanked the man and continued through the crowd along the tree-lined path of stalls.

"You know," Wacko said, tossing a hazelnut into the air and letting it arc into his mouth, "I bet I can teach you all you need to know about the universe with nothing but your imagination and these hazelnuts."

"You shouldn't talk with your mouth full," Strawberry said. "It's impolite."

Wacko popped another hazelnut in his mouth.

"So," he said, munching louder, "manners trump your curiosity to know the secrets of the universe?"

"Of course not. I'm just saying ... What if you spit food?" Wacko laughed.

"I promise not to."

"I meant by accident. You may not mean to—"

"Do you want to know the meaning of the universe or not?" Strawberry rolled her eyes.

"Okay, whatever," she said. "But not with a mouthful of food."

Wacko pinched a hazelnut between his thumb and index finger and held it out between them.

"How many nuts do I have?"

Strawberry squinted an eye at him.

"One," she said.

He tossed the hazelnut in the air and caught it with his mouth, then chewed with his mouth closed, smiling. After he swallowed he took two more hazelnuts from his palm.

"Now how many?" he asked.

"This is a strange way to learn the secrets of the universe."

"How many?" He thrust his hand outward.

"Okay. Two."

Wacko lofted them into the air. He hovered his upturned face underneath as the nuts reached their apex and started down. One clinked off his teeth, but they both found their mark. He smiled and chewed with his mouth closed.

"Okay," he said, swallowing, "one hazelnut and then two hazelnuts. So, how many hazelnuts do I have?" He held out two open palms.

"None, silly. You ate them."

Wacko tilted his head and grinned.

"Eureka!" he said and signaled a touchdown.

"Eureka what?"

"Don't you see?"

"No. What?"

"One plus two equals?"

Strawberry puffed a red tuft of hair out of her face.

"You're crazy."

"Come on. What's the sum of one and two?"

"Three."

"Are you sure?"

"Yes."

"Well, I had one hazelnut, and then I had two more. But now I have none. Hmm. How can that be?"

"You ate them. That's why."

"And where are they now?"

"Well, they're gone, but I can still see them in my mind."

"Aha!"

"What?"

"They're gone, but still in your mind?"

"Uh-huh."

Wacko bit his lip and raised his brow.

"What?" Strawberry said.

"Uh-uh," he said. He poked her forehead. "Use this."

Strawberry's face wrinkled by itself as she thought. Then her eyes opened wide, and she cupped her hand over her mouth.

"Do you see?" Wacko asked.

"I think so. One plus two maybe equals three. Or maybe it doesn't. But it's all in my mind anyway."

"Bingo! And that's the meaning of the universe—it's all in your mind." Wacko wiped moisture from his eyes with his arm. "Really not that hard, now is it?"

Strawberry smiled and jumped into his arms. He swung her around, her shoes just clipping the legs of a nearby stall. He stopped, and they erupted in laughter.

The elfin woman behind the table they'd kicked was watching with vicarious mirth stretching her dimples. Her glossy, slate-colored hair spilled from her hemp bucket hat like a small bush, juxtaposing pleasantly with her olive skin. The wooden table before her was crowded with a variety of gemstones in wicker boxes; assorted books, pamphlets, and CDs on the psychic powers of crystals; and a bowl of dried flower petals and spices.

Noticing her, Wacko and Strawberry turned and said, "Hello."

"Hello," the woman said, picking up a soft rose quartz from the table. "This is the stone of love." She laughed. The stone rested on the tips of her slender fingers like a diamond on the prongs of a solitaire ring. "Placed on the right chakra, it inspires affection and friendship and removes negative influences such as jealousy and greed. It also eases emotional imbalances and improves fertility."

"I'm as fertile as a crescent," Wacko said with a smile.

"Yes," the woman said, replacing the quartz in its box. "Now if you heat the jade stone"—she pointed at a different box—"it will give off a special energy that helps people relax in a peaceful atmosphere."

Wacko nodded.

"And this one"—she indicated a small chunk of sodalite—"will bring clarity of mind and enhance creativity."

"Ooh," Strawberry said. "I want that one."

"It's also useful in the treatment of digestive disorders," Wacko said.

The woman looked up at him from under her hat.

"That's right," she said. "Very good."

"I'm an amateur crystalogist," he said, referring to the reservoir of knowledge planted in his brain by the diligent programmers at Eeftwat Avatars Company Limited. "I'm interested in anything to do with the occult."

"Oh," the woman said, "this isn't the occult. This is genuine—"

"Bullshit!" said a voice from behind. The lumberjack stepped alongside them, sneering. "They're just a bunch of rocks."

Wacko and Strawberry turned and stared. The lumberjack smiled. Behind him a line of congregation members stretched down the footpath, passing out leaflets and T-shirts.

"Humph," the woman said.

"You're going straight to hell, woman," the lumberjack said, extending a monster hand with a leaflet, "unless, of course, you embrace Jesus into your life." He beamed at Wacko. "Give a HOOT!"

Wacko nearly threw out his back laughing.

Strawberry looked as if the lumberjack had reached across the table and slapped the woman.

"Iridium's rarely found on Earth," Professor Al-Qurashi said. He was dressed in white slacks and a polo shirt, sitting on the edge of a lawn chair. "But it's commonly found in extraterrestrial objects, like meteorites, for example."

"Hot pickin'," Professor Tilford said.

They were under a tarp behind the main stage. Professor Tilford donned his patented cowboy shirt and bola tie, matched with shorts and sandals that had the unintended effect of highlighting the network of varicose veins splayed across his ankles. He was moving his fingers across the neck of his Banjosaurus in dampened scale positions. A warming pint of a local microbrew rested at his side, in front of three other banjos nestled in their stands in the grass.

"Not only that," Professor Al-Qurashi continued, "but it's single-crystal iridium. You know what that means?"

"It's not biodegradable?"

"Listen. A single crystal solid is something in which the crystal lattice is continuous and unbroken to the edges, with no interfacing grain boundaries like you'd find in a polycrystalline structure. They're exceedingly rare in nature and difficult to produce in the laboratory, even ones of this size." He held up his index fingers to indicate a space about five centimeters long. "But these things that fell from the sky are made of some kind of exotic single-crystal material, and extremely malleable like paper or thin plastic. I've never seen anything like it."

"Are you sure?" Professor Tilford asked, taking a swig from

his bottle and wiping the lukewarm suds from his mustache with his sleeve.

"A friend of mine at Reed's Research Reactor independently confirmed the results."

Professor Tilford returned the bottle to its spot in the grass and pushed out his lips.

"Exotic material containing stuff from outer space ... Hmm ..." He hummed with a wily smile.

"Okay," Professor Al-Qurashi said. "I'll admit it. It looks like you were right."

Professor Tilford slapped his thigh.

"Hot damn," he said, and zipped a riff all the way from the nut of his banjo to its pot.

"But you had absolutely no evidence," Professor Al-Qurashi said with a finger in the air.

"Call it scholarly intuition, my friend, buoyed by some local Sarawak brew." Professor Tilford's eyes twinkled like diamonds in the sunlight. "I highly recommend the Ibans' tuak to enhance academic acuity."

"You know I don't drink."

"Did you know," Professor Tilford said, "that no one really knows the origin of the name Sarawak?" He became contemplative. "The best theory I've heard is that it derives from a Malay phrase meaning *given to you*, which is apparently what the first white rajah of Sarawak was told when he was granted the land in 1842."

Professor Al-Qurashi smiled.

"You amaze me, Elgin," he said, sitting back in his chair. He put his fingertips together in the air before his face and tapped them in a slow, contemplative sequence.

"So," he said. "Now that we've ascertained that the slips of paper likely originated from somewhere other than Earth, what do you make of the content?"

"Well, factoring in the Lingdi lad—his abilities are too impeccable and his timing too precise for him not to be connected—it could only mean one of two things. Either a truly omnipotent and omniscient being has decided to bring us all under its wing for purely benevolent purposes, or an alien race is trying to butter us up, so we lie down without a fight."

"It's as simple as that?"

"You think some ancient secret society could pull off this kind of technology?"

"Well—"

"Come on." Professor Tilford cast a stern look.

"Okay, okay. For the sake of argument, maybe not."

"Okay. Now apply science's coveted principle of Occam's razor to those two propositions and tell me which one you think it is."

"If you mean the proposition with the fewest assumptions, I'd have to go with the aliens."

"Voilà!" Professor Tilford said. "To quote one of your scientific prophets, 'We are to admit no more causes of natural things than such are both true and sufficient to explain their appearances.'"

Professor Al-Qurashi shook his head with a grin.

"Where do you come up with this stuff?"

"Isaac Newton, my friend," he said. "He said it. I'm just repeating it."

"And God is an invention of man," Professor Al-Qurashi said.

"Spot on. Same argument, different angle. Another way to look at it would be—"

"There she is." Professor Al-Qurashi stood.

Arabella walked up the pathway between the main stage and a small thicket running its width.

Professor Al-Qurashi extended his hand and smiled.

"*As-salam alaykum*," he said.

"*Wa alaykum as-salam*," Arabella said.

Professor Al-Qurashi indicated a vacant lawn chair.

"So good to see you again," he said. "Please sit down."

Arabella took in the backstage scene, then her eyes alit on the man with the banjo in his lap.

"Professor Tilford, I presume." She suppressed a sudden urge to giggle.

"Elgin, please. Call me Elgin." He staggered up and took her hand with a paternal smile that unnerved her somewhat in its intensity.

"It's always a pleasure to meet a genuine scholar," he said, letting go of her hand and sitting back down. He picked up his banjo and rattled off the beginning licks of "Foggy Bottom Breakdown."

"Thank you," Arabella said, not sure of what else to say.

"The professor here"—he swung an arm toward Professor Al-Qurashi—"was just telling me our little messages came from little green men. Of course"—he winked—"he knows that was my theory from the beginning." He grunted as he repositioned the banjo in his gut.

"Really?" Arabella asked, sitting on the edge of the lawn chair Professor Al-Qurashi had indicated. "Are you certain?"

"It contains large amounts of iridium," Professor Al-Qurashi said, taking his own seat.

"The stuff in meteorites?"

"That's the one."

Arabella squished her face in thought.

"I guess that means it's not God. And kind of blows the ancient secret society theory too." She turned to Professor Tilford, who was nodding his head in approval. "But if aliens are trying to manipulate us, what could be their intentions?"

"Animal husbandry?" Professor Tilford said.

"Sport?" Professor Al-Qurashi said.

Arabella suddenly remembered her conversation with Wacko. "Narcotics," she said with widened eyes.

The professors looked at her.

"Do you think Lingdi's involved?" Arabella asked. "He seems rather otherworldly to me, but you've actually met him."

"I do think he's involved, and rather directly, I'd say. And that's what I was just telling the professor. But why do you ask?"

"Well," Arabella said, then paused. "I've recently met someone who seems to have many of the same wild attributes as Lingdi. Foreign languages, charismatic speaking, and"—she bit her lip—"he knows the cave version of the message. You know, the bits about a hole in the head and lesser gods. And he mentioned some aliens that wanted to turn humans into narcotics factories."

"Now, that's cryptic," Professor Tilford said, suspending his beer bottle before him. "Where is this person now?"

"He's right here at the fair, somewhere. He came with us, but my brother first met him in the mountains. I know for sure that he speaks Japanese and Arabic." She looked at Professor Al-Qurashi with raised brows. "Fluently, as far as I can tell. And what's interesting is that he himself says he's from another planet." She frowned. "He's kind of kooky—I mean, he calls himself Wacko. But, of course, he could be a savant of some sort."

"Can we meet this Wacko?" Professor Al-Qurashi asked.

"Yes, please," Professor Tilford said. "I think we should meet him."

"Sure, he's around here somewhere."

Prophet Wacko

Just then a commotion in front of the stage caught their attention. They stood to witness police officers running from the footpaths, and a struggle between persons who Professor Tilford recognized as organizers of the fair and a group of people in matching light-blue T-shirts, one of them with the stature of Goliath.

Arabella and the professors hurried to the front of the stage. The police were escorting many of the members away. The lumberjack, assuming the position of a wrestler ready to leap from the ropes, was in a face-off with four policemen, who appeared to be mentally debating the merits of such a confrontation.

But what caught their attention was the man spinning on the ground like a dervish and laughing.

Two policemen with unholstered Tasers were poised to subdue him, but a red-haired girl standing between them and the man was making threatening gestures as if to kick them in particular places. A gangly man with long dreadlocks and a sandy-haired woman were waving their arms at the police officers in a frantic attempt at persuasion.

"That's him," Arabella said, rushing up.

Professor Tilford followed in unhurried, diplomatic strides.

"That's Wacko," Arabella said, pointing.

"Sirs!" Professor Tilford boomed.

To most everyone's surprise, all of the involved parties ceased their respective skirmishes and stared. Wacko jumped to his feet and brushed the dust from his pants, smiling.

"Gentlemen," Professor Tilford addressed the police officers with a well-mannered firmness. "This man is with the band." He swung his arm toward the stage behind him. "And," he said, "the show must go on."

The police officers exchanged suspicious glances.

"Can you prove that, old man?" one said. "This guy's one of the worst instigators."

"He's a crazy fuck," the other said behind gritted teeth, through which he somehow hawked an aerodynamic missile of phlegm to the ground.

Professor Tilford raised an index finger, then huffed back behind the stage. He returned with two banjos and two sets of finger picks.

"Here ya go, son," he said, handing a banjo to Wacko with a quick conspiratorial nod.

The ensuing version of "Dueling Banjos" is said to have stopped even the chirps of the birds in the trees.

Chapter 37

BEIJING—Lingdi has not been seen or heard from since Chinese authorities escorted him to the local office of the Ministry of Foreign Affairs in Zhengzhou two days ago.

"Mr. Lingdi doesn't possess a birth certificate or identification records of any kind," said a spokesman for the ministry. "As far as we know, he doesn't even have a surname. We requested his presence to verify the identity of his parents and place of birth."

Many of Lingdi's followers expressed anger at Chinese officials.

"Who do they think they are, abducting God's messenger?" shouted a woman from the crowd gathered at Shaolin Monastery.

Diplomatic demands via multiple embassies that the new Prophet's whereabouts be disclosed have been ignored.

A survey taken last week shows that nearly sixty-three percent of the world's population believes Lingdi is a prophet sent by God and would follow him anywhere. Among the responders indicating reluctance to follow Lingdi, most cited a refusal to abandon their current faith. Indifference to religious developments was another common refrain, as was a plain desire to just not be bothered.

With the backing of influential leaders from many walks of life, a global religious summit is being organized by the International Association for Religious Tolerance and Understanding, a global organization dedicated to promoting freedom of belief and religious tolerance. The summit is meant to be a vibrant confirmation of the world's acceptance of Lingdi's spiritual guidance, and will take place concurrently at various venues across the globe.

Beatrice Windsor, a spokeswoman for the International Association for Religious Tolerance and Understanding, said the summit will go on regardless of the Prophet's availability.

Chapter 38

A hologlobic projection filled the middle of Jelpmittlebong's quarters.

Lingdi was strapped to a metal table in a windowless room with bare lightbulbs hanging from the ceiling. His bare feet extended beyond the edge of the table in front of two polled Huaipi goats leashed to an iron ring in the concrete floor. In the shadows, stone-faced Chinese soldiers stood erect on either side of a heavy wooden door. Between the goats was another soldier holding a pail of milky liquid and a large brush.

"This scene's compressed into a few minutes, but in actuality endured for several Earth days," Gargado said. "Prior to this, the vehicle was subjected to a number of physical inconveniences."

He explained the dripping of water on a forehead, manacling a body in awkward contorted positions, waterboarding, electrical shock, asphyxiation, heat, cold, and loud noises.

"All of which, while unpleasant, leave the victim alive and physically unmarked." He turned to Niukah. "An avatar vehicle will sometimes encounter resistance on a charter, but we've never seen such systematic torture before. It caught us off guard."

Gargado glared at Jelpmittlebong.

"And then this." He swung a foreclaw at the still holographic setting, then pushed some buttons.

The scene began moving in a fast-forward stream. The man between the goats dipped the brush into the milky liquid and began basting Lingdi's feet.

"We've determined that's a highly concentrated saline solution," Gargado said.

The goats licked Lingdi's soles with rapid flicks of their coarse tongues. The prophet wriggled and thrashed against his restraining straps in spasmodic fits of involuntary laughter, only managing to shout between gasps that it tickled and to please stop.

As the basting and licking continued, Lingdi's laughing tapered into unembodied moans. The torture was only interrupted to usher in fresh goats and basters, or to encourage Lingdi to repent his religious inclinations and confess to being a spy, or worse, a revolutionary. Incensed by his repeated insistence that he was neither, his tormentors replaced the salty water with sweetened sesame paste.

In time, Lingdi's feet turned the consistency of parboiled turkey skin, then blistered, then swelled in various shades of purple and blue. By the time the bones of his toes began to glisten in the artificial light, the moaning was replaced with shallow wheezing and laborious heaves of his chest.

The goats were lapping over the exposed metatarsalia when more Chinese soldiers burst through the door and halted the exercise by slapping and insulting their colleagues out the door. In their wake, a team in surgical scrubs entered with a blowtorch and proceeded to scorch Lingdi's feet into black stumps stretching halfway to his knees.

The remote audience in Jelpmittlebong's quarters stared with slack jaws and raised brows.

"What the hell they do that for?" 8-1-21 asked.

"From what the linguistic team's been able to piece together, the torturers were berated for being excessive and, in particular, leaving physical marks on the body."

Gargado nudged his chin in the direction of the holoimage.

"The logical conclusion is they're worried about being held accountable for the torture and killing of a prophet as beloved as Lingdi."

"Then why fry his appendages?" 8-1-21 asked. "Don't make sense."

"We haven't quite worked out the motive for that," Gargado said.

"This is outrageous," Jelpmittlebong said, hovering into the holoimage to stare at Lingdi's lifeless, contorted face. "Is this kind of violence typical?"

"Unfortunately, yes," Gargado said.

"I thought the vehicle was programmed to be peaceful. Did it deviate from the program?"

"No. But, given the arbitrary national boundaries dividing Humans, and their long history of interspecies conflict, they live in constant mistrust of each other. The Chinese authorities undoubtedly deemed his actions a threat to the social stability of their state. And Humans commonly use torture to obtain confessions or information, although there also seems to be an added element of sadistic gratification. In any event, as excessive as their actions may seem, in the context of their worldview, they weren't necessarily being unreasonable."

"That's one way to put it," 8-1-21 said. "Another would be to say they just toasted the poor bastard's legs."

"In any event, it's appalling." Jelpmittlebong shook his head.

"It certainly doesn't bode well for the success of the charter," Gargado said.

Jelpmittlebong turned to him, but remained hovering in the holoimage.

"Debrief the channeling Hoo'qqai as soon as it's out of stasis—"

"We lost the Hoo'qqai."

"What?"

"We had good contact until the ruminants appeared, but as the vehicle began to degrade ..." Gargado paused. "For lack of a better metaphor, it spooked. It was overwhelmed by the trauma and couldn't follow our instructions. It didn't detach."

Jelpmittlebong stared.

"The imposed timetable was aggressive," Gargado said. "And the Hoo'qqai handpicked by Swaq was inexperienced, to say the least—"

Jelpmittlebong held up a foreclaw.

"How many charters have resulted in the loss of a Hoo'qqai?" he asked.

"None, until now."

"And now one's been hijacked and another destroyed?"

"That appears to be the equation," Gargado said.

"I don't consider that cost-effective."

"Lordy," 8-1-21 said, "ya startin' to talk like a TEX."

Thoughts of discontinuing the charter floated through Jelpmittlebong's mind, followed hotly by Niukah's voice.

"If you give up so easily, the Horde will deem you weak-willed," it said.

"I know," Jelpmittlebong thought. *"And this species is making it difficult to sympathize with them."*

"The Horde has and continues to do things far more reprehensible. Establish yourself with the Horde, then worry about the Humans."

"Yes," Jelpmittlebong thought, then turned to Gargado and said aloud, "Suggestions?"

Gargado rubbed his chin. "Well," he said, "we could try to salvage Chubij's vehicle, now that we know the reasons for its malfunctioning."

Jelpmittlebong turned to Niukah. "Can you talk to Zawt, as a fellow mute?"

A broad smile spread across Niukah's face. He leaned back and clasped his foreclaws behind his neck.

"Zawt plays by his own rules," he said. "But he does have a fondness for betting."

"A gamblin' mute monk?" 8-1-21 said.

Niukah laughed. "He considers it toying with the probability restraints."

"So," 8-1-21 said, "we just bet him he can't do it? What's in it for him?"

"Let's ask him," Niukah said.

"If we're going to salvage his vehicle," Gargado said, "we'll need to terminate the bigfoot assassin."

––––––––––––

Gwoot fo Krog, head of Eeftwat Avatars' Reconnaissance & Contingency Department, peered out from the other end of a holocamera.

"Krog here. Who be that?" he said.

"My dear Krog," Jelpmittlebong said. "Good to see you again."

"Aye!" Krog said over a small vapor bong, splattering saliva onto the lens of the holocamera. His pupil squirmed under a cloudy film. "Who're ya, and where's Lord Swaq TEX?"

"Don't you remember? I'm Fumb fo Jelpmittlebong, current Topmost Executive Xenkonian of Eeftwat Avatars Company Limited."

"Fumjelpung Twat?" Krog said as he groped for something off camera, shoving his nose into the lens in the process. He looked up with his monocle strapped aslant his dominant eye. "Oh!" he said through the fuzzy transmission image. "Jelpmittlebong? Yow!" he said. "Ya look different, son. Ya gettin' enough R&R?"

"Krog, please call off the bigfoot assassin," Jelpmittlebong said. "Circumstances have—"

"Eh?" Krog said.

"I'd like to request that you decommission the bigfoot assassin you've dispatched in connection with the Earth charter. We've had some unexpected developments, and we'll need to salvage the original vehicle."

Krog tilted his head.

"Ya really the TEX of this outfit now?"

"Yes," Jelpmittlebong said. "Malgorp TEX has been indisposed, and Lord Swaq has graciously—"

"Well, I'll be damned. This place goes through TEXs like hormones through a slink lizard."

"Krog," Jelpmittlebong said, "can you please decommission the bigfoot assassin?"

"Umm," Krog said. "Not really sure I can do that."

"I'm sorry?"

"Uh, well …" Krog said, "the schedule was aggressive, ya know. Didn't really have time to add in remote control functionality. But, Lord Swaq TEX said, 'Make a predator.' He said that bigfoot critter'd make a good predator. Everybody heard him. Just did what I was told. And it's a damned good predator, if I do say so myself. Have ya seen it rompin' through the woods, howlin' at their moon? It's a badass, all right. It smacked—"

"Thank you," Jelpmittlebong said, switching him off.

A cold stiffness filtered through the room.

"I could talk to Pomple-phat," Gargado said.

"Pomple-phat?" Jelpmittlebong asked.

"My Skook contact on Earth. His last transmission did express confusion at the recent events on Earth. Maybe I can segue from that … offer him some sort of esoteric information in exchange …"

"Something about mute monks?" 8-1-21 offered.

"We're as esoteric as they come," Niukah said.

"I leave it to you," Jelpmittlebong said.

"Okay," Gargado said, lifting into the air to leave.

"Oh, I almost forgot," Jelpmittlebong said. "Please also prepare a sanctum for an ad hoc charter."

"Ad hoc?"

"Yes. And program the vehicle to be a perfect facsimile of a real-time Lord Swaq."

Chapter 39

"So," Frick said through a mustache of buttery suds. "How'd you know he played the banjo?"

His dreadlocks jangled over the murmur of the backyard beer garden as he nodded across the table at Wacko, who was bent over a basket of complimentary condiment packets. Wacko slurped a red, gelatinous square of strawberry jam out of its pack and downed it with a glug of chocolate stout.

"Call it a hunch," Professor Tilford said, adjusting the angle of the bill on his cap. "The Lingdi lad was able to do it, so I thought, if he's in any way connected"—the professor swung a thumb in Wacko's direction—"he'd be able to too."

Wacko looked up at the professor, then hunched back over the basket.

Professor Tilford quaffed the remainder of his stout and ran his sleeve over his mouth.

"You really think Wacko and Lingdi are connected?" Arabella asked.

"Yes, I do. But let's ask the man himself." Professor Tilford narrowed his eyes in the vicinity of the avatar vehicle. "Wacko, son, are you connected with this lad in China?"

Wacko looked up and said in a lazy Midwestern drawl, "I guess y'all could call him my little brother."

"The new savior of the world has a big brother?" Carmen asked.

"You don't look Chinese," Rock said from the other end of the table.

"The more you think on this, the further from the truth you'll be," Wacko said, examining a sticky packet of orange marmalade.

"It's really not such a novel idea for the founder of a religion to have a family," Professor Tilford said. "It's just that we're used to thinking of our prophets in relative isolation from their kin."

"Well, big bro," Carmen said, placing an affectionate hand on Wacko's shoulder, "my bet is you'll be edited out of the next big book on the first run."

"Or transformed into *Wacko the Just*," Arabella said.

Carmen laughed.

"Next thing you'll be telling us Lingdi's a swinger. A real tiger."

"Or that he frequents public restrooms," Frick said to an outburst of guffaws from the younger generation at the table.

"Just past the bar, first door on the right." The willowy waitress smiled through cherry lip gloss. She wore a "Lingdi for President" T-shirt.

"Excuse me?" Frick said.

"The restroom," the waitress said.

"Madam," Professor Tilford said. "Your timing is impeccable. The conversation was rushing headlong into the gutter. A refill all around, please." He swept his arms over the table in both directions.

"And some more of these gourmet confections please," Wacko said with the artlessness of a small child, a mass of jelly glistening from his chin.

"Umm," the waitress said, glancing back toward the kitchen, "the first basket's free and all, but the manager's a stingy little fart ..."

"Say no more, Kimani," Professor Tilford said, glimpsing at her nametag. He shifted his face skyward. "Kimani ..." He looked back at the woman. "Hopi?"

"No," she said. "But I'm impressed. It's Shoshone. Means *butterfly*. I'm a distant relative of Sacagawea."

"Very good stock indeed." Professor Tilford's eyes were twinkling.

"Thank you."

"Well, Kimani, descendant of the honorable Sacagawea and Monsieur Charbonneau, your generosity is as magnanimous as your smile is delightful. Rest assured, your secret's good with us, and we're more than willing to compensate you for any additional jelly packs via the customary means of voluntary gratuity."

"In other words, you're promising a big tip?"

"That would be a reasonable interpretation," Professor Tilford said. Then, as if remembering something, "And please tell us if a motley crew in light-blue T-shirts shows up. We think we lost them, but they're rather the persistent type."

"Groupies?"

"Yes, something like that."

"Deal," Kimani said. "Fresh pints of stout and one jelly basket coming right up."

"And another ginger ale, please," Professor Al-Qurashi said, hoisting an index finger.

"And one ginger ale."

"*As-salam alaykum,*" Professor Al-Qurashi said in the direction of Wacko after Kimani left.

"*Wa alaykum as-salam,*" Wacko said in the precise dialect of the professor's native soil.

"Is it that we are now in a time when keeping our faith is like holding a hot coal?" Professor Al-Qurashi asked, continuing in Arabic.

"There are indeed signs of the end of time."

"A time when false prophets will arise in the world? Perhaps one sits before me, and your brother Lingdi is the Dajjal."

"Impersonating the antichrist is surely a sin before Allah," Wacko said, closing his right eye and bulging out the left in a grotesque version of Popeye.

Professor Al-Qurashi sat back.

"Where did you learn your Arabic?"

"The wanderer cannot stay."

"What?"

"Bees making honey."

Professor Al-Qurashi placed his hands on the table and sighed.

"He talks like a madman," he said in English, "but his Arabic's fluent."

Wacko held up a packet of strawberry jam and lolled his tongue like an Irish setter.

"Wacko, my boy," Professor Tilford said, "what exactly is your story? We have reason to believe you're not of this world, that you are, indeed, from outer space. Pray tell, son, what are you?" He thumped the tabletop. "Where are you from?"

An awkward silence settled on the group as just then Kimani appeared with a tray of mugs and a teeming basket of condiments.

"Where is anyone really from?" Wacko asked.

Kimani eyed the group as she slid one hand under the tray and shifted its center of gravity so her other hand could distribute the fare.

"I'm from Pocatello myself. But I've lived here in Eugene most of my life."

"Pocatello, huh?" Professor Tilford said, filling the void. "I wonder what's the origin of a name like that?"

"Named after Chief Pocatello of the Shoshone, who made peace with the early settlers," Kimani said as she circled the table. "And Eugene's named after Eugene Franklin Skinner, founder of a trading post here around 1846. Used to be known as Skinner's Mudhole. Lot of towns around here were named after settlers. Veneta's named after the daughter of a settler, and Lane County itself was named after the first governor of the Oregon Territory."

"And Corvallis?" Professor Tilford asked with the lofty pitch of a game show host.

"Means *heart of the valley* in Latin. Used to be called Marysville after the Virgin Mary, who I don't think qualifies as a settler of the Oregon Territory, no matter how you stretch it."

"Enraptured," Professor Tilford said, accepting a frosty mug with both hands. "There is nothing in God's creation more attractive than a woman of knowledge."

Kimani blushed.

"And Portland was named by a coin toss," she said.

"How's it you're so well-informed?"

"I'm on the slow track for a PhD in history, specializing in the Pacific Northwest," she said, placing the empty tray under her arm. "Ask me something about quantum physics, and I'm afraid you'd be fairly disappointed."

"Not to worry. Our Professor Al-Qurashi here is the resident expert on physics, although I expect Brother Wacko here would give him a run for his money." His thumbs were pointing at different parts of the table. "But, if you're ever in need of a banjo sonata—"

Kimani's gaze settled on her high-top sneakers.

"Um ..." she said.

"What?"

"I've been a fan of Pickin' Elgin for years," she said, looking up. "I used to watch you on *Hee Haw* as a kid. Oh, I know you're a scholar these days and all, but you'll always be little Pickin' Elgin to me. Keep pickin'!" she said, lifting an imaginary pom-pom.

Professor Tilford smiled.

"Indeed, my dear," he said. "Indeed."

Kimani returned to the kitchen with an extra bounce in her step.

"I'm from a multistar system called Xenkon V'rpq, many light-years from here," Wacko said after a swig of fresh stout.

"Excuse me?" Professor Al-Qurashi said, his ginger ale suspended before him.

"Xenkon V'rpq," Wacko said, his aura roiling like a lava lamp from the onslaught of sugar and hops. "More exactly, an antiquated abattoir on Mwookt Qor, twelve parsecs inward core of Xenkon V'rpq Proper, but I consider the Gok'l Nebula home.

This vehicle"—he brought his right palm to his left breast—"was sent by a Xenkonian business enterprise called Eeftwat Avatars to unite the Human race through religious manipulation, but their ultimate goal is subjugation for commercial exploitation. However, my unexpected presence has caused them to deem the vehicle irreparably defective. You see"—he brought his left palm to his right breast, crossing his arms in the process, and drew his face into a puppy-dog frown—"I'm a wayward abbot of the Idiot Doubt-Seeking Order of No-Abiding Xenkonian Mute Monks, a dispersed monastic order that eschews one-dimensional logic and embraces absurdities. The diligent engineers at Eeftwat Avatars consider me unreliable, so they sent Lingdi in relief."

He smiled and signaled a touchdown.

"And a bigfoot is trying to kill me."

Proceeding in a rambling cadence, Wacko then explained the details of the charter's purpose.

After a lengthy pause, Professor Tilford asked, "Is there no way to avoid it?"

"Oh, I'm afraid the Xenkonians are as unrelenting as they are industrious." Dregs of stout sloshed skyward as he pumped his near-empty mug toward the ceiling in mock salutation. "It's been nice knowin' y'all," he said.

The toast was greeted with sullen frowns and puckered brows.

"Can't they just cull the undesirables?" Frick asked. "You know, general evildoers and criminals."

"Or rabid sports fans?" Carmen said.

"Or self-righteous zealots?" Arabella said.

"Yeah," Frick said, "maybe you can convince them—"

"You overestimate my leverage."

"But why do they have to take the entire human race?" Arabella asked.

"The business model calls for the whole population. I assume that decision was run through adequate probability restraints, and no doubt contemplates a few stragglers. In any event, their retort would be that, despite occasional individual insight, the Human species is *fundamentally inclined to gullibility*—at least that was the conclusion of the senior target world analyst at Eeftwat Avatars, who appears to be a pretty smart cracker and very influential among his colleagues."

"Come on," said Professor Tilford, "there've been—and are—many able human philosophers who've championed logic and reason over authority and dogma. Nietzsche, Hume, the new atheists—"

"Imperfect diamonds in an enormous rough," Wacko said with a laugh. "Their most salient feat is writing a lot. In fact, according to the Eeftwat diligence team, the purest unimpeded sentio-intelligent minds among living Earth creatures belong to a one hundred-twenty-four-year-old shaman from a lost tribe in the Amazon rainforest, a mutant lowland gorilla in the Nouabale-Ndoki National Park, and most mature cetaceans, not necessarily in that order. That's it. And none have written a book." Wacko slurped down a packet of maple syrup. "I'm afraid the Xenkonian's plan is based on reasonable assumptions."

Professor Tilford scoffed. "Ridiculous."

Rock looked at Arabella. "Cetaceans?"

"Dolphins," she said.

"I don't buy it," Professor Tilford said. "Look around this table. After listening to your story, and considering all the other things we know—Lingdi, uncanny messages, what have you—I don't think any of us are prepared to go willingly."

"That's right," Arabella said. "I bet if everyone in the world heard your story, they'd never go along with this."

Prophet Wacko

"Agreed," Professor Tilford said. "I bet the human race would back away from a lemming-like leap to alien servitude if they knew the truth."

Wacko smiled. "A bet?"

"I just don't see it." Professor Tilford shook his head. "There's got to be something we can do."

Wacko pointed at the plastic basket before him. "Perhaps a lifetime supply of these sugary condiments would be fair compensation for reining in Humanity's march to eternal bondage."

Professor Tilford sat back, still holding his beer mug. "Are you serious?"

"As serious as a mind in a blender."

Professor Tilford stroked his mustache. "If what you've told us is true, you are in a unique position to affect the outcome."

Wacko smiled. "So are you, Professor."

Professor Al-Qurashi, who seemed oblivious, furrowed his brow.

"So, how exactly did you get here?" he asked from the other side of the table.

Wacko turned. "I don't know," he said over the lip of his mug.

"You don't know?"

"Like I said, I'm a stowaway—not privy to the flight plan. But I imagine they used dimensional shift technology and topological space-time molding to scan and exploit a reasonably malleable wormhole." He smiled. "Doesn't everybody?"

"Are you suggesting that stable Einstein-Rosen bridges are reality?"

"Oh, they're all over." Wacko grabbed a pen from Professor Al-Qurashi's shirt pocket and started writing equations on a napkin. "See?" he said. "The universe—or, more precisely, the multiverse—is like an infinite block of Swiss cheese, you know. Those particular vacuum solutions to Mr. Einstein's equations make for a silky ride through the Higgs field, so long as you maintain adequate negative density in a stable quantized field." He held up the napkin. It had tiny scribbles on both sides.

"Here," he said, "look at these at your leisure."

"Exotic matter?" Professor Al-Qurashi asked, accepting the napkin.

"More specifically, negative inertial mass and positive electric charge."

Professor Al-Qurashi put on his reading glasses and peered over the equations.

"These are ... well, er—"

"Advanced? Brilliant?"

"Well ... perhaps."

"Remember, Professor, they're just equations. The real universe is out there." Wacko grinned and pointed toward the ceiling. "You know, galaxies, stars, planets, and all that."

Professor Al-Qurashi stared at the napkin and pushed out his lips like a boy puzzling over a kite stuck in a tree.

"Or he could just be talking shit," Frick said from across the table with mischievous, glistening eyes.

Wacko stood and signaled a touchdown.

"It's all in the mind."

"You mean—" Professor Al-Qurashi said.

But before he could formulate his next question, Wacko announced a sudden need to excuse himself. He grabbed the basket of condiments and trotted in the direction of the restroom.

Chapter 40

Gobbling jellies and studying the toilet-stall graffiti, Zawt questioned the charter team's unusual request that he take the transmission in private.

"I can do it all in my head, you know," he told them. "I've gotten quite good at multitasking."

"Zawt," Gargado said, "there's someone here we want you to talk to."

Zawt chuckled.

"A hostage negotiator, eh? I dare not inquire about his illness." He devoured a square of apple jelly.

"Old fool," Niukah said into his interface.

Wacko's mouth stopped in midmastication as Zawt ran his mind through multiple probabilities.

"Is it the wind ringing?" he asked. "Or is it the chimes?"

"It's only your mind that rings," Niukah replied.

"My mind abides neither here nor there," Zawt said after a pause. "Who is the monk to whom I speak?"

"Niukah of the here and now."

"The universe is a mysterious place, old friend," Zawt said, propping the soles of the vehicle's sneakers against the wall of the stall. He sucked down another jelly. "So," he said, "what is your quest?"

Niukah nodded to Gargado.

"Um," Gargado said, leaning into the interface, "your cooperation on this charter."

"There's a running bet among the charter team that says you can't do it," Niukah said.

"Phooey," Zawt said. "I've just been tendered an excellent offer by the Humans to sabotage this little mission. You'll have to do better than that."

A pithy bartering session followed that pitted the comparative merits of a lifetime supply of jams and jellies against an enduringly stable galactic community.

"How about if we match the Human's proposal?" Jelpmittlebong said.

"Acquiescence is key," Zawt said.

Gargado muted the transmission and raised his brow.

"That was an acceptance," Niukah said.

"What would something like that cost?" Gargado asked.

"Don't worry about it," Jelpmittlebong said. "We'll put it to Qoohx and stipulate it as reimbursement for the added expense of a second Hoo'qqai."

Gargado smiled and unmuted the transmission.

"Any specific requests?" Zawt asked.

Gargado said, "We'd be grateful if you'd take guidance from the Hoo'qqai Chubij going forward, at least with respect to the fulfillment of the charter."

"Okey-dokey," Zawt said, fishing for an orange marmalade. "Anything else?"

"Um, can we talk to him?" Gargado said.

"Ahoy, Hoo'qqai," Zawt said as if shouting through a tunnel. *"Up and at 'em."*

Chubij's consciousness shook itself to the surface.

"Looks like we're a team now," Zawt said. *"And they want to give us a pep talk."*

It was explained to Chubij that the young Hoo'qqai channeling Lingdi perished due to its inexperience, that Zawt had graciously agreed to cooperate in achieving the mission's objective, and that it would be prudent to stay away from the woods for a while, especially the area around Frick's tree house, until the bigfoot assassin could be decommissioned.

Chubij was silent as he mulled the situation.

"Can I make a suggestion?" he finally said.

"Of course," Gargado said.

"Resurrect the Lingdi vehicle."

"But the channeling Hoo'qqai's gone," Gargado said. "We can't just—"

"I know what you're thinking, Chubij," Jelpmittlebong said, placing a hand on Gargado's shoulder, "but expending another Hoo'qqai on this charter is not the most economical—"

"There's an elder Hoo'qqai, appellation Ulluoi, who's evaded your detection," Chubij said. "She's one of the Hoo'qqai's best channelers, and you'll find her counseling invaluable."

Jelpmittlebong turned to Gargado with a lift of his brow.

Gargado raised then lowered his shoulders. "Umm, excuse me," he said, "we thought we rounded up all the Hoo'qqai."

"You didn't. I suggest you use her as the channeler. It would be like gaining a new Hoo'qqai at no cost, and she'll more than make up for the lost one."

Gargado muted the transmission.

"It could be another ruse," he said.

Jelpmittlebong scratched his chin.

"It doesn't sound like it," he said, "and another elder could boost operations." He signaled for Gargado to unmute the line.

"Chubij," he said, "as a sign of our good faith and desire to create a more constructive working relationship with your species, we will consider your suggestion. But may I ask: why the sudden willingness to expose one of your fellow Hoo'qqai?"

Chubij sighed.

"It's because she's loyal and faithful," he said, "and deserves the right to define her own freedom."

"Well, okay then," Gargado said in a tone that barely contained his skepticism. "So, how do we find this Ulluoi?"

Chubij allowed himself a chuckle. "Ulluoi, my sister?"

"Oh, thank you, my patriarch!" Ulluoi said. "I will cooperate, as you wish."

The two Hoo'qqai laughed.

"Woo-hah!" Zawt said. "*E pluribus unum!*"

Wacko ended the transmission by bolting out the door of the toilet stall. Empty condiment packages littered the floor behind him.

Gargado looked flabbergasted.

"That was mute talk," Niukah said with a blink, "for 'over and out.'"

Chapter 41

Wacko returned to an empty table. Most of the pub's patrons were piled around the bar, craning their necks at a television braced to the wall. He trundled to the fringe of the small crowd and watched a newsflash from The Lingdi Channel.

Grainy footage of Lingdi strolling on a bed of glowing embers graced the screen. Suddenly, the Great Prophet's lower legs erupted in flames. Despite the ostensible expression of pain on his face—though difficult to make out, given the poor quality of the recording—he continued to stroll with two small infernos at his feet. By the time he was pulled from the coals, his lower legs were black, smoldering stumps.

A glitter-fringed-ivory-lounge-suited newscaster with tousled hair gawked from an inset in the bottom left-hand corner of the screen. He was providing frazzled color as the footage repeated itself.

"… is dead. I repeat, dead. This footage is just coming in … from Beijing. And, um, as you can see, it appears the Great Prophet is walking on hot coals or, uh … those look like hot cinders, Matilda … Then, as you can plainly see, his legs just burst into flames … Oh! Geez! Doctors declared Lingdi dead a few hours ago. The cause, shock and trauma from severe fourth-degree burns to his legs and, uh, lower extremities. Unbelievable …

"Chinese authorities are saying Lingdi suggested the fire-walking stunt when they invited him to a banquet thrown by Premier Xu in, uh … honor of the new Great Prophet to demonstrate his divine status … Um, it's hard to tell from this clip, but it looks like … Hey! Can you slow down that idiot board? The teleprompter, slow the damned thing down … This is big news, damn it, and I'm affected, okay?

"A reliable source, speaking on condition of anonymity, told our reporters on the ground that Premier Xu is now questioning the Great Prophet's divine status on the grounds that a true prophet's legs wouldn't have succumbed to the simple earthly element of fire. Oh! What a fucking idiot! Jesus fucking Christ! Matilda, can you believe this scum bucket? That's like saying Jesus' hands and feet should've been impenetrable to nails. Do I have to keep going with this shit? Somebody should just shoot his yellow—"

That particular newscaster was replaced in the inset screen by Matilda, also glitter-fringed and ivory-lounge-suited, but primly so. Matilda was glaring bug-eyed off camera as the sound of grappling in the background intensified, then went silent.

Prophet Wacko

She forced her face back to the camera with a synthetic grin, fretful eyes rolling toward the shadows for guidance. The footage of Lingdi igniting continued on a loop.

"Okay … thank you, Bill …

"In other Lingdi news, it appears that the upcoming Global Religious Summit will concurrently serve as what religious leaders are calling the beginning of the Ascent. According to the Great Lingdi, prior to his, um … untimely demise, he prophesized that little angels would descend from the sky like the paper flood to assist us in our journey to paradise. Beatrice Windsor, spokeswoman for the International Association for Religious Tolerance and Understanding, the organization coordinating the summit, told The Lingdi Channel that they plan for each summit venue to be centered around airports—apparently in accordance with Lingdi's explicit instructions—as they'll also serve as an embarkation point for the Ascent."

As the screen changed to a prerecorded interview with Beatrice Windsor, the group headed back to their table. Upon reaching the veranda, Professor Tilford turned to Wacko with the urgency of an inspired man.

"Wacko, my boy," he said, "are you willing to go on national TV and repeat everything you've told us about these alien critters?"

"Unfortunately," Wacko said, "the Xenkonians tendered a better offer."

"What?"

Wacko winked and said, "May the best species win."

"But—"

277

"Pickin' Elg—er, Professor—" Kimani said, running up.

"Shit!" Professor Tilford clenched his jaw.

Kimani's smile faltered. She touched her fingertips to her bosom.

Professor Tilford turned to face her.

"I didn't mean you, my dear," he said, taking her hand.

Kimani's smile returned. Her eyes morphed into imploring little searchlights.

"Oh!" she said, remembering her initial mission. "I think your light-blue T-shirt gang is gathering on the front porch. They're chanting something—sounds like 'Hoot for Jesus.'"

"Thank you, my dear. That's our cue."

He dropped some one-dollar bills on the table. Then, recollecting, he dropped two twenties.

"Follow me," Kimani said.

They shadowed her through the kitchen and out the back door. As the rest of the group tumbled into their respective cars, Wacko dashed back. After a quick chat, Kimani wrote something on her order pad and handed it to Wacko. She was beaming.

Wacko passed the note through the passenger window of the Professors' car as it pulled to a stop beside him in the parking lot.

"Divorced with two grown children," Wacko said. "Delighted if you'd call."

"You sure you won't change your mind?"

Wacko smiled. "Flux is the natural state of any mind, Professor."

Professor Tilford tightened his lips. "Yes," he said, "I guess it is."

He looked down at the slip of paper, then toward Kimani. She was waving from the doorway. He winked and toodle-ooed with a paternal flick of his hand as they accelerated away.

Prophet Wacko

Thirty seconds later, the Rolls-Royce rolled out in the same direction. It had traveled no more than a kilometer before Wacko was snoring into Frick's jangled dreadlocks.

When he awoke it was evening on a narrow, winding road lined with dark, encroaching vegetation.

"Where are we?" He yawned.

"Good morning, sleeping beauty," Frick said.

"We're in the forest on a full-moon night," Strawberry said from his other side. "Isn't it beautiful?"

Wacko's eyes bulged.

"The forest?" He bolted upright and stretched his neck toward the window. Pale moonlight streamed over the black treetops.

"Whoa, brother, relax," Frick said. "Just need to pick up some stuff from the tree house. Decided to move in with the girls for a while. Starting to feel sort of cut off as a hermit."

"But I don't want to go back to the tree house."

"Relax, dude. We'll just spend the night and go back in the morning."

Wacko fell back in his seat, visions of bigfoot dancing in his mind. He felt sick.

"Maybe there'll be some nice animals to talk to," Strawberry said.

279

Chapter 42

Niukah and Jelpmittlebong sat on worn aasmamyl-hide mats in a table-less void on a Horde officer frigate. Other than some vapor bongs lining the wall behind them, the quarters were spartan—standard for officers under Swaq's command.

Meters away—in their dominant line of sight—a pile of gelatinized aasmamyl offal jiggled in an accoutrement alcove to the hum of the ship's engines. Iron morinurk-head wall urns flanked the alcove like sentinels. The gauzy smoke that curled from their nostrils nearly, but not quite, countered the pertinacious odor of livestock guts.

"Looks like the show's about to start," Niukah said.

The offal blob was squirming like a mollusk.

"We must've come out of dimensional shift," Jelprnittlebong said. He tapped a remote console at his side, and a small holo-globe appeared out of the floor. A live stream of the Xenkon V'rpq System materialized in 3-D, distant but identifiable, with

Xenkon V'rpq Proper in the center. A blotch of brightness—a huge Lord Swaq spotlight—could be seen stretching from a small artificial satellite orbiting the planet.

A subtransmission crackled in the lower right quadrant of the holoimage. The old envoy's face stared back at them.

"We're point zero three parsecs from the home system," he said. "Holding pattern in the Samoth Asteroid Cloud."

"Why'd we come out of shift prior to destination?" Jelpmittlebong asked.

"Target world analyst Goonhopple fo Gargado informs that they need less velocity to align the avatar's program."

"How long before detection?" Niukah asked, grabbing a metal rod that lay beside his mat and then buzzing over to one of the morinurk urns. He poked the rod through a flaring nostril and stoked the smoldering mloshfruit-oil-soaked pebbles. An orange glow flashed through the thickening smoke.

"Approximately zero point nine hours," the envoy said.

"This is a Horde-issued vessel, yes?" Niukah asked, as he flitted over to the other urn and prodded its nose.

"It is. Registered as one of Lord Swaq's personal frigates. We should be able to neutralize initial reconnaissance challenges, but if we can't produce a convincing Lord Swaq within a reasonable time, they're sure to get plucky."

"Rest assured, my friend," Niukah said, returning to his mat and laying the steaming poker on the floor, "upon perfection of the divine appearance, you'll be the first we call." He cut the transmission and buzzed toward the alcove, settling down about a meter away.

Jelpmittlebong joined him.

The aasmamyl offal steadily transmogrified into a reasonable facsimile of the late Lord of the Great Intrepid Horde—lacking vestures, but no less impressive. The completed Swaq vehicle stepped from the alcove and roared, then looked down at its audience and began flexing its muscles.

"Hello," it said in midflex.

"Umm," Jelpmittlebong said. "Hello."

"Hoo'qqai Ulluoi, at your service." She stopped flexing and stretched her foreclaws toward the ceiling.

"Pwond fo Niukah," Niukah said. He nodded toward Jelpmittlebong. "This is your adversary, Fumb fo Jelpmittlebong. The pleasure is ours."

Ulluoi smiled. "They thought this would be a short engagement to get me back in the swing of things."

"Well, welcome aboard."

"Thank you," Ulluoi said, interlocking her foreclaws behind her head and pulling her chin to her chest. "I've been programmed to describe the typical Horde badass challenge, and recommend some supplementary twists that may serve to impart a more indelible mark on our audience." The vehicle fell into rhythmic leg-squatting. "Shall I begin?"

"When the student is ready, the master appears," Niukah said. "By all means."

"Thank you. Do you mind if I circumambulate as we talk? A new vehicle's muscles can be tighter than a virgin slink lizard."

She suspended herself in midsquat and exposed her fangs, mimicking one of Swaq's more habitual mannerisms.

"Did I use that analogy correctly?" she asked.

"Flawlessly, your lordship," Niukah answered.

"Thank you." The vehicle began high-stepping around the edges of the rounded room. "A typical Swaq rally will employ deafening black metal music and pyrotechnics."

"Already arranged," Niukah said.

"And an energetic entrance, usually via a thrust stage."

"That too."

"Good. It's been suggested that in order to make it look as real as possible we should choreograph some—"

The old envoy's head popped into the hologlobe.

"They're here," he said. "And they're asking for the Lord."

"Shit," said Ulluoi, spitting on the ground with a thunderous shake of her head.

"That was quick," Jelpmittlebong said.

"My lord?" the envoy said, training his dominant pupil on the Swaq vehicle.

Ulluoi stomped to the screen.

"Tell those fuckers if they interrupt my meditations any further, I'll have their brains for tea."

"Yes, my lordship," the envoy said with a smirk. "Your bounty is unsurpassed." His face slipped from view.

Ulluoi turned to Niukah with a mischievous grin.

"Was that convincing?" she asked.

"Very," Niukah said. "But I'm afraid we really shouldn't keep them waiting."

"But what about the choreography?" Jelpmittlebong asked. "It would be helpful—"

"We'll just have to wing it," Niukah said, standing. "Are you ready, your lordship?"

Ulluoi buzzed over and spread her muscles, upsetting some vapor bongs. She let out a perfect horder howl.

"Yes," she said with a smile, and headed toward the door.

"My lordship," Niukah said. "Aren't you forgetting something?" He pointed at the assortment of protective apparel hanging in the alcove behind her.

Ulluoi donned an aasmamyl-leather cuirass with a fine-stitched Lord Swaq profile sewed across its chest and matching limb accessories. Then she flitted into the air, tensed her muscles, and howled. Minutes later she was in the commandant's chair of the frigate.

"Escort us to the Exalted Chamber," she said into the holoscreen with a jittery, mucose snarl. "And prepare for a major rally."

The commander of the scout ship lowered his head.

"Yes, your lordship," he said.

As the transmission terminated, the old envoy pointed Ulluoi to another holoscreen behind her with the face of a horder officer frozen in hold mode.

"That's the commander of the Earth fleet. He's wondering how long until they can start the boarding process."

Ulluoi twirled to the screen and switched it live. "Hold your position, you fucking idiot," she said. "This God business takes time."

"Yes, your lord—"

She terminated the transmission and smiled. "Oh, this badass program is so wearisome."

———

In a noteworthy deviation from customary pyrotechnics, the interior of the Exalted Chamber was pulsing like a plasma globe. Roiling filaments of colored light slipped from the hollow, transparent orb floating in the center of the chamber. They cut through purple gas geysers shooting from the floor and across the mob of howling horders like whipping lasers. Holographic Swaqs floated in the haze, flexing their muscles and baring their fangs.

The black metal power chords pounding through the metal structure reached Ulluoi and Jelpmittlebong as repetitious, bouncy patters. They were a few meters apart, swaddled in the bottom of parallel vacuum tubes underneath the chamber. Niukah and the old envoy stood in the space between them.

"The Chamber is primed, my lordship," the old envoy said. "Whenever you're ready."

"Build them into a frenzy," Niukah said to Ulluoi. "And then give us a sign that you're ready for his entrance." He jutted a foreclaw toward Jelpmittlebong.

"What kind of sign?" Ulluoi said, her voice tinny and nasal through the speaker on the console.

"Well, perhaps something—"

"Why don't you call me a stupid fucker?" Jelpmittlebong said, his voice also tinny and nasal. "For challenging such a badass like yourself."

All heads looked at him.

"It would be in line with Swaq's vocabulary and mannerisms."

"Fine," Ulluoi said, "I'll call you a stupid fucker, you stupid fucker." A metallic chortle echoed from her speaker.

"Well, there we have it," Niukah said. "The cue will be 'stupid fucker.'"

He nodded to the envoy, who poised a foreclaw over a button.

"Whenever your lordship is ready," the envoy said.

Ulluoi bared her fangs and inhaled.

"Ready," she said.

She sluiced through the twisting vacuum tube to a simultaneous dimming of the lights and music in the chamber. She barreled into the orb with a flash and an explosion. Silver smoke billowed. A collective roar erupted from the horders. She hovered in the center, flexed her muscles, and howled.

A million-plus horders howled back.

Prophet Wacko

Throughout the Empire, horders and non-horders alike were glued to the Mhowr.

"Horders!" Ulluoi shouted. "A stupid fucker challenges me."

Before he could give it further consideration, Jelpmittlebong swished through the tubing like a spider in a garden hose. He smashed against the orb's glass wall and slid to its base. Bright lights and howls accosted his senses. He rubbed his temples with the flat of his foreclaws.

"Here's the stupid fucker now," said Ulluoi, her voice booming above the din.

"Stupid fucker! Stupid fucker!" resounded through the chamber.

Ulluoi leaped on Jelpmittlebong and threw him across the orb, the crown of his head ramming against the opposite wall. The horders shouted and jeered.

Ulluoi was quickly on top of him, pulling his forelimbs back into unnatural positions, two hindclaws digging into his buttocks. She lifted him with a jerk, buzzed into the air, and lugged him to a hover in the center of the orb, rotating to give all the horders a decent view.

"Some badass, eh?" she huffed, tugging on his forelimbs. Jelpmittlebong groaned and whipped his head backward in an attempt to butt her off. Ulluoi shoved him away, but held fast momentarily with one foreclaw so that Jelpmittlebong spun to face her. She slashed a violent foreclaw that grazed his left cheek. He fell on his back to the bottom of the orb. Violet blood oozed from his face.

The crowd erupted.

"Stupid fucker! Stupid fucker!"

Ulluoi dove down and assumed a quick head-tearing-off bearing. She kneed his abdomen and grabbed his nape with two

287

foreclaws. She tensed her muscles to create the appearance of pinning him to the floor, but applied nominal pressure.

The cheering ceased as if displaced by an internal vacuum, anticipating the kill.

"I think you should start fighting back," Ulluoi whispered in his ear.

Jelpmittlebong stared. Though the wound to his cheek was superficial, the flow of blood suggested otherwise.

"We have to make it look real, don't we?" she said, jutting a hindclaw backward in an attempt to steady her gait. In the process she gashed Jelpmittlebong's tail.

Jelpmittlebong yapped like an aasmamyl pup caught in a hauler's door. He burst from Ulluoi's grip and hopped along the periphery of the orb, yelping in pain. Blood trickled from the wound to his tail.

Ulluoi picked herself up and assumed an immediate attack position, foreclaws tensed and extended.

Jelpmittlebong stopped and faced her.

In the momentary pause, Niukah's voice rang out in his head. *"Now, my student,"* he said.

"What?" Jelpmittlebong thought.

"Exterminate it."

Niukah followed his words with a mental projection of images from some of Swaq's more egregious atrocities, ending with the destruction of the Qanjivians' home world.

The immensity of it all caused Jelpmittlebong to drop his arms at his sides. But a primal rage quickly swelled in his gut. Righteous anger filled his heart. His entire being coalesced into one obsessive thought—the ending of a tyrant.

He lunged at the advancing Swaq vehicle and severed its head with a swipe so furious it was a Horde legend before the torso stopped twitching. He towered over the decapitated body with quavering muscles and thrust the head into the air.

Explosions and power chords followed. The hovering Swaq holograms flickered and became Jelpmittlebong holograms.

Jelpmittlebong bared his fangs and howled.

And the Great Intrepid Horde howled back at their new lord.

Chapter 43

The Rolls-Royce pulled to a stop off Forest Road 19 near an abandoned logging road that had not yet succumbed to the encroaching foliage. The full moon was high and bright, tinting the vegetation in a hoary glow. Frick and Wacko hopped out and began stretching their limbs.

Strawberry stepped out behind them.

"Where do you think you're going?" Wacko asked.

"With you," Strawberry said.

Wacko pointed his flashlight down what was left of the logging road.

"There could be bears in there."

"Nah," Frick said, "I doubt it. Besides, they'd probably scat when they heard this." He shook his head to a burble of jingles. "Better than a bear bell." He smiled.

"Or bigfoots," Wacko said.

Silence.

"Your grandparents will worry."

"Come on, you guys." Frick headed into the forest. "We got a hike ahead of us. They already said she could come, when you were sleeping."

Strawberry stuck out her tongue and sallied after Frick.

After an hour they reached the creek. Thirty minutes of moss-covered stones and gnarly roots later, they veered from its banks up the hill to the base of the two western red cedars that hosted the tree house. As they reached level ground, Frick took a deep breath and smiled.

"Here we are," he said, panting. He shined his flashlight around the trees' trunks and then up at the underside of the tree house. "Welcome to my abode."

"Wow! A real Magic Tree House."

"Yep. Come on, let's get—" A coincidental swing of his arm cut a swath of flashlight beam across a wall of Douglas firs on the far side—each nearly three meters in height. He recoiled the beam back and moved it from tree to tree. They appeared to be lined in two-deep rows, at least a couple dozen.

"I don't remember those being there," he said, looking at Wacko.

Wacko lifted his shoulders.

"The ancient pine was once a seed."

"Yeah right … Or maybe somebody planted them there. And it smells like manure. You smell that?" He scrunched his nose. "Maybe Ranger Noid's found a new way to harass."

"An enlightened farmer cultivates the mind," Wacko said. He lodged the flashlight under his chin and bugged out his eyes.

Frick gave him a dirty look. "Don't be weird, Wacko," he said.

"I think they look nice," Strawberry said.

Prophet Wacko

"All right, what the hell," Frick said. "Landscaped forest, whatever. I'm too tired to think about it now. Let's check them out in the morning." He shimmied up the ladder, turning around at the top to light the ladder for his guests.

After a quick tidying of the loft to accommodate three people, they were soon nestled on the camping mats with the smell of blown-out candles wafting over them, Strawberry in the middle. Minutes later Frick was snoring.

Strawberry rolled to face Wacko.

"I can't sleep," she said.

Wacko stared, visions of bigfoot retreating in waves as her shadowy features came into focus.

"Shall I tell you a story?"

"Tell me about Xenkon V'rpq."

———

"Don't lie to her," Chubij said.

"Empty-handed I go," Zawt said.

"She's just a child."

"And how miraculous this."

———

"It's a very old world," Wacko said, "with a long history. What would you like to know?"

"History's boring. Tell me about the animals."

———

Zawt smiled to himself.

293

"I think we're safe now."

"Anything can be spun to serve a purpose," Chubij said.

"Ah! The master evangelical revealing his secrets?"

"There's only one true Mother-God, whether you acknowledge it or not."

"Ha! What's one plus two?"

"In that case," Wacko said, "I'll tell you about the Great Maze-Jungle on Hurm IV. There are many animals there."

"Okay." She wrapped her thin arms around his forearm and nuzzled her cheek against his shoulder. "What's a maze-jungle? Is it colorful?"

"It's just a descriptive word that's become conventional, but it represents one hell of a natural—and colorful—wonder. And as far as I know, there's just one in the whole galaxy, which is why it's called The Great Maze-Jungle, with big capital letters. But we could call it anything we wish. Poo Poo Skadoo, for example. Or Strawberry's Imagination."

Wacko looked down and smiled.

"Anything you like."

"Being flippant with tradition will only encourage future insolence."

"I rather think it will free her from the bonds of dogma."

"There are things a mature sentio-intelligent being must respect."

Zawt laughed.

"Like avoiding fish without scales?" he asked.

Prophet Wacko

"Excuse me?"

"Or pork?"

"What are you talking about?"

"The cold shadows of your traditions move over the stone steps of the universe as if to sweep them, but no dust is stirred."

"That makes no sense."

––––––––––

Strawberry giggled.

"The Great Maze-Jungle is fine."

"Okay, the Great Maze-Jungle it is. Hurm IV is one of eight moons of a gas-giant planet in the Gok'l Nebula. Poo Poo Ska-doo—I mean the Great Maze-Jungle—occupies all of Hurm IV, except for its large hexagonal lakes, which, by the way, come in every shade of blue imaginable."

"Cerulean? Cobalt? Aquamarine?"

"Yes, all those, and more. From space the moon reflects many shades of green, but emerald is predominant."

"Sounds beautiful. But why are the lakes hexagonal?"

"Artificial, of course. The moon's an environmental and technological wonder."

Strawberry closed her eyes and squeezed Wacko's arm as she imagined a verdant world dotted with blue hexagons skirting an alien Jupiter.

"Sounds like a Christmas-tree ornament," she said.

"Or a psychedelic soccer ball."

"Oh, that too." Strawberry smiled. "Why do they call it a maze?"

"Because it's easy to get lost in. The undergrowth's dense and tall, but full of pockets—some big enough for a city—and there

295

are lots of caverns and underground tunnels. They say the roots of the oldest trees reach to the core. But no one really knows."

"'Roots to the core' is an interesting analogy," Chubij said. *"Don't we all trace our source—our roots—to the Mother-God, the First Cause, the Compassionate Deliverer from evil?"*

"'Roots to the core,' my misguided Hoo'qqai, is based on empirical observation. You'd do better to find evidence for your First Cause in your own psychological makeup."

"An omnipresent God is everywhere. Her mercy is our salvation."

"Creative visualization is the key to any fantasy."

"Do you deny the possibility of a First Cause?"

"The big bang may have initiated the beginning of space and time in this universe—as the practical evidence indicates—but nothing suggests the attributes you ascribe to your Mother-God."

"And what might those attributes be?"

"An unsurpassed ability to heed the niggling pleas of a zillion self-righteous globs of atoms and the unflagging magnanimity to give a shit would be one ... Or is that two?"

"You draw sweeping conclusions."

Zawt signaled a touchdown in his mind.

"One plus two equals zero!"

"Are there howling monkeys there?" Strawberry asked.

"No. But there are some chatty little creatures that flit through the treetops like little helicopters. They twist their antennae on their heads then let them go with a *whee*. They can hover or propel themselves like that for minutes. They're silver, and when light glints off them, they glitter like crystal."

Strawberry grinned without opening her eyes.

"Are there snakes? Jaguars? Tapirs?"

"No snakes like you're used to, but there are some pretty big millipedes that would dwarf a fire hose. They don't move around much, and you'd have to walk right up and kick it in the snout— assuming you could figure out which end was the snout—before it would think of eating you."

"Mmmm," Strawberry said.

"Lots of creatures live in the caves—slippery and eyeless. But, the unquestionable king of the Great Maze-Jungle is the morinurk—big and scary, with a tough black hide, six eyes, and a huge mouth of sharp teeth. There aren't too many left, though. The Xenkonians have been accelerating their extinction."

"Why do they want them gone?" Strawberry asked, her voice full of sleep.

"Because morinurks think we taste good. They could eat many of us at one sitting if we allowed it. And they don't have good table manners."

"Have you ever seen one?" Strawberry asked, yawning.

"Just once. It came through a thicket and interrupted my meditations. But it apparently didn't find me appetizing. It probably thought I was dead—a fully absorbed mute monk sometimes has that effect—so it just peed on my head." Wacko laughed. "The advantages of being a mute come in assorted packages."

"Sounds like the devil to me."

"Show me a god, and I'll show you a devil."

"You deny there's evil in the world?"

"An orb knows not the limits of two dimensions."

Wacko looked down. Strawberry's chest was rising and falling in soft succession, her breaths warming his shoulder. He stroked her hair.

"Good night," he whispered, wiggling from her grasp.

She suddenly clutched his arm and looked up with a stare as cool as a black rocky crevice in the jungle.

"Why do the Xenkonians want to hurt us?" she asked.

And then, as if being pulled back into the dream from whence the question came, she slid onto her side and slept.

"What do you say to that?" Chubij said.

Zawt cleared his mind. In the empty space that resulted, Strawberry's question flitted like a firefly in a jar. It sparked unfamiliar thoughts until he realized he was experiencing a phenomenon that was, for mute monks, as uncharacteristic as prayer.

He'd grown fond of her.

Wacko smiled and whispered, "Oh, this crazy life."

Chapter 44

Professor Tilford, Arabella, and Professor Al-Qurashi stood before a log-cabin structure in a shady grove of oaks and conifers just outside Sweet Home, Oregon. A wooden sign hung from the eaves of the wraparound porch. It was engraved with the words "Rough-Skinned Newt."

"So, how do you know this place?" Professor Al-Qurashi asked as they ascended the timber steps.

"Harley and I go way back. He was my first road manager—got me my first gig at the Opry. But he quit when it evolved to the point of needing a passport—not that there was a lot of international demand for teenage banjo hicks." Professor Tilford laughed as he reached the porch. "He settled here after meeting his wife. They put me up whenever I play at the Oregon Jamboree."

"Well, look what the cat dragged in," said a man behind the

bar, squinting at the haloed silhouettes in the doorway. He suspended his task of wiping down the countertop by putting his knuckles on his hips. "And still toting the Banjosaurus."

Professor Tilford set his banjo at the foot of the bar.

"Trustiest friend I'll ever have," he said as they shook hands over the counter.

"Sorry I missed your gig at the fair," Harley said, "but from what I hear it was a real humdinger."

"We improvised."

"I'm sure you did."

Professor Tilford stepped aside and gestured to his companions. "My partners in crime these days. Abdul Hazem and Arabella."

Harley reached across the bar to shake their hands.

"You can call me Harley," he said. "Welcome to the Newt." Thin strands of gray hair escaped the rubber band of his ponytail and dangled over his face. He brushed them aside and smiled.

"Harley was one hell of a road manager, back in the day. Now he's just a lazy, old fart."

"Speak for yourself, Doc."

Professor Tilford smiled. "Give us a cool one, Harley," he said. "Your best fermented hops for me, ginger ale for Abdul Hazem, and um—"

"Just a Coke, please, thanks," Arabella said.

"And a Coke," Professor Tilford said.

"Coming right up." Harley turned around to fetch the sodas from the refrigerator. "You coming to the Jamboree this year?" he asked over his shoulder.

"If humanity's still the dominant species on this planet, I wouldn't miss it," Professor Tilford said. "You got Wi-Fi in this joint?"

Prophet Wacko

"Except for the clientele, the Newt's as modern as they come. By the way, you're about eight hours early for open mike."

"Got some homework to do." Professor Tilford helped himself to a handful of shortbread from a glass cookie jar on the counter. "Mind if we take over one of your tables, Harley?" he said through a mouthful of crumbs.

Harley placed their drinks on the counter. "Sure. But use one over there." He pointed toward the far end of the room. "This half's still sticky from last night's beer."

"Obliged."

"Can I make you some lunch?"

"Nope," Professor Tilford said with a huff, lifting his gear. "Just ate." He dipped his head at the cookie jar.

"Shoot yourself, Doc. How about you two?"

Arabella and Professor Al-Qurashi declined.

The three sat at a table next to the window and set up their study area: laptops, books, and notepads. For the next hour, the three flipped pages, surfed websites, took notes, and pecked at their laptops.

Harley busied himself behind the bar, and then began wiping down tables.

"All right," he said, finishing with the neighboring table, "am I gonna have to pull your teeth, or you gonna tell me?"

"We're saving the human race, Harley."

"From what?"

"Well," Professor Tilford said without looking up, "you're aware of this recent flood of paper from the sky, yeah?"

"Damnedest thing, Doc, but ain't actually seen one myself."

"You're small market—off the guest list." Professor Tilford reached into a bulging manila envelope in his bag and dropped a fistful of fortune cookie-size slips of paper on the table. "Have as many as you like."

301

"Yep," Harley said, examining one with a squint, "damnedest things."

"They all say pretty much the same thing, allowing for subtle differences in translation."

"I'll take your word for that, Doc. Look more like chicken scratch to my untrained eye."

Professor Tilford looked up. "That's Persian. Most of the world doesn't speak *Inglés*, Harley." He sifted through the small mound as if cheating at a game of Go Fish. "Here," he said, "here's one in Gooberspeak."

Harley skimmed it with a grin.

"Well, I'll be damned."

"We're of the opinion that these"—Professor Tilford swept his hand over the pile—"and the Lingdi phenomena are all the work of a superior race of space aliens hellbent on enslaving every last man, woman, and child."

Harley placed his hands on his hips and stretched his back.

"You know," he said with a smirk, "our good neighbor Reverend Crawley says it's all the work of the Lord. But guess you already thought of that, huh?"

Professor Tilford looked at Harley over his half-eye reading glasses.

"Exactly to which lord was the learned reverend referring?"

"I assume he meant the Christian big guy," said Harley, "since that's the one he's always in a huff about. One thing his flock don't have to worry about is dialing up the wrong lord in a pinch."

"No doubt they sleep better than I," Professor Tilford said, returning to his laptop.

"Me too, Doc," Harley said. "Me too." He stuffed his towel in his apron. All three of his customers had their eyes back on their work.

"Well, anyway, better let you get to it then—saving the world and all." He started toward the bar. "Mind if I call the boys and tell them you're gigging tonight?" he called over his shoulder. "They always love picking with the master."

"That's fine, Harley. Just don't be bothering us for the next few hours while we brainstorm this piece from people brain to electric brain."

"Uh-huh," Harley said, disappearing through the kitchen door.

As the sun's rays began to skim lower through the trees, men with musical cases of various shapes and sizes began drifting into the Rough-Skinned Newt.

Arabella yawned and stretched her arms into the air.

"Wow," she said, "what a marathon."

"I'm afraid I need a bit more time," Professor Al-Qurashi said.

"Me too," Arabella said.

"Okay," Professor Tilford said. He had already completed his part. "Let's call it a day then. Take a break and send me yours in the morning."

More customers and musicians filed in as the three scholars closed their laptops and gathered their materials. Professor Tilford escorted Arabella and Professor Al-Qurashi to the porch.

"Do you think it will work?" Arabella asked.

"It'll at least get the ball rolling," Professor Tilford said.

"And we can work off it as we go forward," Professor Al-Qurashi said. "The technology part is bound to get the attention of the scientific community. When I get home, I'll make some phone calls to some of my colleagues to make sure they read it as soon as it's uploaded."

Arabella smiled at their enthusiasm, and for a moment forgot the impending doom of her planet. She felt lucky to be in the company of such dedicated and intelligent men—kindred spirits, she dared think—and imagined herself at the start of a meaningful academic career.

The article was the brainchild of Professor Tilford and was meant to be a reasoned look at the mass reaction to the Lingdi movement, blending religious and folkloric themes with the hard-core facts of science.

Professor Tilford was to dissect the popular notion that the strange events of the last few months were the result of divine intervention with a critical analysis of faith and miracles. Professor Al-Qurashi's task was to boil down the science and technology—relying heavily on Wacko's notes. Arabella would summarize Wacko's story, then postulate that the plethora of modern myths involving space aliens represents a belief system as valid as any traditional religion, essentially putting space aliens on equal footing with any supreme being in terms of possible responsibility for recent events.

Professor Tilford remained on the porch as Arabella and Professor Al-Qurashi drove away. He ran his fingers over his mustache and stared into the twilight. A slight breeze strummed across the branches of the surrounding trees. After a moment, he reached into his shirt pocket and pulled out a frayed photograph of his departed wife and daughter.

"Storm's a brewin', Blanche darlin'," he said to the photograph, stuffing his white hair under his cap, "but nothing to worry your pretty little head about." He ran a thumb over the photograph in the vicinity of their touching cheeks. Then he inhaled suddenly through his nose, as if having made up his mind about something, and reached for his cell phone.

"Hello," Kimani answered.

"My dear, this is Pickin' Elgin. Are you available tonight for an authentic bluegrass hoedown?"

"Oh yes! Where?"

"The Rough-Skinned Newt, in Sweet—"

"The Newt!" Kimani said. "Harley's place in Sweet Home?"

"Um, yes, that's the one."

"On my way."

Professor Tilford reentered the Rough-Skinned Newt with a fresh spring in his boots.

"It's Not God: It's Aliens!" would be uploaded on *Nirvana Thru Bluegrass* the next afternoon, after breakfast.

Chapter 45

Not sleepy, Wacko sat on the floor of the tree house, dangling his legs through the square hole in its middle. He looked down at the night and kicked at the ladder. The biological hum of the avatar vehicle gurgled, well tuned, as always.

A sudden rustling of branches caught his attention, given the windless night. The rustling was interspersed with an occasional gruntlike trill. Wacko grunted and trilled in tentative imitation. The rustling stopped, followed by a quick series of warbles, then a tramping of heavy footsteps. Formless shadows hastened across the lower rungs of the ladder.

Wacko descended cautiously. He began tiptoeing in the direction of the creek, craning his neck at the shadows, when a high-pitched trill burst behind him, followed by a lower trill from the forest beyond the creek.

Wacko twisted his head to witness a pine tree undulate into a big, furry monster. Within seconds he was in a viselike grip, his feet suspended a meter from the ground. The uncloaked Skook grunted a sequence of monosyllables, the intonation and delivery of which the avatar vehicle's pattern recognition program quickly mapped.

Wacko smiled through the black tuft of fur and grunted back the sequence. Thanks to the diligence of the Eeftwat Avatars linguistics R&D team and his own supernatural brain, he emulated the Skook's words impeccably.

"Weird fucking honky," he said.

A rumble not unlike laughter escaped the Skook's throat as he tightened his hold on Wacko's torso and started down the hill. He crossed the creek in bounding strides, rounded a moss-covered boulder, and marched into the middle of an impromptu Skook strategy powwow.

Wacko hit the ground like a medicine ball.

A large, grizzled-faced Skook stepped up. His black coat was laced with patchy streaks of silver. He studied Wacko with red, button-like eyes.

Wacko swallowed, then smiled.

"Weird fucking honky," he said.

Giggling ensued. The elder commanded silence with a raised fist.

"You are a most unusual Human," he said. It was obviously a different language, with a rolling cadence that suggested sonority, but it dribbled from the old Skook's tongue like slush from an iced-up pipe. "I am Pomple-phat of the Skooks," he said. "May your quiggly hole overflow with game."

The vehicle's brain had no need for the pattern recognition program this time. The full lexicon of the Chinookan languages was already planted in the main program, courtesy of the foresight of the right head of SkroSkro-Bleep.

The vehicle jumped to its feet and signaled a touchdown.

"I am the savior of this planet," it said in fluent Chinook.
The Skooks exchanged glances.

"What're you doing?" Chubij said. *"We're not here to manipulate this species."*

"They speak like Humans," Zawt said.

"Do they look Human?"

"They're bipedal, aren't they?"

Chubij bristled.

"Trust me," he said, *"you can back off the savior spiel."*

Wacko twisted his head at Pomple-phat and said, "May your canoe be steady in the wind."

Pomple-phat crossed his arms over his chest.

"You really are a weird fucking honky. How do you know the dead language of the Chinook? And your skin is not copper."

"It's not dead yet," Wacko said. "There are twelve elderly Humans who preserve it. In, er …" He struggled for the right words in Chinook, then said in pidgin mid-nineteenth-century English, "Somewhere near the settlement of Astoria."

"Astoria?" Pomple-phat said in the same old pidgin English. "That is far away, and long after the great Chinook civilization."

Wacko grinned and said, "You speak wisely, Pomple-phat of the Skooks."

Pomple-phat snorted.

"All Skooks speak wisely compared to the white Humans—even our women."

The sniggering that followed was interrupted by a diminutive Skook who dashed out of the pack and smacked Pomple-phat upside the head. Pomple-phat snarled. The female Skook tried to land a strategic kick, but Pomple-phat snared her ankle and held fast.

"Pig!" she said. She was hopping with her free leg to keep from falling over.

"Do you see what the white Human's television has done to our females?" Pomple-phat said. He drew his arm in an arc toward the pack. "These bucks have learned their language. But I refuse."

Wacko's eyes roamed down to the hopping Skook's foot. A sizeable footprint was forming in the mulched earth.

"Big foot," he said with a gulp. Internally, he sent a distress signal to the charter team.

Pomple-phat tossed the snared Skook into the pack with a flick of his arm.

"Hers are actually small for a Skook, poor dear," he said, extending a hairy foot to within centimeters of Wacko's face. "Here's a real dog."

He wagged it. It was easily sixty centimeters if a millimeter.

"That's a very big foot," Wacko said, trying not to gulp.

The pack huffed and stamped the ground with their big feet.

———————

The recruit on monitor duty looked up from his digimag and rubbed his dominant eye.

"What's the problem, Chubij-Zawt?" he asked, looping in Gargado.

"The vehicle's surrounded by bigfoots."

"Yeah, well," he said, locating the current position of the vehicle on the holoscreen, "we told you to stay put. Why the hell did you go back into the woods? All you had—"

"They appear to be predisposed to violence. They're attacking each other."

"Cool," the recruit said.

"Chubij-Zawt, Gargado here." He was patched in from his quarters.

"Stop calling us that. We're Wacko."

"Roger that, Wacko. Looks like you found the Skooks. They've agreed to help dispose of the bigfoot assassin. Ask to be taken to their leader."

"Isn't that a bit trite?"

"He's called Pomple-phat of the Skooks, a friend of sorts."

"Your friend is the one doing the threatening."

"What luck. In that case, offer him greetings from Gargado of the Eeftwat. Tell him you're the vehicle that needs protecting and that you're prepared to provide the requested information. He'll know what you mean."

"What kind of information?"

"Uh, just tell him something interesting about yourself. You know, as a sophisticated mute monk, and all that."

"Huh?"

"He's a social scientist. Anything speculative, controversial, and unsubstantiated will do."

Wacko looked up at Pomple-phat and licked the beading sweat from his lip.

"Gargado of the Eeftwat, chief of our clan, wishes upon your clan the fattest salmon in the river," he said.

Pomple-phat stepped back.

"This vehicle"—Wacko ran his hand from his head to his feet—"is the one for which Gargado speaks of needing protection."

"The vehicle is biological? In the form of the local dominant species? Outstanding."

"I understand you desire information in exchange for its protection," Wacko said.

Pomple-phat assumed a serious air.

"My dear, er, uh … What shall I call you?"

"You may call us Wacko."

"My dear Wacko of the Eeftwat," he said, "In all fairness, we were already aware of the errant creature masquerading as one of us, though we quickly discerned it was an imposter. It rants and raves like a lunatic. And look." He grinned, exposing his full set of flat teeth. "No fangs. We're mostly herbivores, although we do like the local fish."

He let out a throaty laugh. The surrounding Skooks joined in, until he raised his fist.

"That thing out there"—he swung his arms outward—"is a blot on our genetic landscape. We made the decision weeks ago to take it out the next time we come across it."

"Yeah, right," came a screech from the pack. It was the female Skook. "You sissies take out that humungous piece of male virility? Hah!"

Pomple-phat smiled.

"That's Miko, our resident shamaness and keeper of oral traditions," he said. "She's also prone to colorful delusions. Pay her no mind. She can actually be charming."

"Such is the purified mind," Wacko said.

"Yes, well, in any event," Pomple-phat said, "I insist that the information flow both ways. Then we can see about that imposter. We've been studying this planet for centuries. Is there anything you'd like to know?"

Wacko curled his lips. "Why don't you tell me about the Chinook?"

"Ah, such a noble people. They're the reason we relocated here from the Himalayas, you know." Pomple-phat looked at Miko the shamaness, who had edged herself to the front of the pack.

"Woman," he said, "get over here and tell Wacko of the Eeftwat about the Chinook." He turned to Wacko. "Then you can tell us something about you."

"I can do it simultaneously."

Pomple-phat raised his brow.

"I'm pretty good at multitasking. Have her whisper in my ear."

"You heard him, woman," Pomple-phat said.

Miko the shamaness pulled Wacko to the ground and buttressed his backside with one of her beefy legs. She flopped her other leg over his crotch, then buried her muzzle in his ear.

"Before the white Humans took this land with their brute force and jejune chicanery," Miko the shamaness said, decaying salmon wafting on her breath, "the Chinook lived this land and partook of its bounties, careful not to disrupt the sacred web of life …"

Wacko listened for a few minutes, then looked up at Pomple-phat, who was now sitting cross-legged across from him.

"Until recently," he said, "I lived on an antiquated abattoir on Mwookt Qor, twelve parsecs inward core of Xenkon V'rpq Proper, but I consider the Gok'l Nebula home …"

Chapter 46

Arabella sat in bed, thinking. The article she and the professors crafted was up on Professor Tilford's website. She'd checked it hours ago. But she couldn't help thinking there was more they could do than write an article and wait for people to find it.

Maybe she should tweet about it to her friends and grad school colleagues, or even some celebrities she admired. She grabbed her laptop from the bedside table and opened it against her knees. Something entirely unexpected greeted her tired eyes.

BloogerSNot121: *This is fucking catshit.*

QuarkButt: *Why would an accomplished physicist choose a religious rag to publish a self-dubbed breakthrough in astrophysics? It doesn't make sense.*

MeekShallInherit: *Unless it's pure crap with an agenda!*

LingdiMySaviour: *Finally a real savior comes along, and some ivory tower limp-dix start raging.*

Tweed&more: *jihad the bastards!*

Mockpoodle: *quarter em!!*

TheScientistMan: *Even as a physicist, I have to say the Lingdi postulate is far easier to suppose than these convoluted equations.*

BloogerSNot121: *Can you say, "monkeys at a typewriter"?*

LingdiMySaviour: *Not to mention more satisfying ...*

TheScientistMan: *... I mean really, what are their credentials?*

Tweed&more: *they're hacks. no doubt about it! devil sent.*

LingdiIsGod: *May Lingdi shine his light on their troubled souls.*

Nirvana Thru Bluegrass never had so many hits. Professor Tilford's blog post was inundated with comments. At least a third were from scientists scrutinizing the scientific and technical merits of Professor Al-Qurashi's part. He did say he was going to tell his colleagues.

But what really caught Arabella's eye was this:

BanjoManElgin: *... alrighty, you irrational, insipid whippersnappers! Ha! Take this and snuff it! www.youtube.com/watch?v=njci7fowieQig*

Mockpoodle: *What's that, banjo dick?!*

Tweed&more: *Infidel!!!*

BanjoManElgin: *It's my response to you snaggletooth imbeciles ... May you rot in Xenkonian hell!!!*

Arabella clicked on the YouTube link with a tepid flick of her fingertip. Before it even fully uploaded, something told her that she was going to feel sick to her stomach.

Professor Tilford's face was crimson and sopping. His chest hair flared through his unbuttoned cowboy shirt. His bola tie was wrapped crookedly around his head like an unruly headband. Fat fingers holding a wine bottle pointed at the camera. He slurred a few sentences that were mostly incomprehensible, but peppered with words like *thick-headed, riffraff,* and *gobshite.* Then he fumbled his banjo across his lap and fell into an ad-libbed ballad about the end of the world.

Giggling and shrill harmony emanated from off camera. Arabella twisted her head as she considered who it might be. Then Kimani rolled behind Professor Tilford and wrapped her arms around his neck. Her face was as red as Mars. She swigged from the wine bottle, then kissed him on the cheek.

They ended their performance by simultaneously making raspberries at the camera and shouting, "Lingdi dipshits!"

Arabella clenched her fists to stop from screaming. She rolled her eyes to the ceiling and said, "Oh, shit."

Chapter 47

Strawberry stirred in the tree house's loft, a drumbeat invading her dreams. She yawned and rubbed her eyes, then realized the drumbeat was something tapping the floor. She peeked over the loft's railing through the predawn shadows.

A man was standing on the entrance ladder—his chest even with the floor. He was rapping out measures with a bludgeon-like instrument.

"Hello," Strawberry said.

The beat halted. Ranger Noid looked up from under his Stetson. His face blanched.

"Are you a Boy Scout?" Strawberry asked.

Frick sat up and peered over Strawberry's tousled red mane.

"You fucking pedophile," Ranger Noid said through clenched teeth. He braced the Anus Hercules across his forearm and stared down an imaginary sniperscope. "You're dead fucking meat now, freak."

"Oh my!" Strawberry said.

"Little lady," Ranger Noid said, keeping Frick in the cross-hairs of his mind, "put on your clothes and get your tail down here."

"I'm already dressed."

"Well, get on down here anyway."

Strawberry jumped from the loft just as Ranger Noid lifted himself inside. Her eyes landed on the tool in his hand.

"What's that?" she asked.

"Get," he said, pointing the vibrator at the hole in the floor.

"What are you going to—"

"Get!" He stomped in her direction.

Strawberry shrieked and scurried down the ladder. She stopped at the edge of the incline toward the creek and turned to witness Frick tumble down the ladder. Ranger Noid followed like a rappelling Navy SEAL.

Strawberry fled down the hill, calling for Wacko.

"Good morning." Wacko was waving from the top of a boulder across the creek.

"Wacko! Hurry! Some man's hurting—"

A loud stomping resounded behind her. A young Skook was bounding down the hill. A chirp escaped her lungs but lodged in her throat. The Skook stamped closer with each giant stride, then, just as she leaped into Wacko's arms, rushed past.

Wacko laughed as he watched the Skook disappear behind the boulder.

"It's okay," he said, brushing the hair from her face.

"B-b-but—" she said.

"They're frightful, but friendly. Don't worry. Just take some deep breaths."

She squeezed his neck, but continued to tremble. Wacko carried her back to the group. Her eyes bulged as the Skook entourage came into view.

"Eek!" she said and went limp in his arms.

The young Skook stood in the middle of the group. "Rapist-of-Deer buggers Jangly-Hair!" he said.

"What?" Pomple-phat said.

"Killer-of-Animals-for-Fun assaults Hermit-Who-Jingles," the young Skook said in the lingua franca of his elder.

The Skooks clambered across the creek and up the slope. Pomple-phat whacked the wide-eyed Ranger Noid across the clearing with one massive swoop of his arm.

Wacko knelt down and cupped Strawberry's cheeks in his hands.

"Are you okay?" he asked.

"Were those really bigfoots?"

"They prefer to be called Skooks."

"You really are Doctor Dolittle."

"They're our friends. They won't hurt us."

Just then, the bigfoot assassin stepped from the shadows of the boulder behind them and tapped Wacko on the shoulder.

Wacko pointed up the hill. "They went that way," he said in Chinook.

The bigfoot grabbed him by the hair with both hands and twirled like a hammer thrower.

Wacko landed on his coccyx some fifty meters away on a large, flat stone by the creek, with only a thick layer of moss between him and serious injury.

The bigfoot chomped at the air, then doubled over from the impact of Strawberry's foot in his scrotum. It put a palm and one knee on the ground and sucked wind through a low range of octaves. When it straightened up, it stared at her with indifference, then clomped off along the creek.

Minutes later the Skooks sauntered around the boulder. Strawberry backpedaled. Pomple-phat raised his hand to halt the pack, then approached alone. He ran his hands over the scrambled footprints—and one large handprint—then lifted each finger to his nose, sniffing as if comparing colognes. He stood, pointed toward the creek, and grunted.

Strawberry shook her head, then pointed in the same direction, but ended the gesture with a swing of her arm to indicate along the creek and not across it.

Soon the full entourage of Skooks was on the trail, Strawberry mounted on Pomple-phat's shoulders. He gripped her shins, and she the silver tufts of his nape.

Frick hobbled furtively behind, still not sure if he was hallucinating.

Wacko stopped at the base of a sequoia and bent over, panting. As he caught his breath, he trained his attention on the sounds of the forest, but the howling that pursued him had ceased. He smiled and was soon mimicking the chirps of a mountain chickadee when a pronounced series of hoots resounded from above.

The owl was perched on the branch of a nearby western white pine, stretching its face at Wacko. It twisted its head and chucked the remains of a woodrat. Wacko mimicked the hoot sequence. The owl hooted a new pattern. Wacko copied it. And so on.

"Quit flubbing around and let me drive," Chubij said. *"I speak this language."*

"Ah!" Zawt said. *"Your hooting partner?"*

"She's asking why I keep mocking her like an idiot."

"Well, by all means, have a casual conversation." Zawt granted limited control of the vehicle's vocalization functions to Chubij.

———————

"... done something to your brain? You speak, but make no—"

"My sister," Chubij hooted, "I'm here."

"Oh! My patriarch," Ulluoi said.

"I thought you were channeling the resurrected Lingdi vehicle."

"I've managed to keep this line open. Hurry! The bigfoot has lost your trail, but will soon advance." The owl pushed off the branch and glided low. "Follow me."

Chubij told Zawt to follow it, and Wacko was soon trotting behind.

"Where're we going?" Zawt asked Chubij.

"Where're we going?" Chubij hooted.

"Some railroad tracks, just over the ridge," Ulluoi said. "We must hurry."

"We're going freight-hopping?"

"I think it's a passenger train, but yes, your best chance—"

Chubij translated the plan to Zawt.

Wacko signaled a touchdown and said, "Oh! This crazy world."

The owl looked back as it flew and hooted with apparent mirth.

"What did it say?" Zawt asked.

"She thinks you're a strange seer mind," Chubij said.

Wacko shouted, "Hip, hip, hooray!"

Somewhere in the forest, the bigfoot turned its head and howled, then headed in the direction of the avatar vehicle's shout. Somewhere farther into the forest, Pomple-phat cocked his ears, then swung his arm for the pack to follow in the direction of the howl.

Wacko burst into a swath in the forest where Union Pacific had had its way with the trees.

"The train must be late," Ulluoi hooted. "I'll go check where it's at."

The owl lifted over the treetops. Wacko watched it disappear, then turned to examine the shadows of the forest. Nothing seemed afoot. In fact, the stillness was almost palpable. He laughed and dove into a clump of wildflowers. He was soon hopscotching along the railroad ties, brandishing a corroded rail spike he'd found among the pebbles between the rails.

When the bigfoot assassin stepped from the shadows of the adjacent forest, Wacko was walking one of the rails like a tightrope, and dueling a make-believe gang of bad guys with the rail spike as a sabre—and winning.

With neither howl nor snarl, the bigfoot bounded along the railroad ties. Wacko did not register the events unfolding behind him, but a fortuitously timed bad-guy strike from the rear resulted in a reverse flying lunge and a rusty spike through the bigfoot's eye. The bigfoot swiped at the spike in its head and chomped at the air.

Prophet Wacko

"My patriarch! The train, the train." The owl swooped down, emitting a shrill sequence of hoots. "Quick! Now's your cha—"

The passenger train rounded the bend. It was traveling faster than normal in an attempt to get back on schedule. The bigfoot straddled the tracks and howled.

When the clouds of dust cleared, the locomotive was resting on its side in a thick swad of wildflowers. The bigfoot's mangled torso was imbedded in the train's leading axle. Black smoke billowed around the crinkled frame.

All but the foremost passenger cars remained on the rails, experiencing only minimal damage. The foremost car, however, lay crumpled and twisted, resting on its side against the smoking locomotive, which had also derailed.

The owl landed on Wacko's shoulder.

"That fire is near the fuel tank," it hooted. "It will explode."

A muffled voice came from the overturned passenger car.

"Help!" it said. "We can't get out!"

———

From the shadows, a regiment of small pine trees lined the perimeter of the surrounding forest. Beside them, uncloaked, was Pomple-phat.

Strawberry pulled on his ears and whispered, "Please, help them."

Pomple-phat swung his arm in a circle and shouted a grunt sequence. He was the first into the clearing.

The small crowd of disembarked passengers stood aside with uncertain faces as the towering Skooks rammed their elbows through the aluminum of the overturned passenger car. They were soon pulling on the outstretched arms of survivors too shocked to refuse the hairy helping hands.

325

Five minutes later, as the last passengers and their rescuers hunkered behind the caboose, the locomotive exploded. Metal, grease, and rubber rained from the sky.

"Oh! This crazy world!" Wacko said, jumping into Pomplephat's arms.

A young boy with an iPad had already taken more in-focus photographs of unabashed bigfoots than any devoted cryptid hunter had imagined possible. CNN was downloading them before the engines of the first rescue vehicles even ignited.

"It's times like this that we must come together in the name of God," Wacko told the traumatized Amtrak riders. "God is sending you his love and strength right now." He swung his arm at the smoldering train. "Accept God's gift to you."

The crowd gazed, transfixed. Wacko motioned for Pomplephat to come up and stand beside him, which he did, waving a shy hand. Wacko wrapped an arm around his waist.

"Is it not a miracle that our brother bigfoots appeared when they did?"

Faint murmurs of concurrence floated on the morning sunshine.

Frick rambled out of the woods and joined Strawberry, who was standing at the back of the gathering. They exchanged glances, then put their arms around each other's shoulders.

"God loves you," Wacko said, acknowledging Frick with a lift of his chin.

A few "amens" peppered the air.

Wacko stepped forward. "Lingdi loves you!" he shouted, throwing his hands in the air. Then he repeated the shtick several dozen times in a random order of the world's most spoken languages.

"Now what?" Zawt asked. *"They seem rather subdued."*

"They've just experienced a tragic accident," Chubij said. *"What do you expect?"*

"Can't they just get over it?"

"Tell them Lingdi will be resurrected," Gargado said through the transmission interface. "Use that word, *resurrected*. It has subliminal connotations."

"Okey-dokey," Zawt said. "So, how'll it be resurrected?"

"We're thinking of having him descend from a radiant cloud."

"Well, now, that's not corny at all."

"Just get them in a tizzy. The journalists will be there soon with the main pulpit."

"Pulpit?"

"Live video streams. We're hoping they take you global."

Wacko stared them down. "Lingdi will be resurrected."

A man wearing a Lingdi T-shirt shouted, "Amen."

"Resurrected," Wacko repeated with a pump of his fist. "The Holy Spirit is eternal."

A communal wail swelled.

"That's right, brothers and sisters. Are you ready for your judgment day?"

"Yes!"

"An afterlife of bliss?"

"Yes!"

A great wind shifted down from the sky.

"Armageddon may befall this planet," Wacko shouted over the sudden blasting current of air, "but the Great Lingdi will rise from the dead and lead you to salvation."

"Amen, brother!"

"Lingdi chooses you." Wacko signaled a touchdown, his hair and shirt ruffling in the wind. The owl alit on his outstretched hand, sinking its talons into his knuckles. It spread its great wings into the rushing gale. Wacko cried, "Lingdi! Lingdi! Lingdi!"

The former Amtrak passengers jumped to their feet.

"Lingdi! Lingdi! Lingdi!" they answered, their hands skyward.

A tall, blonde woman with an aquiline face leaped from a helicopter. She marched through the chanting crowd to the magnetic man with the owl.

———

"That's right, Jane," the newswoman said, squaring her eyes at the camera. "We're in Oregon with the most unlikely of stories. A passenger train derailed here early this morning. We're told there are fatalities and many injured, but we're also told the numbers would've been much worse had it not been for a passing group of bigfoots. Yes, Jane, you heard me right. Bigfoots. Not only are we reporting a fatal rail accident—tragic as that is—but perhaps more significantly, we have conclusive evidence that bigfoots actually exist. I mean, the real story here has to be the bigfoots, right?"

The camera panned over the mingling humans and Skooks.

Prophet Wacko

"Apparently one man is responsible for the bigfoots' sudden appearance and magnanimity." She turned toward a beaming Wacko. "Sir—"

"You may call us Wacko."

"Eh? Wacko?"

"Yes."

"Well, er, Mr. Wacko, what can you tell us about this ... this, well, frankly, incredibly wild and shocking scene? I mean, to discover the bigfoots. How long have you been hunting them?"

"Actually, one was hunting me."

"And they seem to have no problem with English."

"God works in mysterious ways—"

"Now," Gargado said.

"Now?" Zawt asked.

"He means," Chubij said, *"you can start the spiel now."*

Wacko stared into the camera with the sultry carriage of a snake oil salesman.

"I am Lingdi's prophet brother and a messenger of God," he told the world. "It is God's will that Lingdi be resurrected and lead you all to salvation."

Then he repeated it in Mandarin, Spanish, Hindi-Urdu, Arabic, Russian, Japanese, and was halfway through in Bahasa Indonesia when the newswoman blurted a question.

"All this has to do with Prophet Lingdi?"

"Yes."

"He'll be resurrected?"

"Yes."

"When?"

"Soon, I'm told."

"Um, by God?"

"Yes."

"And you're his messenger?"

"Yes. Lingdi's my brother."

There was a pause.

"What does all this have to do with the bigfoots?"

"I don't know."

The newswoman stared.

"God loves you," Wacko said.

Arabella stared at the television, chin in hand. The phone rang.

"It's your banjo professor," Carmen said, tossing the phone.

"Are you watching this?" Professor Tilford said. "It's on every channel."

"It's bizarre," Arabella said. "I mean, Wacko and the bigfoots?"

"It's his prediction of Lingdi's resurrection that I'm concerned about. It'll surely hamper our efforts to shine a rational light on the whole situation."

"Kind of like your YouTube video, Professor?"

Arabella's stern undertone landed sharply.

Professor Tilford sniffed.

"A mischievous Delilah with a vintage Oregon Pinot put me up to that," he said. "Not one of my better performances. But I'm afraid, my dear, these bigfoots have changed the equation. I think we need to up our ante."

"I know. But how?"

"I just had a chat with Abdul Hazem. Arabella, have you ever been on TV?"

———————

As the news team packed up its gear, Wacko, Frick, and Strawberry approached the helicopter.

"Um," Wacko said, "can we hitch a ride back to Eugene?"

Chapter 48

Arabella and the professors sat in a dingy green room. They were in a small paid-programming television station in a business park in suburban Portland.

Professor Tilford looked down at the paper cup in his hand and watched little metallic sheens swirl in the coffee.

"Maybe we should've held out and, well, paid the extra money for a real production company—"

"Stop it, Elgin," Professor Al-Qurashi said. "We agreed we have to get our message out as soon as possible. And the prime-time stations think you're a kook after that last article, remember?" Professor Al-Qurashi pointed his thumb at the door. "They said they can play it tonight, and we'll get the disc too, so we can upload it ourselves, then make copies and distribute it. We just need to focus on our message."

A dumpy teenager with thick glasses and a Lingdi T-shirt rapped on the door with the knuckles of a hand that was holding a clipboard. The door swung open with a creak.

"Claudia here'll do your makeup." He swung the clipboard toward a fleshy woman with ratted black hair and a chest full of skull rosaries. "Then she'll escort you to the studio. We can start in fifteen minutes. Any questions?"

They looked at one another.

"Okay," the teenager said, looking at the clipboard, "just so we got it straight, your program's called *Manipulating Aliens* and—" he looked at Professor Tilford "—you're going to start with a banjo tune, right?"

"Well, that's what we were thinking," Professor Tilford said.

"Cool. Is this thing sci-fi?" the dumpy teenager asked.

"If only."

"Like a how-to for controlling little green men?" Claudia asked, as she stood in the doorway, fingering her bone earrings.

Professor Tilford stroked his mustache.

"Hmm," he said. "That would be a reasonable interpretation, wouldn't it?"

"Let's make it more clear," Professor Al-Qurashi said. "Something like *The Aliens Are Here and They're Trying to Manipulate Us*, or *The Xenkonians Among Us Are Manipulating Us*, or something along those lines."

"How about *Aliens Are Manipulating Us*?" Arabella said.

"That's it," Professor Tilford said, slapping his hands on his thighs and pushing himself out of his chair. "Make the change. Now, Claudia, my dear. Fifteen minutes. Not much time to make us pretty."

Arabella scratched something on her notepad.

They sat behind a folding banquet table with a red crochet tablecloth draped over its front to hide their legs. Professor Al-Qurashi and Arabella watched with polite stiffness as Professor Tilford winged through an abridged medley of "We Are the World" and "We Shall Overcome" on his Banjosaurus. He finished with a flurry of arpeggios evoking "The Star-Spangled Banner," then rested his banjo against the wall behind him.

"Welcome to our program," Arabella said, her hands clasped over her notes, "*Manipulat*—er, *Aliens Are Manipulating Us*. Our goal is to convince you within the next thirty minutes that the Lingdi movement is an alien ruse to prepare humanity for slaughter."

She glanced at her notes, then looked back at the camera.

"The aliens in question are known as Xenkonians, and they possess superior technology and questionable morals. How else can we explain the events of the last few months?" She folded her hands on the tabletop and smiled. "God?"

The professors shifted in their seats and cleared their throats, no doubt wishing they'd read Arabella's introductory notes more carefully.

Arabella extended a hand toward Professor Al-Qurashi, but kept her eyes on the camera.

"To my right is Professor Abdul Hazem Al-Qurashi, a Saudi national and long-standing professor of nuclear physics at Oregon State University."

Professor Al-Qurashi nodded and raised his hands without lifting his wrists from the table.

"And to my left"—Arabella extended a hand the other way— "is Professor Elgin Patterson Tilford, renowned scholar of comparative religions—and author of countless articles on the subject—at Indiana University."

"And the truth shall set you free," Professor Tilford said.

"These two men transcend vastly dissimilar religious and cultural backgrounds. They come together tonight to urge you, us—brothers and sisters of the world—to look closer at the Lingdi movement and question its purpose in the name of rationality and the common good of all human beings. Professor Tilford will start us off. Professor?"

Professor Tilford straightened his back and stared into the camera. The studio lights glinted with equal intensity from the sterling edges of his bola tie and his glistening forehead.

"The very future of the human race is at stake," he said, the camera worming in his direction. "First, some inexplicable ancient messages show up in caves around the world. The same basic message appears in a bizarre flood of paper from the sky. A charismatic Chinese boy-genius starts yipping about the unification of our religions. Another young genius discovers the bigfoots, then boldly predicts that Lingdi will rise from the dead. And now we're on the verge of a mass lemming suicide.

"Alarmist, you say? Bah humbug, you say? Friends," he said as he put his elbows on the table, "hear me out. I've heard it in the press and countless blogs and chat rooms, and from the full range of self-proclaimed spiritual pundits, and even our religious and political leaders. The general explanation of the extraordinary events of the last few months is that we're witnessing nothing less than divine intervention.

"To deny that something odd's going on would be obtuse. I concede that someone or something's playing fast and loose with the known natural laws of the universe, but I challenge the interpretation that that someone or something is a benign and omnipotent supernatural being. We have good reason to believe"—he swung a hand across the table at his colleagues—"that, despite what we'd like it to be, it's not God, but an advanced species of aliens called Xenkonians." He stroked his walrus mustache.

"Notice I said 'reason to believe' and not simply 'believe.'

336

Our theory's based on rational speculation as applied to the facts—and some pretty explicit details over beers from the Wacko fellow— but I'm getting ahead of myself."

He smiled then cleared his throat.

"What exactly is faith?" he asked. "The Bible calls it the substance of things hoped for, the evidence of things not seen. A modern dictionary defines it as 'belief that doesn't rest on logical proof or material evidence.' A famous new atheist recently compared it to a weapon on par with tanks and bombs, given its influence on impressionable minds with terrorist inclinations."

Professor Tilford let out a snort.

"I wouldn't go that far, but I will say that I'm not one to easily subvert my rational mind to unsubstantiated claims. Faith can be a great personal comfort, but if left unbalanced can lead to actions that cause incredible suffering."

He took a deep breath and tightened his lips.

"I, like most people, harbor a rational and an irrational mind. Most of the time they live in harmony. One balances my checkbook or fiddles with the carburetor of my Land Cruiser, the other offers imaginative solutions when the intellect fails to explain something, or soothes when a hurt becomes unbearable.

"It's the rational part of our minds that keeps us from being overrun by our innate wishful tendencies. It's why when we're sick our first instinct is to go to a doctor, not a clergyman.

"So, while my irrational mind takes pleasure in the mystery and pageantry of the Lingdi movement, my rational mind counsels—insists on—caution. Folks—" his hands clenched into fists on the tabletop "—the events of the past few months call for vigilance and self-defense, not rallies and parades."

"Professor Tilford," Arabella said on cue, "what do you make of all the assertions that we're witnessing multiple miracles?" The

337

cameraman panned out so that Arabella and Professor Tilford filled the screen.

"Good question, Arabella." He drew a cardboard smile, as the camera zoomed back on his face. "What exactly is a miracle? What are we discussing when we talk about miracles? Are we in fact witnessing them now?"

"Yes," Arabella said, off script. "That's what I'd like to know."

The camera jerked back to take in both of their faces.

Professor Tilford looked askance at Arabella, then turned back to the camera.

"We've all seen the flood of paper from the sky, the off-the-chart intellectual abilities of not one, but two individuals. The sudden appearance of bigfoots. And now Wacko's dramatic prophesy of Lingdi's impending resurrection. While our irrational minds embrace these as signs of Providence, our rational minds struggle to place them within a logical framework of the known universe.

"But we do love a good miracle."

He described how some scientists were vilified for attempting to debunk a centuries-old ritual in Naples, Italy, where an archbishop holds a vial before a large crowd. The vial is said to contain the dried blood of Saint Januarius, Naples's patron saint. If the substance liquefies, good fortune follows for the city. If not, disaster. The scientists had suggested that the substance wasn't blood but hydrated iron oxide, a red substance easily available since antiquity, the viscosity of which increases if left unstirred but decreases if moved.

From the shadows of the studio set, the dumpy teenager in the

Prophet Wacko

Lingdi T-shirt was staring at Professor Tilford. His expression was frozen in a sulfuric snarl.

He said, "Ugh!" and slipped into the hallway. He was soon jabbing at the touchscreen of his iPhone under the ardent shimmer of a naked lightbulb.

"Folks, I've met both of these lads, Lingdi and Wacko," Professor Tilford continued. "Their abilities are admittedly peculiar, reflecting an inexplicable intelligence that does, indeed, appear miraculous. Hell, they can both out-pick me on the banjo. But is the appearance of such gifted individuals a miracle? First there's one. Then another. Are more on the way? When an apparent miraculous event becomes recurrent and no longer outside the realm of experience, is it still considered a miracle?

"So how, you ask, do we know this is an alien scheme? How do we know the Xenkonians are trying to submit us to their will?" Professor Tilford lifted his shoulders and grinned. "The Wacko lad told us—quite candidly, I might add—about their mission."

He extended a hand toward Professor Al-Qurashi, and the camera panned back to encompass all three of them at the table.

"Abdul Hazem here will provide the scientific details of what we know about the Xenkonians and the purported miracles that have allegedly taken place on Earth over the last few months."

Professor Al-Qurashi propped up a large artist's conception of the Milky Way Galaxy from the viewpoint of someone hovering over the radial plane, the spiral arms clearly distinguishable.

"Thanks, Elgin," he said into the camera. "We're of the opinion that the slips of paper from the sky are extraterrestrial in origin."

"From aliens?" Arabella said off camera.

"That's right." Professor Al-Qurashi pointed to the Orion-Cygnus Arm on the chart beside him. "We're here." He slid his finger a few centimeters across the galaxy and circled it over a fat part of the Carina-Sagittarius Arm. "The Xenkonians hail from here. They got here"—he slid his finger back to the *we're here* spot—"by using advanced technology called dimensional shifting and topological space-time molding. According to Wacko, they used exotic matter to harness an Einstein-Rosen bridge—better known as a wormhole—to form a time-compressed conduit between our two worlds …"

He proceeded to explain, with the help of charts, drawings, and photographs, the processes involved in traveling through a wormhole, leaning heavily on the equations Wacko scribbled on the napkin at the pub. He then explained the scarcity of large single crystals and iridium on Earth.

"So," he said, "as you can see, the slips of paper are most likely extraterrestrial in origin and reflect a technological aptitude far in advance of our own. Couple this with the unprecedented sophistication of the delivery system—not to mention the improbability of two ultra-gifted individuals appearing simultaneously—and it's easy to see how so many of us are willing to accept the miracle theory."

The director signaled that only five minutes remained. The camera shifted back to Professor Tilford.

"I know," he said, "we've reached some conclusions that differ from the prevailing thoughts of the day. But we're bound by our consciences to do so. Thus, we'll end with an undoubtedly unpopular suggestion that instead of preparing for an Ascent of angelic proportions, we should be arming ourselves to the teeth."

"Amen, brother," Professor Al-Qurashi said off camera.

Professor Tilford held his smile for an extra moment, then reached behind for his banjo. The camera pulled back and settled on all three of them.

Arabella looked up from her notes and smiled.

"You can find out more about our presentation on Professor Tilford's website at the address on your screen now," she said. "Thank you."

Professor Tilford ended the program with a sober rendition of "Auld Lang Syne" as the brief credits rolled, superimposed on the screen.

In an unfortunate show of improbability, the address of Professor Tilford's website was misspelled.

"Okay," the director said. "That's a wrap."

The bright studio lights over the table lowered to a moderate glow. Arabella and the professors stood and removed the microphones clasped to their shirts.

"Congratulations, Professors," Arabella said. "I think we did it."

"This is just the first step, Arabella," Professor Tilford said. "Now we have to make sure it gets enough airplay."

"Well, the first show's tonight—"

"Mr. Tilford," Claudia called, running up to the set.

"Elgin please, my dear."

"Okay, Elgin. You were awesome."

"Well, thank you."

"Do you go for chubby little goth girls?" she asked with a demure twirl of her skull rosary.

"Darling," he said. "Forty years ago you'd already be slung

over my shoulder, and we'd be out the door. But I'm afraid that nowadays I'm just a fat bag of bones."

"But the things you could do with those fingers," Claudia said, gazing at his hands and biting her lip.

"Yes, well—"

"Professors." The dumpy teenage kid stepped in front of Claudia. "Here's your DVD." He handed the disc to Professor Tilford. "Now, if you will," the teenager said, "please follow me. We need to prepare the set for the next show."

"What show?" Claudia asked. "I thought they were the last—"

"Go look at your schedule, Claud," the teenager said, scrunching his nose. "You should be more prepared." He turned to Professor Tilford, his teeth jutting like a hyena's, and pointed his clipboard toward the door. "Professor, if you will."

They piled into the hall. Claudia jogged toward her dressing room.

"This way," the teenager said, leading the professors and Arabella in the opposite direction. They hurried through a dim passageway cluttered with boxes and idle equipment to an industrial-grade fire door. He thrust himself against the crash bar in a manner not unlike a body slam. The door swung open and a slight breeze scampered in.

The building was long, one story, and U-shaped. They stepped into the large, grassy area that filled the void inside the U.

"This is a shortcut to the parking lot," the teenager said. "Just go along the building toward that light." He pointed his clipboard toward a dim floodlight attached to the building's exterior in the distance. "Then turn left at the next corner. You can't miss it."

They squinted along the dark wall.

Prophet Wacko

"Are you sure?" Professor Tilford asked, turning back. But the door had already slammed shut. They heard the latching of its lock and what sounded like a profane whoop from the other side.

They trudged single file down a dirt path that ran along the side of the building and turned at the indicated corner. But, instead of a parking lot, they found an alleyway lined with Dumpsters.

"What the Dickens is going on?" Professor Tilford said.

"This isn't the parking lot," Arabella said.

Just then, a figure in a Lingdi T-shirt, military fatigues, and a Spider-Man mask stepped out from between two Dumpsters. He was holding a billy club.

"Nope," he said, his voice raspy and muffled by the mask on his face, "this ain't the parking lot, you heretics." He strode toward them, slapping the nightstick in his palm. "This here's hell, and I'm the fucking Grim Reaper."

"Excuse me?" Professor Tilford said.

"No, fat man," the man said, "don't think I will."

In one swift motion, he whacked the shins of each professor. They fell on top of each other, sucking in spit. Arabella huddled at the foot of a Dumpster as the man proceeded to bash the snot out of them.

Afterward, he rifled through the professors' clothes as they lay moaning on the asphalt. He relieved them of their wallets and cell phones, as well as the DVD of their broadcast, then turned to Arabella with a wicked grin.

"Now it's your turn, bitch," he said, yanking her up by the arm. He pulled a gun from a side pocket in his fatigues and pressed it against her forehead.

Arabella gasped and squeezed her eyes shut.

343

"Bye-bye," the man said and pulled the trigger, but instead of the small explosion of gunpowder, there was only a damp, metallic click.

Arabella snuffled and stole a one-eyed glance.

"Bang, you're dead," the man said with a laugh, stuffing the toy pistol in his pocket. Then, with eyes fervent and vacuous, said, "You're one lucky bitch. Consider it a sign to repent your satanic ways and embrace the teachings of Prophet Lingdi."

Arabella sank to her knees and covered her face with trembling hands. A gagging sound seeped through her fingers.

"That's more like it," the man said. "God be with you." He walked away, slinging the DVD across the parking lot like a Frisbee. "And oh," he said, turning as he walked, "I slashed your tires too."

Arabella raised her head. The surrounding darkness pulsated into a constricting tunnel with the man's fading figure at its center.

Chapter 49

Arabella cradled her knees, her back against a Dumpster. Her jaw was clenched, as she rocked slowly on her buttocks. It was raining, but she made no attempt to find shelter.

The professors sprawled over each other on the pavement before her, unconscious but breathing.

The trauma of the beating battled for airplay in Arabella's mind with the imminent Xenkonian attack. She shook her head in an attempt to align her thoughts into some sort of rational order—to make some sense of everything. But instead of explanations, anger filled her mind.

But really, what did it matter? So what if honorable men with love in their hearts had been brutally beaten when the whole human race was rushing headlong to the brink of extinction? If people wanted to be mindless cows in a herd, what did she care? If a ploy as transparent and cockamamie as the Xenkonians' was all it took, then let the Xenkonians scramble their brains. Didn't they deserve it for being so stupid?

She lugged her fingertips through her matted hair and gazed skyward as if to question the streetlight shining on her. It flickered through the drizzle. A burning question barreled down her cheeks that would no longer accept denial as a retort.

Could it be that her species was not built to survive?

"Fundamentalism upon fundamentalism begets fundamentalism ..." she whispered with an inward stare. She squeezed her fingers into fists and snarled at the rain, trying not to think the unthinkable.

A moan brought her eyes back to the professors. With effort, Professor Al-Qurashi dragged himself off of Professor Tilford, so the men lay prone next to one another on the asphalt.

Arabella hastened over.

"Are you okay?" she asked.

Professor Al-Qurashi looked up. His eyes were puffy and bruised, but not allayed of their gravitas. He tried to smile but only winced.

"I think so," he said.

Professor Tilford groaned and twisted onto his side, holding his gut.

"Worse than moonshine," he said with a gasp.

Arabella smiled despite herself.

The patter of the rain intensified, accelerating the professors' return to consciousness. They were both in bad shape, but didn't appear seriously hurt.

Arabella eventually got them on their feet and, with one on each arm, hobbled with them toward the main thoroughfare.

From the sidewalk they looked up at an oblong building sporting a giant bowling pin set at an angle on a rotating pedestal.

Prophet Wacko

Blinking neon letters on the base of the pedestal declared the name of the establishment to be Crankers Bowling World. They cut across the parking lot and entered.

No one was bowling. In fact, the clatter of pins, thudding balls, and general social chatter associated with a bowling alley were noticeably absent. They'd walked the length of the alley— still arm in arm—past the check-in counter, a children's play-room, and a billiard room, when they saw a large gathering in a cocktail lounge set off the main area. Everyone was staring at a large-screen TV in the corner.

The professors dropped into oversized, cushiony chairs at a table on the other side of the lounge and closed their eyes in exhaustion.

Arabella approached the crowd and stiffened her arm to push in for a view, but stopped on noticing Lingdi's silhouette and the words "Crankers for Lingdi Bowling League" embroidered on the backs of their bowling shirts. She wrinkled her nose and stood on a chair instead.

On the television she saw an Asian newscaster speaking into a microphone beside a huge burning structure. The flames began to swirl, then bent unnaturally toward the ground like a ring of drooping lotus petals. The newscaster looked over his shoulder, tossed his microphone, and fled. From the center of the flattened bonfire a figure appeared, small at first, then larger, as if approaching from a distance.

A perfect facsimile of the Great Prophet Lingdi walked out of the flames.

"See!" one of the bowlers shouted. "I told you!"

"Oh my God!" shouted another.

"Shut up so we can hear."

The resurrected Lingdi raised his arms skyward. Golden wings fanned out over his shoulders. They fluttered, and he lifted

347

into the air. He settled into a graceful hover above the roiling flames and smiled. He began speaking in Mandarin. His voice was effortless, sonorous, commanding.

———

Back in the Sphere, Gargado was feeling smug.

A recruit sitting next to him at the control panel said, "Nice touch, sir—especially the wings."

"Thank you," Gargado replied with a smile, keeping his dominant eye on the monitor.

———

The bowling alley patrons released a collective gasp.

"What's he saying?"

"Shit. It's Chinese."

"Shhhh," said a rotund man behind the bar. The scene withdrew into a smaller screen, and the set of The Lingdi Channel appeared in the foreground. The rotund man pointed the remote control and raised the volume. A glitter-fringed-ivory-lounge-suited newscaster was talking excitedly.

"… is alive … I repeat, alive. Lingdi's been resurrected—as an angel!—just as Brother Wacko predicted. In an apparent attempt to quell the civil unrest in China that's been growing increasingly violent over the past few weeks—ever since the Great Prophet's controversial death—the Chinese government held a symbolic public funeral pyre and cremation. Lingdi appeared out of the flames like a phoenix! He hovered like a spiritual being and repeated an important message in every major language ... This is surely the sign we've been waiting for. Here's the message in English. Listen ..."

The hovering Lingdi again filled the screen and spoke in English.

"My children, as my soul brother Wacko prophesied, I am reborn, brought back from the dead by the strength of your faith. And now, it is time. As predicated in the message from the sky, glory is yours. The big Gods will now unite and guide you to paradise. The Ascent will commence soon. You will shortly be requested to make haste to your nearest Global Religious Summit venue. And, my children, go civilly. Go respectfully. There shall be no one left behind."

The screen switched to a map of North America, showing the scheduled locations of the Global Religious Summit. But Arabella couldn't see it from the floor. The Crankers for Lingdi Bowling League members had stampeded in their joy. She hoisted herself onto her elbows. The Crankers were dancing and high-fiving in the lanes. She tasted blood. They'd crunched her nose.

———

In the washroom, Arabella rinsed the blood from her face but couldn't quell the contusion swelling across the bridge of her nose. She set some dampened paper towels across it and went to check on the professors, stopping at the bar for two glasses of ice water.

"What happened to you?" Professor Tilford asked, struggling upright. He accepted a glass of water with both hands and sipped.

"Occupational hazard," Arabella said, handing the other glass to Professor Al-Qurashi.

"What occupation is that?" Professor Al-Qurashi asked. He was sitting on the edge of his chair, feeling around the edges of a scrape on his forehead.

"Saving the planet from aliens," Arabella said, "of course." She sat across from them. "Which just got harder, I might add." She gestured toward the mingling bowlers, whose wild dancing had wound into spirited discussions. "Lingdi's been resurrected."

"Is that what the commotion was about?" Professor Tilford asked, dropping back in his chair. He sucked a breath of air as if it contained needles.

"They're celebrating their impending trip to heaven."

"Hallelujah," Professor Tilford said with a grimace.

"Resurrected?" Professor Al-Qurashi asked. "How?"

"He appeared from a big flaming lotus flower—with angel wings. It was quite impressive."

"They're mixing religious motifs perfectly," Professor Tilford said, then coughed and grabbed his ribs.

"Yeah," Arabella said. "Wacko's got some pretty informed colleagues."

"What did Lingdi say?" Professor Al-Qurashi asked.

"He basically said it's time for the Ascent."

"Now?"

"Uh-huh."

"Well, come on then," Professor Tilford said, laboring to his feet. "We can't just sit here."

———

Arabella stood next to the reception counter of the Beaver's Lair Motel, which was just a few hundred meters along the boulevard from Crankers Bowling World. Her clothes were rumpled and wet. The bump on her face shone like a waxed eggplant.

The professors waited outside, cognizant of the awkwardness of two grown men showing up with a young woman at a motel at such an hour.

"Just a minute," came a voice from behind a curtain draped over a doorway on the other side of the counter. A hefty woman in curlers and an avocado face pack appeared. A cigarette hung from her lips.

"You all right, honey?" the woman asked. "You look like somebody beat you up. Want me to call the cops?"

"No," Arabella said. "That won't be necessary. Just a room please, for three people."

"Sure, honey," the woman said, glancing at the silhouettes through the smiling beaver logo on the front window. "No questions asked here." She slid a guest card across the counter. "But you don't seem the type."

Arabella narrowed her eyes at the woman, as she reached for a pen on a stand in the form of a bobble-head Lingdi. The head jiggled as she removed the pen. She began filling out the guest card.

"Honey," the woman said, removing the cigarette and exhaling smoke out the side of her mouth. "Don't you worry none about the bastard who done all that." She pointed her cigarette at Arabella's face. "He'll get what's coming to him. God'll make sure of that."

Arabella looked at her.

"Yes," she said, brushing a clump of hair out of her eyes and handing the card to the woman.

The woman glanced at it, then grabbed a key off a hook on the wall.

"Here you go, Arabella honey—what a sweet name. One-sixteen, just down the sidewalk. Nice and clean, with a king-size bed and two singles, right next to the ice machine. Now, you get yourself cleaned up. If you need a ride to the airport, you can come with me."

"Airport?"

"To Seattle," the woman said. "That's where the closest Ascent pad is. The airlines are taking everyone for free. We're going to heaven, honey." She smiled and patted Arabella's hand. "Paradise."

"Thank you, ma'am," Arabella said. "Paradise sounds nice."

"It sure does, honey." The woman pointed at her own face. "I haven't prettied myself up like this for years." She giggled and snuffed her cigarette in an ashtray on her desk.

Arabella nodded.

"Lingdi'll be pleased, I'm sure," she said.

The woman smiled. She had two teeth in her head.

Arabella sat on the edge of the king-size bed in a robe, with her hair wrapped in a towel. The clock radio on the bedside table read 1:16 a.m.

The professors were asleep on the single beds. They all agreed that one room was best under the circumstances, so they could spontaneously powwow, given the urgency since Lingdi had been resurrected. But the professors had fallen asleep as soon as they hit their beds.

Arabella called Carmen to tell her what happened.

"Wow," Carmen said, "are they okay?"

"I think so, but they'll be feeling it for a while."

"This whole Lingdi thing is out of control. Leah even called to try to get me to repent my sins. I'm worried about her."

"I'm afraid it's soon going to be every woman for herself, Car. People here are just freaking out."

"Same here. Listen, Bella, Frick and Wacko are back from the woods. And that Strawberry girl's with them. They're crashed, but if Wacko's really connected to this, you guys should probably get here as soon as you can."

"I know," Arabella said. "But that crazy guy slashed our tires."

"Maybe we can come get you?"

"Let me see what I can do first. I'll call you in the morning."

They hung up.

Fatigued, but still charged from the day's events, Arabella turned on the TV. All the broadcasts were about Lingdi and the Ascent. She pressed her finger on the channel button, and the images progressed in rapid succession—reruns of the resurrection, Lingdi talking heads, some clips of Wacko and the bigfoots, maps showing locations of Global Religious Summit venues, artists' renditions of paradise—even an animation of all the world's deities dining together, Last Supper-style.

She stopped on Channel 93 and quickly surfed back to the Infomercial Channel at 89. Her own face looked back.

"Welcome to our program," the TV Arabella said. Professors Tilford and Al-Qurashi stared at her from the screen, their faces full of determination.

Her vision narrowed on the television. She wrapped her arms around her head at the foot of the bed and an involuntary moan escaped her gut. Her hope felt impelled to scurry, as if chased by a shadow as big as the sky. But when she looked up at the zenith in her mind, it wasn't a horde of alien invaders staring down at her, but a sky full of faceless humans.

Her mind went suddenly blank. She slid to the floor and fell asleep.

_____

Just then and for the next thirty minutes, as nearly every television in the world was tuned to a channel carrying the Great News, a dozen elderly Chinook were alert and curious in the recreational common room of a nursing home in Astoria, Oregon.

"What's the young man with the banjo saying?" a wrinkled Chinook woman asked from her wheelchair. She was one hundred-twenty-two years old.

"Something about miracles, I think," said a man next to her, who was also wrinkled, and older.

The old woman laughed.

"Oh my," she said.

Eleven other wrinkled Chinook laughed too.

Chapter 50

The Horde fleet that Swaq ordered to Earth came out of dimensional shift just inside the asteroid belt between Mars and Jupiter. To camouflage their arrival, the ships appeared in successive sequences, like twinkling lights among the small celestial bodies. But events on Earth being as they were, the strategy proved superfluous—no Human noticed.

The fleet dispersed among the junked satellites in Earth's graveyard orbit. In an attempt to pay tribute to their new lord, and to alleviate their boredom at having to wait to commence the boarding process, the horders aligned their lasers and glow-chiseled in unison on the light side of the moon.

"The Horde's glow-chiseled your profile into the Humans' moon," Gargado said from the screen of a hologlobe. 8-1-21 stood beside him. Earth's moon glowed behind them from a holoscreen imbedded in the wall.

"I know," Jelpmittlebong said from a transmission cube in the Exalted Chamber of the Great Intrepid Horde. Niukah stood behind him. "Old habits die hard, it seems. The commander of the fleet just called to apologize for the errant deeds of his subordinates, then ripped off his own head."

"Really?"

"Yes. In line with their code of honor, I'm afraid. But how does this impact the charter?"

"The Humans be spooked, Lordy," 8-1-21 said with a wry smile.

"They're definitely flustered," Gargado said. "The Ulluoi elder is channeling the resurrected Lingdi. I've highlighted their main eschatological theologies and asked her to improvise."

Jelpmittlebong smiled. "You're a natural born TEX."

Gargado nodded.

"As a matter of fact," Jelpmittlebong said, "I'm abdicating that title as of right now."

"Excuse me?" Gargado said.

"Congratulations, Goonhopple fo Gargado. You're the new Topmost Executive Xenkonian of Eeftwat Avatars Company Limited."

"But—"

"I'm afraid my destiny lies elsewhere, my friend. And if anyone can manage Eeftwat Avatars the way it's supposed to be managed, it's you."

"Thank you," Gargado said, smiling, "Lord Jelpmittlebong."

"What'll ya do, Lordy?" 8-1-21 asked.

"Train and hone certain skills that I'm told will serve me and the Empire well for many seasons."

Niukah put his foreclaw on Jelpmittlebong's shoulder.

"And," Jelpmittlebong smiled, "keep a watchful eye on the Horde." He stepped closer to the hologlobe for a better glimpse of his profile glowing from Earth's moon over Gargado's shoulder. "So, Gargado TEX, what's your strategy for the Humans?"

"I suggest stimuli that focus them back on the exodus. May I assume you have command of the Horde fleet that surrounds Earth?"

"You may."

"It would help if they could make some strategic laser blasts onto Earth's surface and hack into their global communications systems."

"What are you thinking?" Jelpmittlebong asked.

"A geological event that would threaten them with extinction—"

"Oh," 8-1-21 said, "that should light a fire under their butts."

"We won't actually trigger the event," Gargado said. "We'll just simulate its initial symptoms. Then we can transmit a global monition to the effect that it's now or never."

Jelpmittlebong inhaled slowly. Despite their self-destructive, irrational tendencies, something inside him still wanted to give the Humans a fair shake.

"What percentage of the population do we expect to board the ships?" he asked.

"Roughly eighty-nine percent, according to the probability restraints. Six billion individuals."

"Eleven percent of 'em still ain't convinced after all we've thrown at 'em?" 8–1–21 asked.

"It's a calculated estimate, but yes," Gargado said. "There's a fairly consistent ratio of Humans across all of their disparate cultures that's hardwired against divine pageantry. They just don't see the point."

Niukah laughed.

"There's hope for them yet," he said.

"Gargado," Jelpmittlebong said, smiling, "open a line to Zawt."

"Master Zawt, on behalf of the entire Xenkonian Empire, I'd like to express my gratitude for your efforts on this mission."

"Does that mean I won?"

"Well, there's a very high chance not all of the Humans will board the ships," Jelpmittlebong said. "We're looking at an approximate eighty-nine percent success rate. The other eleven percent just can't be bothered."

"Ha! There's hope for them yet."

Jelpmittlebong laughed. "That's what Niukah said."

"As he should."

"My advisors are recommending eradicating the remaining Humans, as an act of euthanasia—"

"Who said that?" Gargado said, turning a wide eye to Jelpmittlebong from his holoscreen.

Jelpmittlebong raised a foreclaw and continued.

"We'll put them out of their misery, so to speak. It would be done compassionately, of course. But I wanted your—"

"They dream."

Jelpmittlebong squared his dominant eye on the holoscreen. "Excuse me?"

"Their dreams are just involuntary visions while they sleep," Gargado said, "relatively primordial in nature, according to our analysis."

"Have you ever had one?" Zawt asked.

"Um, well, I've seen simulations."

Prophet Wacko

"Is there something remarkable about their ability to dream?" Jelpmittlebong asked.

"*Remarkable*, young monk, is in the mind," Zawt said.

Jelpmittlebong grinned.

"But, Lord Jelpmittlebong, their dreams invoke intuition, and transcend reason," Zawt said.

"Umm," Gargado said, "and the significance of that is …?"

"Humans are mute-inclined," Zawt shouted.

"Oh great," 8-1-21 said. "Just what we need—a new species of mute butts."

"The universe was once a seed," Zawt said.

Niukah's voice rang softly in Jelpmittlebong's mind.

"That's mute talk for 'they need a teacher.'"

"When the student is ready …" Jelpmittlebong thought back.

"Indeed."

"Perhaps, Master Zawt," Jelpmittlebong said aloud, "instead of eradicating them, we should help the remaining Humans evolve into something—in our joint minds—remarkable."

"A teacher?"

Jelpmittlebong grinned.

"I bet you can't."

359

Chapter 51

Arabella lifted her head from the carpet to the sounds of shouts and honking cars. She'd been dreaming about an Earth culled of fanatical, God-fearing people—the slate on religion wiped clean of all its barbarous history. The new society she saw was compassionate and visionary, strangely guided by a small group of bald women. There were also bigfoots and giggling children.

She smiled.

Passing headlights flickering through a gap in the curtains pulled her out of her reverie.

The professors were snoring on their beds. A newsman was talking on the television screen but producing no sound. Arabella forced herself into a sitting position and braced her back against the footboard of the bed. She looked around for the remote control, then discovered she'd been lying on it. She wiggled it from under her thigh and turned up the volume.

"… and forest rangers throughout the park have reported an unusual exodus of wildlife away from the caldera. Tremors have been occurring with increasing frequency, causing many geysers to explode, including the famed Steamboat Geyser, while Old Faithful has gone silent for the first time since its discovery in 1871.

"Compounding concerns is that similar signs of an imminent eruption of the supervolcano in Lake Toba on the Indonesian island of Sumatra are also being reported. Scientists predict that simultaneous eruptions of both Yellowstone and Toba would envelop the globe in a cloud of sulphur dioxide, sending the Earth into a decade-long volcanic winter from which we may not—"

A pound on the door commanded her attention.

"Arabella!" a harried voice said from the other side. "You in there, honey?" This was followed by another series of pounding.

Arabella stood and shuddered from a dull ache that seemed localized in the middle of her chest. Her head began to throb. She hobbled to the door and opened it. The sounds of a modern exodus rushed in.

The motel receptionist stood before her with a stuffed duffel bag.

"Honey," the woman said, "we gotta get going."

"What's going on?" Arabella asked.

"Something bad's going on, honey." The woman's eyes were the size of dessert plates. She was dressed in a black full-slip nightgown and running shoes. "It's Armageddon." She closed her eyes and shook her head. "Oh, Lord Lingdi, save us all!"

"Armageddon?"

"If we leave now, we'll miss the real jam that's sure to hit at daybreak. My man's got room in his pickup truck, if you wanna ride." She pointed her thumb at a Dodge Ram that was idling in the parking lot. Guns N' Roses' live version of "Knockin' on Heaven's Door" cranked from the cab. A German shepherd was panting at them from the bed of the truck, its pink tongue lapping at the predawn air.

Arabella looked over the woman's shoulder at the pickup and then at the passing vehicles beyond it in the street. They were all heading in the same direction, toward the ramp to Interstate 5 North and Seattle. She felt a sudden impulse to follow the woman.

But she couldn't.

"Thank you, ma'am," she said. "But I'm waiting for some friends. They should be here soon. I'll just wait."

The woman frowned.

"Okay," she said, shrugging, "suit yourself."

Arabella swallowed and said, "But do you happen to have a car I could borrow?"

The woman grinned and grabbed Arabella's hand with both of hers.

"Maroon Impala sedan parked out back," she said. "Keys are hanging at reception on a big butterfly key ring. I ain't got no use for it no more, honey."

Arabella smiled back. "Thank you, ma'am. And, um, see you in paradise."

"Oh, praise Lord Lingdi!" the woman said, lurching at Arabella in a spontaneous hug. Then she dashed into the parking lot. The pickup began spinning its wheels as she jumped into the cab, her nightgown getting caught in the cab's door. The black silk streamer flicked at the pavement as they squealed toward the traffic.

The German shepherd howled at the sky.

Arabella closed the door and drew the curtains to block out the passing headlights. She turned the television volume up until it drowned out the growing commotion outside. On the screen was a close-up of the full moon. An incandescent cyclops stared back, exaggerated fangs frozen in a twisted snarl.

"... what to make of it. It looks like a huge hologram of a one-eyed monster, or, er, something. There's general chaos in every city across the globe. Several news organizations are calling it Satan. Oh, God!"

The scene shifted to the studio, where a newsman was looking off camera.

"Shouldn't we wrap this up and get the hell out of here? ... Yeah?"

He ripped the microphone from his shirt and dashed away. In his wake, the camera angle plunged to a blurry close-up of the floor. Frantic, receding voices emanated from the TV.

Arabella stared at the screen. Part of her wanted to laugh at what in any other context would have been a hilarious late-night comedy sketch.

Suddenly the scene shifted.

A seraphic Lingdi floated before a background of gold-tinged clouds in a cerulean sky.

Seconds later, celestial music sprung from the clock radio of its own accord. All over the Earth, every communications and media device was being activated without human intervention.

Arabella turned up the volume and shouted, "Professors, I think you should see this."

She leaped into the space between their beds and shook their legs. They protested with moans and grunts but eventually strained themselves into sitting positions with their backs against the headboards, rubbing their eyes.

The Great New Messiah cast a munificent smile over the room, then spoke.

"My virtuous, suffering children, your planet is facing an irreversible cataclysm. Approximately fifty-two hours and seventeen minutes from now, widespread seismic and volcanic activity will commence. Earth will soon be uninhabitable.

"As rightly foretold in your sacred texts, eventual reunion with the divine is the consummation of God's creation of the world. As God may giveth, so may God taketh away, but His spirit is eternal.

"And now, my children, the end of ordinary reality has arrived. The consummation of God's plan and your own blissful reunion with Him in paradise is nigh. Hallelujah, and rejoice in your good fortune to be alive at this hallowed time in history.

"Board God's ships, my children, and live forever in paradise, happy in His service, free of sin and death. Or rebuff God's will and perish in the blazing fires and eternal darkness that will beset Earth after our Divine Departure. The choice is simple, my children, and the choice is yours.

"It is God's will that you calmly and civilly make haste to your nearest Ascent pad and follow the guidance of His divine winged soldiers. Fear not their repulsive little bodies, for they too are God's children and your humble brethren in service to His will. Their divine supervision will ensure that the Ascent is orderly and economical.

"The safe passage of all God's children is of utmost concern. In particular, it is God's wish that you take extra precautions to avoid undue injury to your pineal gland. It is, indeed, the very seat of your soul."

Lingdi's benevolent face undulated on the screen for a few seconds, then repeated the message.

———

"Well done," Gargado said.

"You don't think the caveat to protect the hormone-secreting gland was too trite?" asked Ulluoi.

"No, no, quite the contrary. Wish I'd thought of it."

———

Arabella and the professors watched the announcement repeat five times before any of them spoke.

"Shit," Professor Tilford said.

Chapter 52

Arabella found the motel woman's Impala without event. It even had a full tank of gas. It was also laden with rubbish, the bulk of which she and Professor Al-Qurashi bailed into the parking lot. Professor Tilford, complaining of a massive headache, nestled into the backseat among empty food containers and dog hairs and fell asleep.

Interstate 5's northbound lanes were bumper-to-bumper, but the Impala was the only vehicle going south. Gambling that the Oregon State Police were active elsewhere, Arabella took liberties with the speed limit. The Impala protested with a relentless flue of black smoke, but they made the usual two-hour trip to Eugene in less than ninety minutes.

They arrived at the house just after daybreak. Carmen met them on the porch, visibly upset.

"Where is everybody?" Arabella asked, ascending the steps.

"Rock and Leah left an hour ago with Strawberry's grandparents."

"Left?"

"Looking for the nearest Ascent pad."

"Rock too?"

"Yeah, he just said if everyone else is going, he might as well too. Frick and Strawberry are asleep upstairs, and Wacko and Masa went shopping."

"Shopping?" Professor Tilford asked, laboring up the steps with both hands on the railing. Professor Al-Qurashi was a step behind, holding his friend's arm.

"Wacko wanted to make breakfast for everyone," Carmen said, "in celebration, he said."

"Oh," Professor Tilford said, putting a palm to his sweaty forehead as he reached the porch, "that boy's got one warped sense of humor."

"I think he was serious," Carmen said.

Wacko and Masa waltzed into the kitchen with grocery bags full of white bread and assorted jams.

Professor Tilford picked his head off the table and looked at Wacko.

"Son," he said, "you sure run a mean ship."

Professor Al-Qurashi nodded, with arms crossed over his chest.

"Professors!" Wacko said, dropping the bags on the countertop. "So good to see you." He smiled and swung an arm at the groceries. "But I'm afraid your wager turned out to be illusory. All of this is free when no one's manning the shop."

Professor Tilford rested his face in his palms. "They're all off to the Xenkonian smokehouse," he said.

"But not you."

"No, but many of our brothers and sisters are," Professor Al-Qurashi said.

"And they're so happy to do so."

"Deceived is more like it," Arabella said, entering the kitchen. Frick, Carmen, and Strawberry followed.

Wacko turned.

"But I did win my bet with the new Lord of the Great Intrepid Horde of Xenkon V'rpq." He signaled a touchdown. "And now the galaxy's safe from tyranny."

The ensemble of eyes bearing down on him yielded the aggregate empathy of a murder of crows.

Wacko smiled limply. His celebration of their rejection of blind faith was not going as planned.

Zawt felt compelled to tell them about his most recent wager with Jelpmittlebong.

"I've made another bet with them, you know," he said.

"Oh great," Professor Tilford said. He closed his eyes and held the bridge of his nose with his thumb and index finger. "That you can convince our brethren to swim in a special sauce to make them taste better?"

"No, no, nothing like that. Besides, they don't want their meat, just some hormone in their brains."

"Then what?"

"They bet that I can't help the remaining Humans evolve into a remarkable galactic species, and I bet I could."

"Why would you do that?" Arabella asked.

"Because," Wacko said, smiling, "you dream." He pushed the grocery bags to make space on the counter and lifted himself up.

"And your dream state is very similar to that of a meditating mute monk."

"You want to help us because we're like you?"

"I want to help you because I like you."

"I dreamed about bigfoots last night," Strawberry said.

"Really?" Wacko said, turning to her with a grin.

"Yes. They were chasing us around the forest. We were screaming, but I didn't feel scared. We thought it was fun, but the bigfoots were all serious and stuff. They were acting like parents or something."

"Actually," Arabella said, "I also dreamt about bigfoots."

They all turned.

"It was in the woods too. The bigfoots were playing with children, and there was a bunch of bald women in robes who seemed to be teachers. Somehow I knew it was the beginning of a new society free of dogma and religious persecution."

"Well," Wacko said, smiling, "let's talk about that."

"Bald women teacher?" Masa said. "Must be Japanese Zen woman monk. They enlightenment, so teaching very good."

"Yes!" Arabella said. "That's perfect. Zen nuns."

"But wouldn't that just be trading one religion for another?" Carmen asked. "I mean, they're Buddhists, right?"

Professor Tilford looked up and said, "Zen's about as far away from faith as you can get and still be called a religion. I'd say it's more a philosophy for living with eyes wide open."

Wacko bugged out his eyes. "Hallelujah!" he said with a laugh. "And Zen emphasizes living from within—bound only by the limits of your own mind. Which for some of us"—he tapped his temple and grinned—"is boundless."

An inspiring discussion ensued that lead to various ideas about how to build a lasting humanistic society. For some reason, the Skooks loomed large in most proposals, as did children of impressionable age, and Zen nuns.

Afterward, Professor Tilford headed out of the kitchen holding his head. He turned at the doorway.

"I think this old man is suffering from a concussion at the hands of a religious fanatic," he said. He winked and let a grin momentarily outshine the menace of his throbbing head. "He may have won the battle, but I think we might have just won the war."

He fell asleep on the sofa with his arm over his eyes.

The rest of the gang feasted on white bread and jam.

Chapter 53

"Lord Jelpmittlebong, sir," Gargado said from his transmission interface, "I thought you might like to know, the first wave of ships has begun loading the Humans."

Jelpmittlebong was expressionless, but inside he felt at the center of a bittersweet whirlwind of sorrow and hope.

"The collective hysteria at the loading pads is greater than expected due to the simulated supervolcano eruptions," Gargado continued, "which has, predictably, proved an effective way of convincing most remaining nonbelievers. But the Humans on board are already in a high state of bliss. They're exhibiting the same brain wave patterns we've observed in specimens who've been successful at gambling or a sporting event."

"Have the probability restraints been realigned as a result?" Jelpmittlebong asked.

"We're now expecting roughly ninety-two point seven percent of the population, factoring in the new crowd models."

"Wow," Jelpmittlebong said with a thoughtful clip. "You should probably refine the Armageddon angle for future charters."

Gargado laughed.

"I'm not sure it will always be so easy," he said. "By the way, Zawt's asked for our help in regrouping the Humans who choose to remain."

Jelpmittlebong smiled to himself.

"Is that so?" he said.

"Yes. He wants to establish an educational institution, under the guidance of the Skooks and some females from the other side of the planet."

Jelpmittlebong grinned.

"Fine with me," he said. "I think it's the least we could do."

Epilogue

The Shokozan Tokei-ji temple in Kamakura, Japan, was established in 1285 and run by Zen Buddhist nuns as a refuge for women who had been abused by their husbands. Its few adherents were among the handful of humans not packing for paradise.

The abrupt displacement of the temple from the wooded hills of Kamakura to the Three Sisters Wilderness in Oregon was nominally done in honor of the humans Wacko befriended there, but was primarily done to avoid radioactive contamination from the abandoned storage pools of spent nuclear fuel rods that dotted Japan's seismically active landscape.

For the nuns, the change in environment was neither here nor there, as their minds were supple and lithe, and not abiding in any particular place.

From among the humans who had chosen to stay, five boys and five girls from every distinct culture—ranging in age from three to four and exhibiting a specific balance of healthy brain-wave patterns—were transported to the relocated temple, accompanied by members of their extended families who had not opted for paradise. The children were escorted into a large courtyard not far from Frick's tree house and greeted by a small ensemble of towering Skooks, wheelchair-bound Chinook, and bald Japanese women in robes.

The children, being children, couldn't stop giggling.

Neither could the greeting committee.

Arabella watched from the stone steps of the relocated seven hundred-year-old temple gate. She had just arrived, having stayed to help Kimani nurse Professor Tilford back to health.

Her eyes flitted about like a child's.

"This place," she said "It's ... it's—"

"It's your new abode," Wacko said, "assuming you're willing to shave your head and eat nothing but gruel."

"It's not that bad," Strawberry said, rubbing her own hairless crown.

Arabella smiled.

The nun escorting them aimed a willowy finger at the children.

"*Kochira wa atarashii sekai de-gozaimasu,*" she said, her shaved head lilting on her shoulders as if floating on the wind.

Masa, who had been walking behind her, stepped to her side.

"She said, 'New world is here,'" he said, pointing in the same direction.

A shrill laugh gushed from the nun's throat.

A short sequence of hoots suddenly echoed from the bushes. Wacko's ears seemed to stand by themselves.

In his excitement, Chubij took advantage of an unguarded Zawt and seized control of the vehicle. He hooted toward the bushes, which rustled, then parted. The Lingdi vehicle emerged onto the steps of the gate and smiled.

"Chubij!" Lingdi hooted. "My patriarch!"

"Ulluoi? My sister?" Wacko's eyes widened.

"Yes, my patriarch! I hitched a ride with the last shuttle of children. I wanted to surprise you."

"Ulluoi! Oh, my Ulluoi!"

Lingdi blushed, then hooted something quick and warbled.

Wacko gulped.

"What's he on about?" Zawt asked.

"Hoo'qqai are built in such a way as to preclude embracing," Chubij said. *"My sister wants to give me a hug."*

There, in the crimson streaks of a budding dawn, two ancient behemoths held each other in brawny alien arms.

Light-years away, the fleet of Human haulage frigates arrived on Mwookt Qor. Paradise had been prepared for them in the old abattoir that Zawt once called home, which had been closed for humanitarian reasons and sold at a discount to Zoggop Recreational Substances. (Zawt, for his part, was pardoned by Lord Jelpmittlebong and set free after his head regenerated. He became the only known Xenkonian with one core personality in two distinct living brains, and the subject of countless books on Xenkonian existentialism.)

Paradise on Mwookt Qor smelled of disinfectants and faint aasmamyl musk.

The new occupants were strapped to the walls like chickens in a coop. Tubes poked from their faces. They sniffed at the holy air and smiled at the Xenkonian angels, who skirted about, adjusting linkages and regulating metabolism.

Everyone was blissful.

THOMAS LEO was born and raised in Indianapolis. As a young man, he forwent formal education, opting instead to travel and collect experiences. He held various jobs to support this lifestyle, including chef, hospital orderly, construction worker, roadie, bookstore clerk, farmhand, flower deliverer, English teacher, and coordinator for international relations for a local government in Japan. Intermittently, he was the occasional student. One community college and five universities later, he had a bachelor's degree in Asian Studies and Japanese Language and Literature and a law degree. Since then Thomas has been based at various times in Tokyo, London, Helsinki, San Francisco, and Singapore.

Thomas is married and has two children. Prophet Wacko is his first novel.